PRAIS

"Smart but lightning ̲a̲s̲..

Brian Evenson, author of Last Days

"[A] brilliant mosaic novel... These stories straddle the lines between science fiction, fantasy, fairy tale, and acute reality."

Publishers Weekly, Starred Review

"Deftly translated by award-winning Halbert, Kim's latest import... again showcases his sly, surreal, dark humor about all the ways humans are, well, not particularly human."

Booklist

"This charming and fantastical book is sure to introduce Kim to a whole new legion of weird fiction fans, ideal for readers of Han Kang's The Vegetarian and the works of Haruki Murakami."

Chicago Review of Books

"What begins as a rather whimsical set of stories turns into a much darker novel, raising issues of difference and acceptance, what people must do to survive, and what is truly monstrous."

the Guardian

"Jealousy was my reaction to *The Cabinet*."

Kwon Yeo-seon, author of Niche of Green

"Like a veteran killer, he's terse. Quickly, coolly, and without hesitation, he commands sentences and stories that stab the reader between the ribs. We've been waiting for this storyteller and his story."

Park Min-gyu, author of Ping Pong

BY THE SAME AUTHOR

The Plotters
Jab
Hot Blood

Un-su Kim

TRANSLATED BY SEAN LIN HALBERT

THE CABINET

ANGRY
ROBOT

ANGRY ROBOT
An imprint of Watkins Media Ltd

Unit 11, Shepperton House
89 Shepperton Road
London N1 3DF
UK

angryrobotbooks.com
twitter.com/angryrobotbooks
Cabinet of Curiosities

An Angry Robot paperback original 2021
Originally published in Korean as *Kaebinit* by Munhakdongne 2006

Copyright © Un-su Kim 2021
English translation © Sean Lin Halbert 2021

Cover by Glen Wilkins
Edited by Rose Green, Sam McQueen & Eleanor Teasdale
Set in Meridien

Angry Robot and the Angry Robot icon are registered trademarks of Watkins Media Ltd. This book is published with the support of the Literature Translation Institute of Korea (LTI Korea).

ISBN 978 0 85766 917 9
Ebook ISBN 978 0 85766 924 7

Printed and bound in the United Kingdom by TJ Books Ltd.

9 8 7 6

CONTENTS

WARNING

All the information contained in this novel has been manufactured, modified, or distorted in some way, and should not be used as evidence in any argument, be it in a respected academic journal or a heated bar fight. Furthermore, the specific names, places, terms, theories, news articles, and historical events appearing in this novel are only loosely based on reality and should not be reused in any form. Please keep this in mind as we are not responsible for any harm that may result from using the contents of this book as factual scientific evidence.

PROLOGUE

It is called Cabinet 13. But there is no particular reason for the number 13. It only means it's the thirteenth cabinet from the left. This would probably be a better introduction if it had a fancier name. But then again, what would you expect from a cabinet?

There is no need to imagine anything grand. If by some chance you intend on reading this book to the end, it would be best if you rid yourself now of any fanciful or romantic expectations, because if you have such expectations, you will only see that or less.

No, this is an exceedingly ordinary cabinet. The kind that was in vogue in government office buildings during the 80s and 90s. It is an unsightly, dilapidated cabinet, mind you. The kind perfect for stashing away smelly gym clothes, lonely tennis shoes, deflated soccer balls, and expired documents. The sort of cabinet that requires no imagination to think of. Yes, that thing you just thought of now, despite saying to yourself, "No, you can't mean this." Yes, that. That is precisely the kind of cabinet we're talking about.

PART 1
The Cabinet

WHY, LUDGER SYLBARIS, WHY?

May 8, 1902. Martinique.

It was here, on this island in the West Indies, that the most violent and powerful volcanic eruption of the last century occurred. When the eruption began, lava and fragments of volcanic rock were launched into the air at 200 kilometers per hour from the crater of Mount Pelée, which towered 1463 meters above the sea. Shortly following the explosion – which resulted from the buildup of high-pressured volcanic gases inside the volcano – the earth and rock that had once constituted the ash-covered summit of Mount Pelée began to fall on the southwestern face of the mountain, enveloping the beautiful city of Saint-Pierre, which stood only eight kilometers from the summit.

For the people of Saint-Pierre, the whole event was over in a blink of an eye. They didn't even have the time to identify the source of the sound. Nor did they have the time to say in warning, "Papa, this is not time to be in the bathroom. Pelée just erupted!" They didn't have the time to make tear-filled farewells such as the ones a grandma might say to her old and decrepit husband: "I know we had to live together out of necessity in this world, but in the afterlife let's go our separate ways." Nor did they have the time to gather their clothes hanging in the yard or jump out of the tub naked and throw on a robe before running for their lives. Sitting on the toilet or lying in the bathtub, unable to fulfill their promises, with perplexed eyes wide open – that's how the people of Saint-Pierre were buried alive.

There had been several eruptions in the past, and there was always volcanic activity in the crater, but it never bothered the people of Saint-Pierre. In fact, because they held the absurd belief that the volcano was their protector, they looked at the smoke coming from the crater like a beautiful landscape painting. Every time a rumbling came from the faraway mountain, the grandmothers of Saint-Pierre would place their terrified granddaughters on their laps and rub them on the back, just as their grandmothers had done for them.

"My child, do not worry. The volcano will not harm us. In fact, it protects our town from the evil spirits. They say having a volcano next door is good fortune."

But nothing fortunate came from the 1902 eruption of Mount Pelée. Nearly all of the town's 28,000 inhabitants died, including the tourists who had come from afar to see Martinique's beautiful crater lake. Numerous flocks of sheep, and the dogs that chased those flocks of sheep, and lactating cows, and birds who couldn't fly away fast enough, and wagons carrying milk, and the fountain in the town square that gave free droplets of water, and streets paved with fine rocks, and the church tower that rang its beautiful bells every hour – all of these were buried in ash, desperately hanging on to their last breath.

The thick, heavy lava marched down the mountain blanketing all of their possessions, and, as it dried, it transformed all of the memories, jealousy, joy, anger, and passion of the people of Saint-Pierre into a giant heap of stone.

But amidst this pandemonium, there was one person who miraculously survived: the prisoner Ludger Sylbaris. This sole survivor's good fortune was thanks to a curious prison located in the middle of Saint-Pierre. Usually prisons that house vile inmates are located on the outskirts of a city or in some dark and damp underground pit. But not in Saint-Pierre; for some odd reason, they decided to erect a tower in the middle of the city, and at the very top of this tower, they put the most despicable prisoner in all of the town. Ironically, it seems that Ludger Sylbaris was saved by being a vile criminal.

The prison tower of Saint-Pierre was very tall. It soared forty-eight meters into the sky, and this dizzying height was enough that there was no need for iron bars on the prison windows, something all other prison windows needed. Indeed, for the last several hundred years, there wasn't a single prisoner who was able to escape from that tower, despite it not having any bars. Of course, that's not to say there weren't escape attempts. In 1864, Andre Droppa the sailor, who was as brave as he was stupid, attempted to escape the prison. Droppa used bed sheets, prison clothes, underwear, belts, socks, and several towels to fashion a rope long and sturdy enough (or so he thought) to reach all the way to the base of the tower. A rope, in other words, that was at least forty-eight meters in length. In order to get materials for his foolish plan, he tore up all of the fabric he could find in his cell. And because he had torn up everything that had even a bit of fabric on it – that is, his pants, drawers, prison clothes, bed sheets, and blankets – he was forced to sit naked on the cold stone floor as he wove the rope. At night, a chilling sea breeze blew through the tower. Butt naked, Droppa endured the cold sea breeze and lonely night, thinking of the rosy future in which he would be sitting next to a beautiful woman as he ate hot beef soup and drank rum. Finally, when not a single thread of cloth was left in the cell and the rope had been finished, Droppa was so excited he was moved to tears.

It goes without saying that Droppa's rope did not reach the ground. But with no more fabric to increase the length of the rope, Droppa naïvely thought to himself, "How short could it be? If I get to the end of the rope and I still haven't reached

the ground, I'll just jump the remaining height!" and decided
to go through with it anyway. Who knows? Such a plan might
have even seemed feasible when he looked down from the top
of the tower. But deciding to risk it all was the most foolish
decision of the many foolish decisions Andre Droppa had made
throughout his life. Sure enough, when Droppa got to the end
of his rope, he realized that it wasn't even half the length of
the tower. And because of the layers upon layers of moss that
had grown on the stone, there was no way he could climb
back up the tower wall. As Droppa hung from his rope and
struggled to not let go, he realized something.

"So this is why they don't have bars on the windows!"

In the morning, it was the old shepherd taking his flock of
sheep out to the mountains who discovered the prisoner wrapped
up in his rope like a cocoon and hanging on for dear life. Looking
at the spectacle, the old shepherd called out to Droppa.

"Andre! What are you doing up there? And why are you
butt naked?"

Droppa tried to give the old shepherd a polite answer, but
because he had been hanging on to the rope all night, not a
single word was able to escape his throat. Instead, the only thing
left his mouth before he plummeted to the ground and died was
two grunts. Perhaps they were grunts of lament or resentment
or regret. Indeed, what could he have said just before dying? I
like to think he might have said something like this:

"You old coot! What kind of question is that in a time like
this?"

After that incident, bars were installed in the windows of
the prison tower of Saint-Pierre. But it wasn't to prevent prison
escapes; rather, it was to prevent the foolish conclusions that
prisoners often came to when they were bored and stared at
things for too long. In other words, it was to remind prisoners
both that any rope they could fashion from their sheets and
drawers wasn't going to be long enough, and that things were
much farther than they appeared.

* * *

French prisons treated prisoners like fine wine. Just as wine is aged in dark, damp cellars, criminals are aged in dark, damp cells until they become sweet and tart. But in Saint-Pierre, they treated prisoners like wet laundry or fish to be dried. They hung criminals up in high places where there was good sunlight and plenty of wind so that the dampness of their crimes would evaporate in the warmth of the sun and be blown away by the breeze.

Thanks to this, the people of Saint-Pierre were able to look up at the prison tower and see the town's most vile and despicable human being every time they took a break from work and straightened their back or laughed so hard from a joke that they had to grab their stomach. Each time they did this, they would take turns saying mean things: "Even if you stabbed that man in the ass with a harpoon it wouldn't be enough"; "They should castrate him and leave his balls out to dry so that he won't be able to spread his bad seed"; "Why stop at that? You should cut off his dick while you're at it and feed it to your dog Wally"; "Don't say that about my dog. What did he ever to do deserve such a thing?"

To the people of Saint-Pierre, the prison tower was a symbol of evil, an object of scorn and resentment. It was also the source of all their misfortunes, both natural and manmade. If your pig ran away, you looked to the tower; if your daughter got pregnant, you looked to the tower; if you lost a wager, you looked to the tower. The people of Saint-Pierre blamed everything on the prisoner at the top of the tower – everything from the largest of natural disasters to the smallest of inconveniences. Whatever the reason, regardless of whether it was reasonable or not, all of the evil and bad things that happened in the town were hung on that one prisoner. The town's priest would even say, "Why curse your neighbors, your lovely wife, your beautiful children? If you really want to curse something, just look to the tower!"

The cell at the top of the prison tower was almost never empty. And that was because if there was no prisoner in the tower, the entire town's moral law would collapse – at least, that's what the town's elders thought. Not to mention the fact that people would become exceedingly bored. So, if there was no suitable successor for the current tenant, that inmate would sometimes have to spend a much longer sentence than he or she deserved – and this was despite the fact that they had probably already turned crispy from years of hanging on the windowsill to dry in the sun.

Now let's return to the story of Ludger Sylbaris, the sole survivor of Saint-Pierre. Ludger Sylbaris was locked away in the prison tower for twenty-four long years. He was put in prison at the age of sixteen, and it wasn't until he turned forty that he was able to leave its confines. In fact, he was only able to escape with the help of the volcano, and not because he had served out his sentence.

The charges against Ludger Sylbaris were for raping nuns and insulting a priest. They claimed that Ludger Sylbaris had snuck into the convent each night to rape several nuns and that he had insulted a priest in a public place. Despite admitting to the second charge, he denied to the end ever raping any nuns. But before Ludger Sylbaris had time to defend himself, the judge had already sentenced him to eighty years in prison.

In truth, the claims of rape against Ludger Sylbaris were dubious at best. The accusation of blasphemy also did not make much sense. Although insulting and shaking your fist at a priest in a public space was worthy of punishment, it wasn't the type of thing for which you would lock up a sixteen-year-old for eighty years.

In spite of the charges' ambiguous and nonsensical nature,

Ludger Sylbaris was locked away in the prison tower for a total of twenty-four years. Then on May 8, 1902, Mount Pelée erupted. A mountain's worth of volcanic ejecta and ash were spewed into the air, and Saint-Pierre was razed to the ground in a matter of seconds. Sticking his head through the iron bars of the tower, Ludger Sylbaris watched as the pyroclastic material from the summit of Mount Pelée engulfed all of Saint-Pierre's 28,000 inhabitants. From that tower in the center of the carnage, he saw all of the city's death and tragedy. And just before the tower was swallowed up by the poisonous steam from the lava, Ludger Sylbaris was saved in dramatic fashion.

How it was that the tower was able to survive the countless number of large and small pyroclastic projectiles that were flung across the sky, and how it was that Ludger Sylbaris was not suffocated by the volcanic gas, remains a mystery. For whatever reason, Ludger Sylbaris, who endured everyone's hatred and ridicule from the top of that lonesome tower, was able to survive with the power granted to him by that very same hatred and ridicule. Because both the laws and customs that had defined his crimes and the people who remembered those crimes were all buried in lava and turned to stone, and because Ludger Sylbaris' crimes were in turn also buried in lava and turned to stone, Ludger Sylbaris was now a free man.

Many journalists wanted to interview him, but Ludger Sylbaris would say nothing of what had occurred. Instead, quietly escaping through the disordered crevices created by the disaster, he disappeared into the night. From time to time, you could hear rumors about a miraculous survivor, but as with all things that garner the interest of the world, the existence of Ludger Sylbaris was soon forgotten.

Saint-Pierre was frozen in time. But Ludger Sylbaris' watch kept ticking. He crossed over to Mexico. And there at the edge of a desert where no one lived, he lived in seclusion for thirty long years. By then, no one was even slightly interested in who Ludger Sylbaris was or what he had endured. But then, some ten years after his death, a book was published in his name in the state of Louisiana. The book – which was five hundred pages long, written in miniscule font, and titled *The People of Saint-Pierre* – recounted in detailed, calm prose from a relatively objective perspective the history of Saint-Pierre, the lives of its people, and the eruption of Mount Pelée. Ludger Sylbaris probably wrote the manuscript one section at a time, day by day over the duration of his thirty years in isolation. But in the pages of this book, there are several questionable sections. You could call them somewhat preposterous, or even illogical. Let's take a look at one such section:

Father Cleore had a badger tail on his ass. Bishop Desmond also had a badger tail on his ass. Bishop Desmond's tail was slightly larger and longer than Father Cleore's. Because I only saw it from a distance, I couldn't be sure whether they were really badger tails. They could have been flying squirrel tails or fox tails. Actually, so much time has passed that I now wonder if they weren't wolf tails or hound tails. But regardless of what kind of tails they were, people should never have tails on their asses. I was only sixteen at the time, but I knew enough to know that badger tails only belong on the asses of badgers.

As Father Cleore and Bishop Desmond were standing in front of the holy cross, they rubbed their asses together and stuck their faces in each other's butts and made grunting sounds as they took large whiffs, and when they got tired of that, they lay down and started fiddling with each other's tails. It looked just like how monkeys pick at each other's fur. As Bishop Desmond started petting Father Cleore's tail, Father Cleore looked pleased and wagged his erect tail several times.

At that moment, the railing I was standing on lurched

forward and let out a loud creak. Bishop Desmond looked my way. I was so scared I didn't look back even once as I started to run out of the church. From behind me I could hear Bishop Desmond shouting at me. But I didn't stop. I ran and ran until I reached the Zelkova tree on the hill. Shaking with fear, I waited there for my lover Alisa until night came. But when darkness fell, it wasn't Alisa who came for me, but the police.

This wasn't the only odd thing that Ludger Sylbaris wrote. He also wrote that the town butcher, Mr Billy, had four testes and two penises, and that because he was unable to suppress his huge sexual appetite, he used one penis for his wife and the other for the pig. There was also mention of the Daley family who, every other generation, gave birth to a child with talons. According to Ludger Sylbaris, to hide this fact from the world, the family cut off the toes when it was a boy and killed the baby when it was a girl, secretly burying the body in the family graveyard. These are just a few examples of the many stories about the eccentricities of the people of Saint-Pierre, each one being depicted in shockingly graphic detail.

Was this Ludger Sylbaris' revenge? Was it his way of getting back at the people of Saint-Pierre who had ridiculed him and locked him away in a tower for twenty-four years for having done nothing?

Many believe so. They say it was Ludger Sylbaris' pettiness and deranged desire for vengeance that wrote these stories. But I have a different opinion. After all, is this really how a man who spent thirty years as a recluse at the edge of world would think about the people from his hometown – people who were so tragically obliterated in a volcanic eruption?

"You locked me in a tower and spat at me. Good riddance! Now you'll get a taste of your own medicine. I'm the only survivor of Saint-Pierre, so I'm going to pin badger tails on all of your asses. With this record of mine, you will all be remembered for eternity as priests who had badger tails stuck to their asses. Hahaha!"

Honestly, wouldn't that be a little childish even for a man in his position?

I sometimes go into my study and take out *The People of Saint-Pierre* to read a few pages. Each time I do this I think about those thirty years Ludger Sylbaris spent away from people and what a lonesome life it must have been. A life in which all the people and places he knew had disappeared. A life in which there were never any visitors, nor anyone to ever visit. A life in which you grew corn and potatoes in a vegetable garden, cooked dinner by yourself, and ate alone by candlelight. A miserably quiet life.

Ludger Sylbaris never once left Saint-Pierre before the disaster. Saint-Pierre was where he was born, the home to everything he ever knew. He couldn't have known how to live in any other place that wasn't Saint-Pierre and he had never imagined leaving Saint-Pierre. So, every day, from the time he woke to the time he went to sleep, there was no way he couldn't have thought about Saint-Pierre and the way it disappeared into the smoldering lava. He would have constantly gone over the memories of Saint-Pierre: beautiful Alisa, and the women who stared and hooted at him; the town at night, when he could hear the ringing of bright bells; the rhythmic beating of the wheels on a horse-drawn wagon carrying milk; the sight of the market with its boisterous and lively patrons; and, of course, the last moments as the town was transformed into a pile of ash. "What was it like down there?" he must have wondered. "And why was I the only one spared to be exiled in this foreign land?"

Ludger Sylbaris had to write about Saint-Pierre. Not out of some sense of duty, but because it was the only thing he *could* do. Each time he wrote about Saint-Pierre, the city that had been turned to stone would come back to life with paved streets and wagons filled with milk. The flower beds would be filled with flowers in full bloom, people would be chatting in the market again, the meek sheep would be bumping up against each other's butts as they followed the shepherd boy. And, most importantly, beautiful Alisa would be waving her hand in the distance and smiling.

"Ludger! Meet me tonight at the Zelkova tree on the hill."

Then why, I wonder, after thirty years had the people of Saint-Pierre changed into monsters? What happened as Ludger Sylbaris walked endlessly through the labyrinth of his imagination? Why, Ludger Sylbaris, why?

SYMPTOMERS

According to the 2005 Manhattan Consulting Report, there are more than 1400 people worldwide who consume gasoline as a food and water substitute. Now, we've all heard those stories of children from developing countries drinking tiny amounts of gasoline to kill parasites, but this is different. The people to whom this report refers are those who religiously drink two liters or more of refined gasoline every day. What's more, these people are, in large majority, affluent individuals who live in high-class apartments in large metropolitan cities like London, New York, or Paris: people who work in elite professions, like accounting or law. And not only do these people drink gasoline as if it were a health drink that abates exhaustion and fatigue, they also use it as common ingredient while cooking.

Terry Burns, an accountant in London who has drunk gasoline instead of water for the last ten years, says he consumes more gasoline than even his BMW sedan. "But no matter how hard I try, my mileage is nowhere near what my BMW gets. Are BMWs really that efficient? Or am I just lacking?" When Terry asked me this absurd question, I didn't have any intention of giving him a polite answer. But if I had to, I guess I could have said not to worry, as with the way things are going in this mess of a world, it was only a matter of time before BMW invented a car that ran on Dunkin' Donuts and McDonalds.

So, why is it that these people – who are as rich and educated as they come – consume something as bizarre as gasoline? Well, the reason they choose gasoline over food like steak or bread is simple: it's because gasoline for them is much more of an efficient fuel source for the mind and body than food. In fact, they even believe that, like a fine-tuned engine, life in a city requires gasoline..

"Any problem can be solved with a little bit of gasoline. We've all experienced sleep deprivation, fatigue, or emotional instability. But you'll never make it in modern society if you let things like that get in the way. So, where did these problems come from? We who drink gasoline believe they have been brought about by traditional diets consisting of carbohydrates, proteins, and fats. Humans become unreliable and lazy when they only eat bread and meat. Gasoline is the way forward for humankind. Just look around you. It's the twenty-first century. The age of speed! We need to be ready to accelerate at a moment's notice."

There's Xin Tiandi who lives in Hong Kong and eats glass. In fact, not only does he eat glass, he eats nothing *but* glass. Xin Tiandi's existence has led some scientists to claim that there are special calories in glass – calories humankind has yet to discover. Of course, this is a bit of an embarrassing claim to make as a scientist. It's well established that glass, as an inorganic material, contains not even a fraction of a percent of a calorie. So, as many have argued angrily, it's preposterous that any human could survive on glass alone. And I tend to agree with this; humans *can't* live on glass. But then there's Xin Tiandi – a man whose ability to live a healthy life in spite of a glass-only diet is like a middle finger to the whole of science. In fact, not only is he healthy, he's also 54 years old, a father of five, and, barring something unfortunate, he'll probably continue to live another twenty, maybe thirty years. Tiandi even does tai chi in the park every morning and has just recently joined a club called the Hong Kong Park Laughing Club where people sit in a circle and laugh like idiots to stay young and relieve stress.

"What's your favorite type of glass?"

"Crystal."

"And what about your least favorite?"

"Mirrors, of course."

"But what ever made you want to eat glass?"

"When I was young, I had a beautiful crystal cup. I was so mesmerized by that cup. It was more beautiful to me than diamond or gold. Sometimes I would even place it on my desk and stare at it for hours at a time. It was so beautiful I could look at it over and over again and never get tired of it. Then one day, I got the urge to taste it. You might say that I wanted to transform its visual beauty into a beauty I could taste. And so I ate it."

"And how was it?"

"Good."

In Australia there is a man named Steven McGee who snacks on steel. He bites off bits of steel with his teeth, softens them with his saliva, and then swallows the softened steel as though he were eating candy. But it's not candy, mind you; it's steel. In 1988 while on vacation in San Francisco, he was arrested for biting off a piece of the Golden Gate Bridge. The case report written by the officer in charge was quite detailed, and *SFGATE* even published an article about it titled "Man ate piece of Golden Gate Bridge: 'Too beautiful to resist.'"

Of course, as manager of Cabinet 13 for the last seven years, I wasn't the least bit shocked or surprised by this story. I was curious, however, about how human teeth could be stronger than steel, and how human saliva could dissolve it. If more people appeared like Steven McGee, by the year 2100, the act of spitting could be considered first-degree murder.

My colleague Professor Kwon and I went to Australia to meet Steven McGee. We wanted to confirm that he really could eat steel, and if that claim was true, we also wanted to inspect his teeth and get a sample of his saliva. Steven McGee was collecting scrap metal in the junk yard when we arrived. He gave us a warm smile before offering a handshake. He looked like your average Joe. We asked him if he would show us his teeth and he readily obliged. But in contrast to our expectations, Steve's teeth were hardly something to write home about. He was actually missing seven teeth, and of the ones that remained, three of them looked like they were about to fall out. He also had horrible breath. His teeth looked like they could hardly bite into a piece of apple, let alone a piece of steel.

"It must be difficult chewing on steel with these teeth, no?" I asked him, somewhat disappointed that we had come all this way for nothing.

"Oh, these? Yes, I have lots of cavities. My missus says it's because I eat too many sweeties. I guess I should cut back. But steel? I have no trouble eating that!"

Shortly after saying this, Steve picked up a piece of scrap metal that was lying on the dirt and stuck it in his mouth. Then after a few seconds, like magic, you could hear a loud crunch as the piece of steel broke apart in his mouth.

In Singapore there is a man who lives off newspapers. By now this one should seem quite normal. Compared to ingesting gasoline, glass, and steel, eating newspapers seems almost cute. He says he eats six newspapers a day. In the morning, he opens the morning newspaper and sips on coffee as he nibbles on the paper. He reads each section before eating it, moving from politics, to culture, and so on. And on Sundays when the paper isn't delivered, he eats a few weekly tabloids.

"I have no choice on the weekends, but during the week I avoid tabloids at all costs. I can't stand the taste."

"Which newspapers taste the best?"

"As long as they're interesting to read, it doesn't matter what the quality of the paper is. So, in that respect, American newspapers don't taste particularly good. They're all so shameless. The *New York Times* is the worst."

"Do you ever eat newspapers without reading them?"

"I don't *need* to read them, obviously. But they taste better if I have read them first. It also keeps me from getting bored."

"What is it exactly that you're consuming? Is it the news? Or the paper?"

"Both, I guess. It's like food: you need both taste *and* smell."

"Then I guess you could also eat CNN news from the TV?"

"Why would I eat that? You can't chew it."

And these aren't the only people in the world who eat strange things. In Inner Mongolia there is a girl who eats more than a kilogram of dirt every day, despite the best efforts of her parents and teachers. In Finland there is a person who consumes 300 watt-hours of electricity every day to supplement their extremely low intake of protein. And in China there is a person who lives off the roof tiles from a house that has been passed down in their family for hundreds of years. There's even a person who eats sandwiches made not from bread but sawdust, and a librarian from the Vatican who was tried in court for eating seven hundred rare ancient documents. When asked in court why he ate the books – books that were so important for not just historians and academics but the whole of humankind – the old man simply said, "I was hungry."

What should we think of phenomena like these? How can people forgo perfectly fine foods like jjajangmyeon, spaghetti, and stir-fried octopus for gasoline, glass, newspapers, and sawdust? Usually, humans (actually, not just humans, but *all animals*) can recognize immediately what they can and can't eat. It's what we call the Garcia Effect. That is, according to the

Garcia Effect, while people can eat sawdust or glass once or twice for fun, they'll soon realize "Ah, humans aren't meant to eat this... As a human I should eat what humans are supposed to eat..." and instinctively stop eating that thing. That's what normal humans do. Why, then, do these people eat the things they do? Is it to prove that humans can actually eat a lot more than formerly believed? Is it to challenge the weak imagination of a world that defines what is and isn't edible? Or perhaps it's all just an audition for *Ripley's Believe It or Not!*

Well, I'm not sure if the problem is as simple as that. When we see things like this on the news, we tend to trivialize the matter and say hackneyed phrases like "It takes all sorts," or "To each his own."

But the fact that there are at least 1400 people in the world who drink gasoline instead of water (a number that increases by five percent annually) cannot be ignored. The fact that there are people in the world who survive off glass – that is, the fact that there are organisms that survive eating only inorganic substances – contradicts the very notion of calories. And the fact that there is a person in Finland who has a daily calorie intake that would starve even a bunny and is able to recharge their bioenergy with massive amounts of electricity, flies in the face of all the basic assumptions in biology. But what if we look at this from the perspective of evolution? Might the existence of these types of people suggest that the human gut has evolved to digest and extract the necessary energy for survival from steel, glass, and even electricity?

Evolutionists Niles Eldredge and Stephen Jay Gould have argued that species can evolve suddenly after millions of years of evolutionary dormancy – a theory they called "punctuated equilibrium." In other words, when there is little environmental pressure, a species will feel no need to evolve and will change very little; conversely, when there is immense environmental pressure, a species will be forced to evolve rapidly. (Of course, when Niles Eldredge said "rapidly" he was thinking about before the industrial revolution, when evolutionary timescales were tens of thousands of years. After the industrial revolution, however, when everything became faster and messier, more extreme and more chaotic, "rapidly" took on a whole new meaning.)

If we follow their hypothesis, altered environments must accelerate evolution. In other words, *Homo sapiens* should be feeling more evolutionary pressure than ever. And just look at the events of the twentieth century and the speed of the twenty-first century; these changes are the greatest humankind has ever experienced. Sure enough, the symptoms of this accelerated evolution are slowly appearing all over the world. But perhaps this was to be expected. When the world changes, the essence of what it means to be a human and the requirements for continuing to live in this changed environment also change. And I'm not talking about philosophical or ethical essence; I'm talking about biological essence.

People are showing the symptoms of an evolving species. Without a suitable term from academia, we have decided to call these individuals "people with symptoms" or just "symptomers." Symptomers break slightly from *Homo sapiens* as defined by biologists and anthropologists. They exist between the humans of today and the humans of the future – that is, they exist on the branch between species. They are both the last humans and the first of a new kind.

Among symptomers there are some individuals who have cactuses or grapevines growing from their fingers, and there are some individuals who have lizard-like body parts. There are even some who can smell, taste, and see with their fingers. And for the last forty years, it has been Professor Kwon who has researched the world's various symptomers. In fact, if it weren't for him, Cabinet 13, which we manage together, would never have become filled with so many records of extraordinary people.

But *why* it is that our cabinet is filled with such impossible documents is a question for which there is no simple answer. The story of Cabinet 13 is a complicated one, and if I make the mistake of simplifying it, you might not believe me. It took Ludger Sylbaris thirty years to write about the people of Saint-Pierre. So, I think it best if I explain Cabinet 13 piece by piece, story by story. Besides, even I still don't understand all of the cabinet's contents.

"Is this some sort of modern *Naturalis Historia*?"

This was the first question I asked after seeing Cabinet 13.

"This is the end of the Bible," Professor Kwon said. "The last stage for the species known as *Homo sapiens*. And the start of a new species."

According to the famous Mitochondrial Eve hypothesis, all modern humans descended from a single African woman who evolved from apes. And from this "Mitochondrial Eve" in Africa, the entirety of humankind set forth, migrating east, toward Western Asia and the Middle East, and then across the Bering Sea toward North America and down to South America. Obviously, these migrations weren't linear, happening in waves as some decided to stay while others left; but eventually, humans spread throughout the entire world, and for 200,000 years they reproduced and flourished. Over that time, they made the Earth into a landfill, cut down a third of the Amazon rainforest to make beef for hamburgers, and even sent spacecraft to Mars and Jupiter.

But now after 200,000 years, at least according to Professor Kwon, the curtain is finally falling on the final act of Homo sapiens. Just as the age of dinosaurs ended, humans are now becoming a footnote in the history of life on Earth. *Why* you ask? We can't be sure, but some say it's because humans can no longer endure the "internal cultural orders" they created. And isn't that a little ironic? It's not some external threat from space, nor is it some internal threat from Earth. No, it's the order we humans made ourselves – an order in which we can no longer survive.

I've imagined all the ways humankind might meet its extinction: an asteroid impact, extreme climate change, a lunatic with nuclear launch codes, the appearance of a deadly airborne virus, or the emergence of artificial intelligence and a robotic civilization. But I never imagined humans would be become fossils because of the order they themselves created. What does that even mean? Is it that the capitalist system, which humans invented two hundred years ago, is now growing into an uncontrollable beast that will devour human society? I'm not sure if anyone knows.

"A new species is emerging. This isn't the evolution of a species; it is the birth of a new one."

"You mean the age of humans is coming to an end?"

"Unfortunately."

"That's so depressing."

"Well, Deok-geun, nothing lasts forever."

"Then I guess ten thousand years from now they will have to go to museums of natural history to see us humans."

"Ten thousand? You think it will take that long, with the way things are accelerating?"

"Then how long?"

"A millennium? Maybe half. And our remains will be on display in their museums only if we also assume they'll even be interested in us. They might, but only as a cautionary tale they tell their children. 'Don't live like *Homo sapiens*,' they'll say. 'They were a truly pitiful species.'"

This is a story about a new species, one that has been hitherto considered an abomination, a disease, a form of madness. It is a story about people who have suffered from the side effects of that evolution. A story about people who have been ensnared in a powerful and nameless magical spell, unable to receive insurance benefits, proper treatment, or counseling. A story about people who have been physically and mentally devastated, and who have willingly or unwillingly lived a lonely and melancholic life away from the rest of the world. A story about people who – because they exist in an intolerant scientific world that brands anything that exists beyond its microscope as mysticism and heresy – must shut themselves in a cramped room to live a hard life, never having anyone to call for help. This is a story about symptomers.

As one last example, there is a man who produces potent amounts of methane gas in his stomach. He can produce a flame as big as that from a flamethrower by holding a lighter to his mouth and burping. In fact, once when he was a little boy, he accidentally singed everyone's hair by blowing out the candles on his birthday cake. He grew up as a shy, introverted child and spent many years hiding in his room with his embarrassing secret. But after much contemplation and searching, he finally left his room and found a doctor. But the only prescription the doctor gave him was, "You'll be fine as long as you don't do anything stupid, like holding a lighter to your mouth when you burp. Oh, and never burp around a large heat source."

That's how helpful our beloved science is. But just imagine how sad and angry this man must have felt after being so insulted. He's not afraid because he doesn't understand why flames come from his mouth. No, he's afraid because he doesn't understand why he's different.

Indeed, symptomers have no way of understanding why such things happen to them. Neither can they receive treatment at medical institutions or counseling at counseling centers. This is because their "disease" doesn't show up in textbooks. They have been left on the peripheries of the world, alone and dejected. How should we understand these poor people? Should we display them like freaks and cackle or gasp at them in shock before abandoning them in some remote place in the city? Or should we group their conditions together with psychological disorders like neurosis, obsessive compulsive disorder, and schizophrenia and lock them away in the dark corners of psychiatric hospitals?

If I can say just one thing before you jump to rash conclusions, I want to clarify that I am *not* suggesting these unique individuals be featured on shows like *Ripley's Believe It or Not!* or *How in the World*. Neither do I want to tell a magical fairytale about flying carpets and toads that turn into princes with true love's kiss. In fact, I'm so averse to such fanciful things that people often call me a "square." Why then am I writing a story like this, you ask? It's to show you that these magical phenomena really do exist in our lives. Whether we accept it or not, whether we comprehend it or not, those illusions and phenomena that we deny the existence of are occurring every day all around us. You can find them every second in every house of this city – even within our own bodies. And they have a direct impact on our lives.

Now that we have that settled, I think this would be as good a time as ever to introduce you to the wounded symptomers of this city.

GINKGO TREE

We once knew a man who had a ginkgo tree growing from his pinky. He was an average forty-year-old man who ran a stationery supplies store in front of a small elementary school in the country. And from July of 1998 to October of 2001 he came to us once a month to receive counseling and tests. Aside from his premature balding, which made him look far older than he actually was, and legs that made him look unbalanced and top-heavy because they were too skinny for his portly body, there was nothing extraordinary about his appearance. But that changed one day when, while clipping his nails, he discovered a tree growing from the tip of his finger.

"At first I thought it was just a splinter. Can you imagine my surprise when I realized it was a tree?"

Indeed, because the tree sprouting from his finger was so small and thin, at first glance it looked like a corn or wart. But if you looked closely, you could see three delicate branches and some adorable little roots growing beneath his fingernail. After looking at the tree under a magnifying glass for some time, Professor Kwon declared, "There's no doubt about it. It's a ginkgo tree." Having been diagnosed by a PhD in biology, you could say that the man was officially a ginkgo tree man. Personally, I thought it a bit ridiculous to call that thing – which looked more like a splinter – a ginkgo tree. To me, ginkgos were huge, magnificent trees that lived for thousands of years.

He was an extremely shy man. During our counseling

sessions he never knew where to look, and he would turn red like a schoolgirl whenever Professor Kwon made a joke. Even the simplest of questions made him flustered and start to stutter. Because he was never able to find the right words, he often misspoke and said nonsensical things. It was only when he talked about the gingko tree growing from his finger that this changed. Whenever the topic of the tree came up, he always became full of confidence, even extroverted. With a face full of pride, he could talk for hours on end about the ginkgo tree.

"It grew a lot this month, don't you think so? Look, the roots are digging deep into my skin. And on the left, there's a new branch sprouting. I was so concerned last month when I started to smell the scent of root rot. I guess the soap I was using wasn't good for the ginkgo tree. These days I've been staying away from detergents all together. And now look at it. It's so much improved. I also relocated the checkout counter at the store to the window. That way the ginkgo tree gets plenty of sunlight. But I have to keep my arm still at all times. The ginkgo tree doesn't like it when I move my arm too much. It stresses it out. You guys better watch out! Now that I know what to do, the ginkgo tree will grow big and strong."

The ginkgo tree, however, only reached 2.8 centimeters before its growth stunted. On the third Wednesday of each month when he came for counseling, I would take a picture of the tree, measure its length with a ruler, and make notes in a file. When I looked at the tree's growth over time, it was clear that the ginkgo tree had stopped growing. But this was good news for us. It would be an unimaginable headache if the tree on his finger grew to be big and strong like a tree in the forest.

With a look of worry on his face, he would always ask me, "Deok-geun, I mean, Mr Kong, why won't the ginkgo tree grow anymore?" And I would say something like, "Well, I'm not sure." It was the honest answer. After all, what else could I say to him? Why it was that a ginkgo tree was even growing from a man's finger and not the ground, was something I could hardly believe, let alone explain. In fact, if it were possible, I would have grabbed the ginkgo tree by its proverbial collar and demanded answers. "Look here, ginkgo tree," I would say, "I don't know what your problem is, but you belong in the ground with the worms and ants, not in this man's finger!"

The man had inherited the stationery supplies store from his father after graduating from high school. He said they were able to survive with the money they made from the store. But as more people flocked to the cities, it was only natural that the countryside population diminished. This was only compounded by the plummeting birthrate. And the town where the man's store was located was no exception; there were fewer children, and as a result, it became harder and harder to make a living running a stationery supplies store for schoolchildren.

"I was really miserable in those days. I spent all day catching flies and watching over the junk food and cheap toys that no one wanted to buy. Now that I think about it, I really didn't do anything back then. Twenty years I spent sitting in the corner of that stationery supplies store, staring off into space. Twenty years! But don't get me wrong; I'm not saying they were tough times. Spending idle time was something I was used to, and it suited me well."

"But being the owner of a stationery supplies store is a pretty swell job, isn't it? Think about it this way: children are the most beautiful things in the world. And every morning, you get to see dozens of children as they walk around and chatter like little birds, so happy and full of life. I bet not a day went by that you didn't hear the laughter of children playing in the alley. They'd call out to you, 'Good morning, mister.' And you'd call back, 'Good morning, children!'"

When I said this, he scoffed.

"You don't know much about kids, do you, Mr Kong? They may look like angels, but that's just a disguise. They're little devils at heart."

The man would always lean over to see the exam results as I recorded them and ask me if there was any good news. I would often say something along the lines of, "Nothing in particular. But it's not getting any worse." Each time I responded this way, he would look so disappointed.

"I look at the ginkgo tree every day. I feel like I should be doing something for it, but I'm not sure what. And every time it crosses my mind that the ginkgo tree might die, I get so unbearably scared."

It really seemed like he felt some sense of responsibility for the lifeform that had taken root in his body. I wanted to say something to ease his disappointment, but, as I mentioned before, I didn't know anything about ginkgo trees growing from people's fingers; so, there was really nothing I could say to him. All I could give was emotional support.

"Cheer up," I said one time. "Ginkgo are resilient trees. It's not going to die. You know, they say ginkgo trees survived through the last ice age."

Giving me a defeated smile, he dropped his shoulders and returned home.

Then, in the third year, the ginkgo tree's growth suddenly began to accelerate. What had been the size of a pea the previous month was now as big as a chestnut. And after two months, it had grown to the size of an orange. And by the third month, it was as big as a watermelon.

"Isn't it splendid! This month it also grew an amazing amount. I guess the manure I applied to it was effective – smelly but effective. But even though I'm so happy it's growing, what worries me is how people are going to start taking notice. I hate that. What happens if I have to go on TV? What if people crowd around me and ask me to show them my ginkgo tree? I hate loud commotions. And I don't think it will be good for my ginkgo tree."

But this was the least of our worries. Professor Kwon and I were more concerned about the man's well-being. Obviously, not being able to take root in the ground, the tree's only source of sustenance was the man's body; if this continued, we had no way of predicting what the final result was going to be. The ginkgo tree had already taken root deep inside the man's body, and as a result, his left hand was nearly paralyzed. But despite our warnings, the man only continued to talk about what he was going to do for the ginkgo tree.

"I think it'd be best if I stop hiding and let it grow out in the open, for everyone to see. I know it'll be difficult, but if I want to continue caring for my ginkgo tree while also being a member of society, there's no other way. Do you think they have an expert on ginkgo trees at Forest Services, Mr Kong? Someone like that will surely be able to give me a lot of helpful advice. I have so many questions. How much light should my ginkgo tree be getting? And I heard ginkgo trees are dioecious; do I need to cross-fertilize my ginkgo tree, then? If I wave my arm in the air, will it cross-fertilize itself? Or do I need bees or butterflies? Oh, but I hate bees. What then? But it should fine. I can stand butterflies."

As time passed, the man became gaunt. He lost so much weight that there was almost nothing remaining of his once portly body but a thin shadow. He had jaundice in his face and the paralysis in his hand had spread to his entire arm. Worse yet, he was having digestion problems and his stomach rejected everything he ate. We told him his only choice was to amputate and extract the roots that had burrowed into his hand. If he let things continue, he was going to die. But he politely rejected our advice. Instead, he started to put all of his affairs in order, like a man preparing for death.

"Have you all lost your minds!" yelled his wife when she came to us in a fit. "He's leaving his family behind for a stupid tree? Another woman I could understand. But a tree? Please, try to talk some sense into him. He can put it in a planter if he likes it that much."

From his wife's perspective, this was all madness. I can't say I disagreed with her. But it didn't matter what we thought; his preparations were decisively quick and simple. After transferring the house and the store to his wife's name, he simply left. We only heard from him when he called us from the bus terminal.

"I'm leaving now. Thank you for everything."

It was a short call. He didn't even tell us where he was headed.

I had heard of plants growing on corpses. But I had never heard of a tree that grows on a living body. So why? Why did that ginkgo tree want to take root in live human flesh, rejecting the fertile, holy ground that had been given to it and blessed by Mother Nature? We may never know.

He would send us letters from time to time. One day he was staying in an underground hut in Mt Songni, the next, he was in Mt Taebaek. He never did reveal how he was able to eat and move around without attracting people's attention. His last letter was addressed from Mt Chiri.

The ginkgo tree is healthy. I'm healthy, too. I think it's ready to stick its roots in the ground. I'll have to go deeper into the mountains before then. I guess I won't be able to send any more letters once the ginkgo tree takes root in the ground. But I will continue to look after the tree, just as I have been. Thank you for helping plant life in my body. And

*don't worry. This is the happiest I've ever been in my entire
life.*

Because I've never tried to grow a ginkgo tree on my body,
I can't really understand how one could be so happy in spite
of (or rather, because of) a terrible tree that survives by
vampirically sucking on one's blood. But he did write that he
was the happiest he'd ever been. If he's not already dead, he's
probably living with that ginkgo tree somewhere deep in Mt
Chiri. And if he doesn't die soon and continues to live, it'll all
be thanks to that ginkgo tree. I can imagine him now, hanging
on like a leaf or a piece of fruit to the branches of a ginkgo tree
many times larger than himself, suckling on the nutrients the
gingko tree has extracted from deep in Earth.

On the other hand, I sometimes wonder if he hasn't himself
become a ginkgo tree. Perhaps his body has slowly elongated;
his toes turning into roots; his arms turning into branches;
fingers to leaves. Perhaps he's hanging from the tip of a tall
branch somewhere, swaying in the wind, watching from afar
the trifling, chaotic life down below.

"Mr Ginkgo Tree, how is the view from up there on your tall branch? It must be wonderful, is it not? This city is so wearisome."

"I'll have you know, it is not all good. Woodpeckers pecking at me all day. The bugs tickle me. And the ants form lines as they eat my skin no end."

PICK UP THE PHONE

Monday mornings are always busy. They're busy because I have to wrestle with the endless calls that come in through the two phones on my desk. Each time I get a call, I'm required to record the call, write down the time and name of the caller, and quickly schedule the next appointment before they hang up the phone. And as soon as I finish one phone call, like magic, another one comes in. Then I repeat the above routine to a T. On some days I get so many calls that I don't even have the time to get a cup of coffee. There can be so many a day that I must hold my bladder until lunch because I don't have enough time to even go to the bathroom. Because of all this, I often think about strange things on Monday mornings – like what is the max volume to which a human bladder can stretch?

Most of my callers are symptomers. And as a result, there are never any normal conversations with normal problems or normal solutions. I mean, how could one ever have a normal conversation with a man who calls saying that he came out of the shower to find that his penis was missing? All you could say to someone like this is something stupidly obvious, like "Did you check inside the shower? Maybe it fell off while you were washing." Every time I have to say something like this, I feel an indescribable sense of misery rising up from deep inside my heart somewhere. But don't get me wrong. I'm not complaining. This is what I do, and I know that complaining won't make my situation any better. It is what it is.

It's 9:25 on a Monday morning. The first call comes in. It's from Reporter Kang. It's never a good sign when I have to start a Monday off with a call from Reporter Kang. Not only is she eccentric and irritable, she's also smarter and more eloquent than I am. Once she begins haranguing me, there's no stopping her. After a phone call with her, I always feel like someone has beaten me over the head with a hammer.

Reporter Kang experiences the unusual phenomenon of time loss. We call such people time skippers. Time skippers are usually unnerved and irritable right after an episode.

"Why haven't you been answering my calls, Mr Kong?"

"Sorry. I got into the office late today."

"I know you were ignoring my calls on purpose. It must be a drag having to deal with a woman like me."

"No, not at all, Ms Kang."

"You can admit it. I don't care either way. But I wish you people would try to see things from my perspective, as someone who is in pain. That's your job, isn't it?"

"Yes, I understand. So, how can I help you today, Ms Kang?"

"I've lost time again."

"Did you notice anything different from before?"

"They're becoming more frequent and longer. And now it always happens just when I'm about to do something important, something with which I can't afford to lose time."

"Would you mind explaining exactly what happened?"

"Several days ago, I was on my way to work to give a presentation to the company executives. Naturally, I left for the subway a bit earlier than usual and boarded the train at Ahyeon Station at 7:40 am. But when I got off at City Hall, it was 11:30 am. Can you believe that? It was only a five-minute ride, but it took me four hours! I swear I didn't do anything else. I just boarded the train, took a deep breath, glanced at the subway map, then got off at City Hall. But by then, four hours had passed. By the time I got into work, it was already lunchtime. Obviously, the meeting was a disaster. My project manager looked at me like I was some kind of hippopotamus at the zoo.

"And then yesterday the same thing happened just two hours before an article was due on my boss's desk. I laid out all my materials in front of me, turned on my laptop, and was nervously staring at the flashing cursor preparing myself to type the first words when it happened. In the blink of an eye, two hours had gone by. Literally, I blinked once, and two hours were gone! Well, one hour and fifty minutes to be exact... but still! Am I going crazy? Now I'd be lucky just to have the boss look my way, hippopotamus or not."

"Are you sure your watch is accurate?"

"Yes, I'm sure. In fact, I carry around two just to be safe. What, are you saying you don't believe me?"

"Of course I do. Of course I believe you Ms Kang. We don't doubt anything our clients tell us. And to be quite honest, it's been a long time since I lost the ability to differentiate between things I should believe and things I can't believe."

"Well, my condition is getting much worse. It used to be manageable, but now I'm so worried and scared. I don't know how I can go on living like this. So that's why I'm asking this of you: I want to meet the other time skippers. I want to ask them how they cope with time loss."

"I'm sorry, Ms Kang. But, as you know, the contact info of other time skippers is confidential. The others don't want their existence to become known to the world. I'm sorry. But we can still make the appropriate arrangements for you."

"Appropriate arrangements? What the hell are 'appropriate arrangements'? I don't need your worthless counseling anymore! You're never of any help. There's no way you can understand what it feels like to have time taken from you. I don't want counseling. I want to talk with other people who have felt my pain. In person! Not through you idiots, but one-on-one."

"Please calm down."

"If you can't even do that, why do you even run a research

institute? Am I your test subject? I've explained all of my episodes in excruciating detail, yet you have done nothing for me. Do you even know how hard my life is?"

"I'm sorry. I'll look for some other way."

"I can't talk with you. I want to talk with Professor Kwon."

"The professor isn't feeling well these days."

"Then I'll call again tomorrow. In the meantime, figure something out."

9:37 am. The phone rings for a second time. It's Kang Shinae. Age 26. Kang Shinae has a doppelganger. That is, from time to time she is visited by a person who looks just like her. And when it's time, the doppelganger disappears. But unlike what you might think, this doppelganger isn't something from a horror movie. To put it in everyday terms, her doppelganger is more like an annoying younger sibling.

"She's a troublemaker."

"What has she done exactly?"

"Before, she would just hang around for a while before silently disappearing. There were a few minor episodes, but nothing serious. It was almost surprising how benign she was. But now she's always making trouble. She's bought whole wardrobes of expensive clothes with the credit card I keep in my drawer as well as a bunch of useless things from those TV infomercials. I mean, honestly! Who thinks that a buffalo hide sofa set is becoming of a 284 square-foot one-room apartment? Recently she even went to my boyfriend's work. And in front of everyone, she slapped my boyfriend and broke up with him. I can't believe her!"

"Were you thinking about breaking up with your boyfriend?"

"No. In fact, we were thinking about getting married. Even if I wasn't sure he was 'the one,' he was still decent husband material. And besides, I liked his personality."

"So why do you think she did it?"

"How would I know?"

"Did you try talking to her?"

"She just shuts her mouth and says nothing."

"And when does your doppelganger usually disappear?"

"It's different each time. It can take anywhere from five minutes to two weeks. This last time she stayed for quite a while. She's got me so anxious I can't function at all."

"I'll consult with Professor Kwon. For now, try to lock her inside your apartment for a few days. Maybe she'll be ready to talk with you when you return from work. For now, that's all we can do."

"I've tried that. But when I lock my doppelganger inside my apartment, strangely enough it's me who ends up getting locked inside."

"You must be joking, right? You mean you don't check to see which side of the door you're on before locking it? Oh! It looks like I'm getting another call. I'm sorry, Ms Kang. Let's talk more next time. Until then–"

9:45 am. Sometimes I also get calls from people who aren't symptomers. And, to be honest, these people are even more insufferable than the symptomers. Hwang Bong-gon. He's been calling me non-stop for the last two weeks.

"I want to turn into a cat."

"You have the wrong number, sir. We don't do anything like that here."

"Mister, please help me. My life depends on it. I'll be good, I promise."

"Please, Mr Hwang! What is wrong with you?"

"I'm alive, but I don't feel alive. Nothing's right: sleep, my work, the food I eat; even masturbating doesn't feel right anymore. My life feels like a giant ditch. Mister, my life is such a mess."

"Mr Hwang, can you hear me? Because of you *my* life is a mess. And because of you, *I* don't feel alive. Eating, pooping, peeing – nothing feels right. I'm begging you. Please, just stop calling."

"Mister, I will be able to find my life's purpose if I turn into a cat. And I heard there is someone who knows the way to do that."

"How many times do I have to tell you before you get it? I don't know where you heard that from, but we don't do that here. And people can't turn into cats. If you keep bothering me like this, I'm going to report you to the police."

"I'm sorry. I'm sorry. I'll call you again later."

"No, don't call again later. Don't call again, ever."

I'm looking at goldfish in a fish tank. Life underwater looks so simple. The air bubbles fizz up to the top and the waterwheel goes round and round, slapping against the surface of the water. The best part is that none of the goldfish call the aquarium manager demanding to be changed into cats. Quietly, and without demanding anything of anyone, they open and close their mouths. *Blub-blub*. That's not how someone would demand something. *Blub-blub*. That's them eating. I bet they don't even have phones or counseling underwater. Sounds like paradise.

The reason telephone counseling is so difficult for me is because I'm too normal. I'm not messed up enough mentally to understand why on Earth a human would want to change into a cat.

10:05 am. I get my fourth phone call of the day. It's Ahn Sae-cheol. Ahn Sae-cheol barely eats any food. He's 5'11" and only 92 lbs. What's more, he's still losing weight. I sometimes wonder if he's trying to become a living mummy, like the Zen Buddhists of Japan who used to prepare their bodies for death by excessive fasting.

"Have you eaten today, Mr Ahn?"

"I'm not hungry."

"Well, people don't have to be hungry to eat. We eat because it's lunchtime. When the lunchtime bell rings, we eat. It's simple, really. Nothing much to it. You simply open your mouth, stick the food in, chew on the food for a bit by moving your jaw, and finally push it down the back of your throat."

"But I'm not hungry."

"What you suffer from, Mr Ahn, is anorexia. Instead of calling us, you should see your doctor."

"It's not anorexia. Anorexia is when you can't eat or won't eat. But I simply never get hungry. Must I say it again? *I never get hungry.* I don't hate food. It's just that I don't feel the need to eat."

"That's what anorexia is."

"It's not anorexia!" Ahn Sae-cheol shouts from the other end of the phone, losing his temper.

"Fine. Let's just assume for the moment it's not anorexia. You say you haven't been eating lately?"

"Actually, I have eaten a little bit. Sometimes I can't help but eat a little, and sometimes I eat just because I'm bored."

"Well, that sounds promising. So how much do you eat a day, roughly, be it for fun or out of necessity."

"It's different each day. Sometimes I can last the whole week on a single carrot. But even then, it's just something I eat for fun. Sometimes I get curious about things, you know. Like, 'Do carrots taste different from erasers?'"

"So, which one tastes better?"

"Erasers, of course."

"Aside from erasers and carrots, is there anything else you've tried for fun?"

"Oh, sometimes I eat things like flower petals or paper fliers or pieces of toothpicks."

"But Mr Ahn, why in the world would you eat such strange things?"

"Is it much different from eating chicken legs or hamburgers?"

"You must be joking… You're telling me you think eating

chicken legs and hamburgers is equivalent to eating erasers…?"

Every time I talk with Mr Ahn, my blood pressure rises and I get a piercing pain in the back of my head.

"Never mind," I continue without giving him a chance to answer my question, "Let's just say that makes sense. Let's assume it's a fair comparison. Are there any other kinds of foods you eat?"

"Recently I've been eating moonlight."

"Moon… light?"

"Bingo. Light from a full moon might be plentiful, but it's not very tasty. No, if you want to know the taste of moonlight, there's nothing better than light from a new moon. There's not a lot of it, but even one bite of it is enough to… how should I put it… enough to know the true taste of moonlight."

"OK. Well, when you eat moonlight, Mr Ahn, do you sprinkle a bit of salt or pepper on it, too?"

"What a great idea! I must try that tonight. Oh, but wait a minute… Today's a full moon…"

"That's enough for today, Mr Ahn."

"But what about my next appointment?"

"Mr Ahn. Until you eat some ramen, dumplings, or bulgogi – you know, things that have carbs and protein – until you eat something like that, please don't call again. I'm terribly busy and you're wasting my time with your stupid pranks."

This is what my Monday mornings are like. And Tuesday mornings aren't much better.

Inside this cabinet are 375 individual files: 375 examples of magic, 375 grievances, 375 bizarre, stubborn people. Of course, this number is a lower bound. What would be the true number of times I've had to listen to the grievances and complaints of those 375 bizarre people who call day after day after day? It's a figure I don't even want to try enumerating.

I've spent seven years rummaging through the files in this

cabinet. And during that time, I've given counsel to each of these ridiculous people three to four times a week. Sometimes I even get drinks with them. How much is my monthly paycheck, you ask? I do get paid a little, but it's barely a smidgen. Most of my income actually comes from a different source. You might not believe me, but I'm actually a normal office worker at a publicly owned company. So, why do I do this? Is it an odd hobby or some form of volunteer work? No, I'm not lucky enough to do that. Then why? Is it because I derive some sense of meaning from helping others? I'd rather jump off a cliff.

Then why? Well, it just sort of happened. One percent of it was the fault of my foolish curiosity, and the other ninety-nine percent was the fault of my wretched bad luck. You might say I was caught in a sort of boobytrap. But the backstory is so involved, so unlucky, that I'll have to tell you about it in the next chapter.

O, SING IN ME, HMS PRINCE WILLIAM, OF THAT AFTERNOON'S BOREDOM

It was boredom that brought me together with Cabinet 13. In fact, I was so desperately bored that I even gave my boredom a nickname. I called it an I-would-rather-eat-dog-treats-than-suffer-this-boredom boredom. Indeed, it was a truly impressive boredom, one to which any creature, from dogs and cats to cows and horses, would throw up their hands (or front legs, I guess) in surrender.

Back then, all I did was sit quietly in the corner of my office, staring out the window like an ornamental plant. For six long months, that was all I did. If someone had actually given me a dog treat, I really would have eaten it. I was bored. Bored beyond words. So mind-numbingly bored.

I work at a research center affiliated with a publicly owned company (we'll call it Y). Whenever I say this, people tend to ask with a slightly surprised expression, "Oh, are you a researcher or a professor?" When this happens, I quickly and honestly answer, "No, I organize documents and files at the lab. It's essentially administrative work." Quickly and honestly. That's critical. If I don't correct them quickly and honestly, by the time the conversation is done, things become uncomfortable and awkward. It's hard to describe, but it's almost like they feel they've been lied to and I feel like I've been insulted.

Of course, this is the unavoidable inferiority complex that comes with working at a research center as a non-researcher. Still, I think people must understand that not everyone at the hospital is a doctor and not everyone in the air force is a fighter pilot. In order for fighter jets to fly straight and not end up in a random field with a farmer laughing at them, someone has to properly replace those big wheels, wipe down the jet, tighten the bolts, and top off the fuel. There also needs to be someone down on the tarmac furiously waving two flags. That jets need more than just a pilot to fly; that there needs to be someone doing the dirty work behind the scenes for everything to go smoothly; that this is the world we live in – these are the things I wish people would understand. That is, when dealing with others, we should treat people as individuals and not rely on common stereotypes. In my opinion, this is the first step toward mature and meaningful human relations. Take for example the following conversation between two people who respect each other:

"Where do you work?"

"At a hospital."

"Do you find your work enjoyable?"

"Sometimes. I work in the radiology department as a radiographer. I guess you could say I find enjoyment in peering inside people."

"The enjoyment of peering inside people? Well, isn't that interesting."

"Did you know that we have cavities inside our bodies?"

"You don't say? I've never heard that before."

"It's true. Your body is absolutely teeming with empty cavities, and no two people are the same. I get to peek into those cavities. Sometimes when I see those cavities, I think to myself, 'I bet that's where people store their most private possessions.'"

"Fascinating."

"And secretive."

"If you have a chance, will you look at my secret cavities?"

"I would like that. Just stop by sometime. I'll give you the deluxe package. All strictly confidential, of course."

Forgive me if I don't follow this conversation to the end; it was getting quite erotic. Anyway, wasn't this conversation so very friendly, amiable, profound, and somewhat decadent? Whether or not you think it was vulgar, you must agree that it has real potential for further developments. This shows how beautiful our world can be made by going beyond perfunctory etiquette and having a bit of fundamental respect for other human beings. The conversations I encounter on the regular, however, are not so wonderful. They usually go like this:

"Where do you work?"

"I work at a hospital."

(*Somewhat surprised*) "Are you a doctor?"

(*Somewhat flustered*) "No, I'm not a doctor."

(*Somewhat disappointed*) "Oh... then what do you...?"

"I work in the X-ray room. So, I'm just an X-ray technician. One that mindlessly takes digital images with X-rays all day."

(*Now visibly disappointed*) "How... interesting."

(*Rubbing foot into the ground, unsure what to say*) "The weather's been dreary lately, hasn't it?"

(*Changing the subject back to professions*) "Do X-ray photographers make a lot of money?"

(*A bit astonished by the forwardness*) "Well, it's nothing to write home about. If you don't make sacrifices, it can be hard to get by."

(*Now having lost all interest*) "Everyone's having a rough time these days. You, me – we're all hurting with the economy the way it is. But I heard specialists make at least 5 million a month?"

"Probably. Those people *are* specialists, after all."

Do you see any potential for further developments in this conversation? I think it's as good as done. She's going to soon forget the dry conversation she had with this uninteresting radiographer who's struggling to get by, and he thinks she's just a shallow woman. This is like so many of the innumerable, pointless, and tedious encounters in this city.

I'm not a researcher, but against very stiff competition I was the highest scoring candidate out of 137 other applicants. Don't misunderstand me, though; I'm not trying to say that the test was as difficult as something like the bar or the CPA. Indeed, if someone expressed doubt that a job as mediocre as mine would be that competitive, I would have to concede, "You're right. I am mediocre." And I could say this without a sliver of doubt.

But to get this job I had to suffer in my own way. I went back and forth like a busy ant between my small one-room apartment and the handful of cram schools I attended; I even developed irritable bowel syndrome from all the miserable food I ate at the student buffet halls. What's more, because there aren't any bathrooms in the cram school center where I could comfortably relieve myself, I suffered from chronic constipation. And no different from any other anemic and malnourished unemployed college graduate, I too was obsessed with hiring rates and felt a sense of dread every time the news reported on the unemployment rate in South Korea. But as a foolish young adult in a pitiful situation and with no connections, the only thing I could do (and the only thing I knew how to do) was sit on my fat ass and wait all summer and winter. But it was what it was. And in my opinion, while some might think the job I eventually landed isn't that impressive, it wasn't something that I got by doing nothing.

So, regardless of what other people thought, when I got the job I cheered as though I had passed the bar exam. And when I learned that this was the type of stable job that I wouldn't be fired from as long as I didn't cause a disaster at the first office party, I really did feel a sense of destiny as though this was the job for me. The only things in my life that ever went right were things that only went right because of dumb luck; but now I had finally accomplished something. In fact, I was so overcome with joy that I even cried. I was now eligible for the national pension, health insurance, and the general income tax; I was now someone who paid attention when the news started talking about boring things like tax deductions, unemployment insurance, and the five-day work week. Coming from that black hole of a life when every day was a holiday, I welcomed this change. Seeing the money from my paycheck go to things like utilities at the end of every month, I even giddily thought to myself that I must be more frugal. I had now become a respectable member of the workforce.

But trouble always comes from where you least expect it. My problem was that my office didn't give me any work. In Korea, where everyone works themselves to the bone before leaving the office in low spirits, complaining about not having enough work must sound to some like bragging. But working a job that has no work to be done is mind-numbing and exhausting in its own way. At the time, all the work I had to do was as follows: At 9:30 am a truck loaded with lab supplies arrives; the truck driver unloads the supplies and hands me some paperwork; as I receive the papers, I engage in small talk, asking about sports or the weather; they're not demanding topics, and the truck driver gives me equally cursory responses; after checking that the number of supplies on the sheet match the number of supplies from the truck, I stamp the papers; then I plod back to my office, sit down in front of my computer, and record the data into my computer. All of this would take less than ten minutes. And then I was done. You mean, done with your morning work, right? No, done with my work for the entire day.

At first, I thought things would change once my probation ended. But as the first month passed and then the second, there was no change in my workload. I spent all day just sitting in my chair. I was an ornamental plant. And the more time that passed, the more anxious I became. Everyone else was busily working at their desks, although I had no way of knowing *what* exactly they were doing. As for me, I just stared vacantly at the ceiling or the fluorescent lights or the fly carcasses on the windowsill. Sometimes I played with my ballpoint pen: I would spin it with my fingers, take it apart, marvel at how simple the construction was, pull the ink cartridge out with my teeth, put the whole thing back together, start pressing the button like a madman, then spin the pen around my fingers again ad infinitum. Occasionally I would have to crawl around my desk looking for the spring when it suddenly ejected from the pen as I took it apart. And if someone called my name at the inopportune moment, I would shoot up from underneath my desk as if I had been caught doing something wrong, and call back to them in a voice that was probably too loud.

I started looking for things to read when the anxiety that people might start to notice became too much to bear. I read things like schematics for a new pipeline or design proposals for new driver's licenses – random documents that I found somewhere and which also served the purpose of covering my embarrassingly empty desk. A couple of people gave me suspicious looks when they saw what I was reading, but this only made me feel like I needed to read more. I started reading articles like "The Effects of Primary School Classroom Gender Ratios on the Sexual Identity of Young Boys" or "Comparing Average Square Footage of Apartments in Gangbuk and Gangnam" or "The Correlation between the Number of Feral Cats and the Number of Traffic Accidents in Cities." A few days later, however, a woman came to my desk saying, "You shouldn't take someone else's papers without permission. I was looking everywhere for these!" When she finished lightly reprimanding me, she took her papers back and left.

No one gave me any work and no one took any interest in me. I could have voluntarily asked if there wasn't something more I could be doing, but if I was going to ask that, I should have done so within the first week. It would have been a bit ridiculous for me to ask for more work after spending an entire month doing nothing. *You'll get more work when the time comes. There's no way they'd keep giving you a paycheck like this.* At least, that's what I told myself. And just like that, the second month went by. When I received my second paycheck, my anxiety had reached its limit.

"According the management system, we have no work for you, Mr Kong. I'm sorry to tell you this, but I think it best you submit your resignation."

This is what I was afraid they might say to me. I imagined all types of scenarios before one day carefully approaching my section chief, Mr Kim, as he drank coffee in the lounge. I thought he of all people would understand.

"Hey, Mr Kim, is there something more I can be doing?"

Section Chief Kim peered through his glasses and stared at me for a moment.

"Is something wrong?"

I confided in him everything that I was going through. I grumbled and mumbled as I told him about my concerns and about what I had been doing for the past two months at the office: how I wasn't doing anything at the office; how I was a good person whose motto was to always be sincere; how I was embarrassed for receiving a paycheck despite having done nothing; how I thought this was such an immoral way to spend one's youth. I even rhetorically said things that were more like philosophical questions to myself than actual questions – things like: What does it mean to '"feel alive"? Who am I and where am I? What does the company expect of me? You don't think they made a mistake, do you? Perhaps they meant to buy a calendar or a coat hanger, but got me by mistake? It took a while, but eventually I confessed everything that was on my mind.

Section Chief Kim – whom I once saw make a face of deep, melancholic existential dread as if he were an unlucky man who had spent the last ten years wandering from one cramped

one-room apartment to the next; as if he had failed to pass the
bar exam despite making it past the first round three times; as
if he often stared out the window and wondered if this place
was right for him, if it wasn't in the courthouse wearing a black
robe and holding a wooden mallet where he truly belonged –
looked like a man who could understand my plight. But after
listening to my confession, he simply scoffed at me.

"Don't try too hard, kiddo. Relax a little. You gotta think
about 'quality of life.'"

Oh! How could I forget? Yes, quality of life! Of all things,
this is the advice he had for me. But that wasn't all, he also
went on about how we Koreans have been trying so hard for
so long. "There's never been a time in history when our people
have tried so hard." I guess it was a convincing argument,
but I still had no idea what that had to do with my situation.
He hadn't given me a satisfying response to my question – a
question which had taken so much courage to ask – so, I asked
it one more time.

"But since I'm getting a paycheck, shouldn't I at least be
doing something?"

Section Chief Kim stared at me and gave me a look as if to
say, "Are you *that* dense?" But for the sake of this dense friend
of his, he kindly explained it again.

"Look, kid. We man our post; that's what we do here. And
besides, manning one's post is hard work depending on how
you look at it."

And he was right. There was absolutely nothing to do here,
despite how big this office building was and despite how many
documents there were. In simple terms, there was nothing else
to do but faithfully man one's post. Clock in before 9 am; clock
out after 6 pm; work late two days at the end of each month
to settle accounts (something which I dare not pretend was
difficult work for fear I might be stoned to death by this city's

salarymen); and man my post – this was the extent of my job responsibilities. That's what my boss does, that's what Section Chief Kim does, that's what everyone else here does. In other words, we man our posts! And if we man our posts, we get our paychecks. You must be saying to yourself, "No way! What kind of job is that?" But that is what we do here. It wasn't until I came here that I learned that such jobs exist in Korea. Another thing I learned while working here is that there are actually lots of jobs like this in the world; you just don't hear about them often because it's hush-hush.

There are places where there's a lot of tedious work, and there are places where there's absolutely no tedious work whatsoever. Not only do stable jobs have no work, you also get frequent bonuses from (what I guess is) taxpayer money. Didn't I jump with joy, you ask? No. To be quite honest, my reaction was something akin to disappointment.

Just manning my post was difficult. At first, I felt anxious, worried, and nervous, but now that I was relaxing and not doing anything, it truly felt like I had become an ornamental plant. One day, Department Head Song suggested I get a hobby. In fact, he was currently into assembling model ships himself – Half Moons, to be exact, which according to him were sailboats from the sixteenth century; Section Chief Kim (who I thought had been working hard in that corner of his) actually spent his time reading up to five trashy martial arts novels every day, and Ms Park surfed the internet, made paper cranes, and chatted with the other women from General Affairs... As for me, I just mindlessly endured.

I endured for six long months sitting by the windowsill and staring out at the three trees – a chestnut tree, a cherry blossom tree, and a maple tree – which took turns blooming. Actually, I wasn't "enduring"; I was simply and mindlessly staring out the window as the time passed. I watched how the trees changed with the seasons. And at night I would open the window and taste the smell of sperm emanating from the chestnut trees as I imagined lewd things. One time I counted how many bungeo-ppang the couple across the street sold in a single day: 752. I thought they must be rich. Back then, things were so surreal.

Sometimes I would lean my head against the window frame which was warm from the sunlight shining down on it and think to myself, "Is this how I'm going to spend my youth? Why is the song of my youth so desolate? Must I live my life in such utter frivolity and mediocrity? Why did such unwelcome misfortune befall *me* of all people? Do the citizens of this city pay their taxes knowing that I'm living like this?"

My soul was as empty as a dry cornstalk in late autumn. They say life should be a battle, so how could I mindlessly go through life like this? Day after day I idled around, and day after day I became more and more tired. By the sixth month, I got used to my job and would go with Section Chief Kim to the cafeteria for bus and cab drivers to have drinks and eat pork duruchigi. Afterwards, being too drowsy from the alcohol to last through the afternoon, we would go to the 24-hour sauna across from the lab, where I would sometimes run into Department Head Song. And when that happened, Department Head Song and I would chummily enter the Russian-style wet sauna together and have awkward conversations while seated on scalding hot rocks:

"I must be having liver problems. I'm always tired these days,"

"Me too. I wake up and don't feel rested,"

"I'll try to give you less work."

Then, when we got out of the sauna, we would plop into the ice baths to cool off our bodies. After that we went to our own rooms and consummated our idle afternoon by taking a long nap. When we finally returned to the lab, it would be time to stamp our timecards and go home.

The research center was always devoid of people. The PIs never showed their faces and graduate students only came to the lab to get things that had been delivered there or on some other useless errand. They would cook ramen in the lab, play a game of foot volleyball in the courtyard, and marvel at how well kept the field was. Weirdly enough, the only thing that was operating in a normal fashion at this research center was the foot volleyball court.

I would sometimes be overwhelmed with anxiety. Was it OK that I was living like this? There was a time I had tried hard, and while I maybe wasn't as hard-working as other students, I still tried my best to suffer like everyone else. More than anything else I was bored. But this wasn't what I had signed up for. I wanted life to be at least a bit of a struggle.

I thought about looking for another job. But in the end I never did look up other employment opportunities or send my resumé. I never wanted to go back there – to the cram schools, the library, the vocational schools in Noryangjin, the classrooms where ridiculous lecturers would stand with microphones as they told us how important it was to memorize the exact height of Seokgatap Pagoda. I didn't have the confidence. Beating out 137 other applicants and getting this job was nothing short of a miracle. I knew for certain that a miracle like that wasn't going to happen twice. So I just stayed put.

And life passed like that for a while. Department Head Song completed one model sailboat and challenged himself to a model of the HMS *Prince William*, an extremely long boat with three large sails that was built in 1665. Because I didn't have any hobbies of my own, I would either help Department Head Song with putting glue on his model ships or play FreeCell before returning back to my nest near the window. Section Chief Kim, who was sitting next to me, looked at the department head's boat from several angles before saying, "How about building the *Titanic*?" To which Mr Song replied, "Modern ship designs are too simple. They're not elaborate enough for me." After nodding his head, Mr Kim stared into the fish tank with its two vivacious goldfish and four somewhat lifeless tropical fish for the next two hours before finally and suddenly muttering to himself, "Maybe I should read a collection of world classics."

It was around this time that I first discovered Cabinet 13. I can't quite remember why it was that I went up to the fourth floor where there was nothing but empty offices, or why it was that I walked to the file room at the end of the hallway on the fourth floor. Maybe there wasn't a specific reason. People do all sorts of strange things when they're bored. Technically I was the assistant manager charged with the safekeeping of those cabinets. But because the cabinets were unable to move from their corner, and because barely anyone used them, the cabinets were safe enough without me. In fact, I thought it a bit silly that they would use the term "safekeeping" for such old cabinets.

What made me interested in Cabinet 13 specifically was the fact that it was the only one that had a shabby old four-digit lock guarding its contents. That lock intrigued me. I couldn't help but feel the urge to unlock it. Was I into lockpicking at the time? No. Like prisoners who obsess over useless things, I just needed something to which to devote my time.

I spent several hours every day dialing numbers into that lock. From 0000 to 9999. But it wasn't difficult. I only had to close my eyes and file through ten-thousand numbers. Fortunately for me the passcode was 7863, so I only had to try 7864 numbers before it opened.

The cabinet door opened with a creak and I stared inside. The inside of the cabinet was packed from top to bottom with a hodgepodge of documents, including everything from medical records to questionnaires for depression and alcoholism. I took one file from the middle and dusted it off. And, without really thinking much about it, I sat down and started reading the file. I wasn't that interested in random medical records, but seeing as I had spent so much time getting the cabinet open, I thought I might as well see what all the fuss was about.

Chimera-7 Lizard
The doctors had concluded that the woman's aphasia was due to psychological factors. However, the real reason she

couldn't talk was because a lizard was growing inside her mouth. From when she was young, the woman was fond of lizards. She believed that she was in possession of lizard-like traits. And as time went on, she eventually began to identify with lizards.

When she turned 20, the woman started raising a Sphaerodactylus ariasae *in her mouth. First discovered on an island in the Dominican Republic,* Sphaerodactylus ariasae *are the world's smallest lizards, measuring only 16mm in length from head to tail.*

When eating, the woman chewed carefully so she wouldn't crush the lizard between her molars or accidentally swallow it with the food. The lizard grew like a weed in the girl's mouth. And every day the girl cut a small portion from the bottom of her tongue with a knife. She did this both to give the lizard more room and to provide it with nutrients. Eventually, the lizard left the space beneath the girl's tongue and began to burrow into the actual root of her tongue.

Little by little, the lizard ate away at the girl's tongue. And because of this, the girl's pronunciation began to change, eventually sounding like a foreign language to others. And all the while, the lizard's cave continued to deepen. As the cave became deeper, the girl's tongue got smaller, eventually becoming an unnatural thing. Once nothing was left of the girl's tongue, the lizard stuck its tail deep into what had been the girl's tongue root and started acting as a prosthetic tongue.

The girl's body craved the foods she used to eat, but the girl's tongue (the lizard, that is) craved the juices of rotting insect carcasses, grubs, and other beasts. And because the girl's palate was now determined by the lizard, the girl had to eat what her tongue desired.

Because all of this developed slowly over a long time, the girl did not think she had become a monster. In fact, she loved her lizard-turned-tongue. Her lizard-turned-tongue, or, rather, her tongue-turned-lizard was not used to language.

So, when the girl talked and flicked her tongue around, it was only natural for the lizard to be thrashed about in her mouth. Realizing this, the girl started to keep her mouth shut. And slowly, she began to lose her language. Because she neither needed to talk nor wanted to talk, and because she was afraid people would kill her and her lizard if they found out a human was colluding with a lizard, she lived out her life never opening her mouth again.

Recorded in detail in this thick file was a timeline of how the lizard merged with the girl's tongue. And in the margins was a chart mapping the genetic sequences for reptiles and mammals, several words like "chimera" and "hybrid species", and some notes about the possibility of combining reptiles with mammals.

After a while, I put the file back where I had found it. The first thing to escape my mouth was this:

"Jesus Christ."

My body shook and I felt disgusted that a human would do that to their own body. Even if it was all made up, I thought it disgusting that someone would even imagine such a thing. I quickly got up and left the file room in a sour mood.

The next afternoon, however, I returned to the file room. I opened Cabinet 13 and took out another file to read. Again, my body shook as I felt a sense of disgust and hatred; I cursed some more, too, regrettably. But even so, by the next day, I found myself back in the file room. And again, I took another file out to read. Something about it was addicting.

As time passed, my sense of disgust and hatred subsided. Perhaps I was getting used to the feeling. There were also several times that I felt pity and sadness while reading the files. The stories contained in the files were captivating. They were interesting, unique, utterly impossible, and, most important of all, they didn't have the stench of administrative work. I went up to the file room on the fourth floor whenever I had a free afternoon. And there in the file room with its whirring ceiling fan, I would smoke a cigarette underneath the DO NOT SMOKE sign as I spent all afternoon leaning against the cabinet and reading files. The more I read, the more I got sucked into the cabinet's world. At least it was better than chewing on dog treats.

"I can't talk anymore," the woman with a lizard for a tongue wrote down on a piece of paper.

"Does it hurt?" I asked.

"Not really," the girl indicated by shrugging her shoulders.

"Would you show me your tongue?"

"I don't want to frighten you."

"I'll be fine."

"Don't use a flashlight. You'll scare it. Just look with your eyes."

"I'll be careful."

The woman slowly opened her mouth. And quietly staring at me from inside the damp, crimson darkness near the back of her throat, were a pair of glowing reptilian eyes.

TORPORER

Torporers sleep for abnormally long periods of time. They can sleep anywhere from two months to two years, not eating anything or waking up once. Some prefer to use the term hibernator instead of torporer, but this is a bit inaccurate, as torporers don't necessarily sleep in the winter. They can sleep and wake whenever they desire, be it spring, summer, autumn, or winter. And, needless to say, because they're not bears, they don't make dens or store fat for the winter. You might be wondering if I'm talking about cryogenic sleep. To that I can only say, no; they sleep just like the rest of us. You know, with a blanket and pillow.

Hibernation traditionally refers to the several-week-long sleep that lizards and snakes enter into by drastically lowering their body temperature to reduce energy consumption. In contrast to this, torpor refers to the winter-long sleep that warm-blooded animals like bears and racoons are able to accomplish with their reserves of fat. The sleep that torporers enter into is unlike either torpor (because they don't require large fat reserves) or hibernation (because instead of drastically reducing their body temperature, they actually maintain a relatively high body temperature of 86° F as well as a high metabolism). It is still unclear scientifically exactly how it is these individuals' metabolisms are able to stay high for such long periods of time without regularly eating.

One thing that all torporers share in common is the fact

that, when they wake up, they are focused and full of energy, compassionate toward others, and more positive and optimistic. Their health also improves and those with diseases are either magically cured or markedly improved. And as torporers sleep, the waste and feces in their bodies is removed, and they become gaunt as they burn through fat. (I'm sure some of you are interested in how it is that their bodily waste is "removed," or how it is their body burns fat; but I think it best if you didn't ask about that. Besides, that's not really important right now, is it? If you really must know about how your body removes waste, I suggest you go see a doctor or a dietician. They will be able to answer all your questions.)

After torporers experience their first torpor, they will continue to regularly experience torpor. Thanks to this regularity, torporers are able to prepare in advance for each state of torpor. The problem is the first happening, which comes unannounced. Because of its unexpected nature, all sorts of strange things can happen during one's first torpor.

Mr Gwak lives in Bonghwa, North Gyeongsang province, and grows specialty crops in greenhouses. One day, while taking a nap in a large Styrofoam box in the attic where he stores seeds, Mr Gwak suddenly fell into his first torpor. He was in that state for 97 days. A few days into his sleep, however, the areas of Bonghwa, Yeongju, and Chunyang were flooded by a large storm; many people drowned or went missing. His family waited for three months before declaring him dead and holding a funeral. They even prepared a cenotaph. But then on the night after his funeral while his family was eating, Mr Gwak suddenly awoke from his torpor and came down from the attic. "Hey, you should have woken me up if you were going to eat. I was dying of hunger." These nonchalant words fell on Mr Gwak's family as they stared at him in utter disbelief.

When they aren't in torpor, torporers sleep just like anybody else – going to bed at night and waking up in the morning for work. Personally, when I first learned this, I thought it was quite odd. If they sleep eight hours a day on top of regular states of abnormally long slumber, wouldn't that mean they spend most of their life sleeping? When I asked this question to a torporer, they gave me a very matter-of-fact answer: "But not sleeping at night is bad for your skin." I guess they're not wrong.

In this day and age when time is money, being a torporer can be a real nuisance. But for some it can also be a blessing. Take Mr Hur, a CEO at a gas machinery manufacturer:

"The deadline for making a deal was fast approaching. It was a contract for supplying manufacturing parts to the last unsigned plant in the Middle Eastern market; the fate of our company was hanging in the balance. I'm not exaggerating when I say that if we closed the deal we would survive, and if we didn't, I would have no other choice than to disband our company. At the time, everything was a mess because of the Asian financial crisis. At first, I would work two or three days without sleeping, come home and sleep a little, and then start all over again by working late another two or three days. But then, one day, I wasn't able to sleep anymore. I was up to my ears in work. And my relationship with my employees was starting to fray. I was irritated. I lashed out at people, picked fights, and was always grumpy. My workers weren't on the same page like I wanted them to be. They didn't seem to care. But, even so, I still thought it was *our* company, not *my* company. So, regardless of how big or small it was, whenever there was excess revenue, I would give it to my employees in the form of incentives. Despite what people might say, I wasn't just in it for myself. Of course, my employees had it tough, too. Working all those hours, there's no way they couldn't have had a hard time. But when your company's in a life or death situation, everyone has to band together. And at the same time, when the company's in crisis, it's also every man and woman for themself. I was overcome with stress. I couldn't sleep some nights. And slowly I found myself sleeping less and less. My body was as heavy as lead, but strangely enough, when I lay down, I couldn't fall asleep. It was like there was a leaky faucet somewhere inside my head. And there were many times when my body felt like it belonged to someone else."

"What came of the contract?"

"We didn't get it. I heard the company that got the deal was a joint venture that used technical support from England and manufactured its parts directly in Vietnam. We were completely outmatched in both technology and price. I had the ability to avoid bankruptcy if I made some sacrifices, but I couldn't get rid of this nagging feeling inside me that it was all for nothing. So, one day when I returned home from work, I thought to myself, "Why go on living like this?" Things weren't so desperate that I contemplated suicide, but seeing my empty house (after my divorce, my ex-wife took the kids and ran off to Australia), my life felt so devoid of warmth. So I packed my suitcase. I had a mountain villa that I had bought for fishing trips a while back. It wasn't anything luxurious, just a cozy cabin. That's where I went. And I took with me ten jugs of pesticide. I lit a candle in this spider-infested cabin and began to cry. I've never cried so much in my life. It felt like I was shedding every last tear I had in me. I cried so much that I eventually cried myself into exhaustion. There was pile of straw in one corner of the shed, so I went there and fell asleep. For 172 days."

"172 days. Not hours?"

"Yes, precisely 172 days. I went there in early summer, and when I came out, it was winter."

"And how was your body?"

"I felt revitalized. Like I had been reborn. I was a little thin, of course, but nothing extreme. So I returned to civilization.

And, when I returned, everything was a mess. But what else would you expect? Leaving so irresponsibly like that, without telling anyone. But I was able to start anew. I was in a really bad situation financially, but I was so happy to just be alive, to be working again."

"I've heard rumors that you've amassed another fortune. Is this true?"

"Oh, that? It's nothing. Just enough to put bread on the table. Oh, and I almost forgot to mention! I got back together with my wife not long ago. I flew down to Australia and stayed at a shabby hotel for a month begging her to get back together with me. Can you believe that? Haha."

Just as bears and snakes enter a deep sleep to get through harsh seasons, torporers usually enter a state of torpor when they face a crisis. And they come out of their torpor rejuvenated. Still not quite understanding what a torpor state was, I asked a question.

"Before you enter a deep sleep, do you prepare anything? Do you pack on weight like a bear?"

The man scoffed when I asked this. He was a veteran torporer, having experienced several different states of torpor and lived as a torporer for about six years.

"It's important that we're well fed when we enter torpor, but we don't need to eat as much as a bear. We do need, however, to prepare dreams."

"Dreams?"

"It was after waking up from my second state of torpor that I realized this. I was so bored the first two times when I went in without any preparation. You don't notice it when you only sleep several hours a day, but when you sleep for three to four months at a time, you become lucid in your dreams. And when that happens, it's reality that becomes dream-like. Anyway, it's a real bore if you don't have material for dreams.

I bet the afterlife isn't much different. It's a world formed by one's imagination, after all. There, happiness and power come from imagination. But when I first went into a state of torpor blindly, I hadn't prepared anything, so I was a little bored."

"Can't you just do it in the dream? After all, it is *your* imagination."

"Easier said than done, Mr Kong. We all live very busy lives. So, when we dream for long periods of time, there isn't much to do. We torporers all ask ourselves at one point, 'I can't believe I don't know how to dream a dream. What kind of life have I been living to not be able to imagine a good dream?' And because everything in a dream happens so quickly, thirty years in a dream can take minutes out in the real world. Of course, there are times when short periods of time are drawn out for extended periods of time in a dream, too. Anyway, in order to dream a dream, you need material for a dream."

"So how do you get material for a dream?"

"Read old journals, peruse picture albums, meet with old school friends and old girlfriends. You know, people you don't see that often. Remember and think about things that happened a long time ago. Recently I've been reading a lot of books. The more enjoyable the things you imagine, the happier your dreams are and the happier you are after waking up."

I like to think I'd be a good torporer. I enjoy sleep, and I hate getting up. In fact, just once I want to dive into that swamp known as torpor. If only I didn't run the risk of getting fired from my job, losing my paycheck and insurance, seeing my savings disappear, and hearing my friends and family judgmentally say, "What are you doing with your life?" I would happily forget everything and fall into a deep sleep for six months. But torporers say many people cannot experience torpor because they care too much about unimportant things.

"If you want to experience torpor you have to be willing to do one of two things: you either have to be fine with everything going to hell, or you have to have a devil-may-care attitude and be bold enough to act completely irresponsibly. You'll never be able to achieve torpor worrying about every little thing that comes your way."

Perhaps they're right. Perhaps the reason we can't fall into a deep sleep despite always being exhausted is because we don't have the courage to risk losing everything, the courage to act irresponsibly.

"Modern people cannot fall into a deep sleep. Ever since the invention of electricity and the emergence of monolithic cities, the modern night has fallen into a state of constant unrest. In my opinion, the most lasting legacy of capitalism will be angst. Insurance, stocks, real estate, investments... The entire modern economy is based on anxiety, and, as everyone knows, anxiety is the mortal enemy of a good night's sleep. And insomnia only leads to more anxiety – it's a vicious cycle. Thus, we are always anxious, internally and externally. Conversely, primitive humans were much more spiritual beings. They worked when the sun was out, and they dreamed and rested once it set. In other words, in order to live properly, you have to follow divine providence and live half your life working, and the other half dreaming."

"You mean to say, all I need to do is sleep when it's dark out...?"

"I went to sleep, and when I woke there was nothing. My bank account, my stocks – gone. I had been fired from my job, and my wife had left me. My life was in complete shambles. Now what do I do?"

"Go to sleep again. Only then will your life start anew."

DOPPELGANGER

"Where did you two meet?"

"We met in Sillim market. I was on my way back from a haejang-guk restaurant. I like their ox blood soup. I often go there to eat. Their soup is unique. I'm not sure how to describe it. It's a little pungent and a bit fishy. You also get the strong taste of blood from the boiled ox blood; it's even a little gamey. You either like it or you absolutely hate it. I guess it's a place only for enthusiasts. I once saw a girl take two sips before spitting it out onto the floor, but I don't think it's *that* bad. The old lady who owns the restaurant has a sailor's mouth and is as stubborn as a rock. When customers complain about it tasting fishy, she tells them, 'Then why come to a place that serves boiled ox blood? Just stay at home and eat cucumbers if you don't like it.'"

"You two must have run into each other often, seeing as how you're both regulars."

"Oh, no. That was my first time, actually. I was just exiting the restaurant and turning the corner when I saw him. He was going right into the restaurant as I was leaving. He looked so attractive from the side. It's not often that you feel so strongly attracted to someone at first sight, you know? You might think I'm the type of guy who will go into a public bathroom with just anyone, but I'm not like that. I can feel love too. But it's hard to find someone you're attracted to more than just sexually. That's why I followed him."

"Do you often follow men like that?"

"Yes, sometimes. But if I'm not at a gay bar or the like, I don't approach them. You can get punched doing that. I want to, but I don't. Anyway, I followed him because I didn't want to miss out. Even if just to observe him from far away."

"I see–"

"Have you ever felt attracted to the same sex? Gay or not, I think we've all experienced it at least once."

"Never."

The man began to blush a bit at my curt response.

"It's not that I'm offended by it. It's just that I've never had that experience..." I added.

"Yes, I understand. It's fine."

"Anyway, continue your story. What happened after you followed him?"

"I sat behind him and watched him as he ate ox blood soup. He was my type of man: slight and bashful from behind. The slope of his shoulders looked so forlorn. I just wanted to give him a hug."

"Were you sitting close to him?"

"About fifteen meters? Maybe ten? I can't quite remember. It wasn't particularly close. Anyway, I watched him until he finished the ox blood soup and got up. But then..."

"But then...?"

"But then he turned around. And there I was, staring back at myself. His face was the same as mine. At first, I wondered if I had discovered my long-lost twin. But no, he was me, not my twin. I could tell just by looking at him."

"That must have been a real shock."

"Oh, it was."

"Did you say anything?"

"No, not at first. In order to calm myself down, I went outside and waited until he came out. My legs were trembling. I smoked two cigarettes to calm my nerves. He came out when I was about halfway through the second cigarette. Standing in the doorway of the restaurant he just stared at me. He must have been quite shocked himself because he stood there frozen in place. So, the two of us just stood there staring at one another. We must have stood there for ten minutes. And I had this thought: If I were him, what would I say in this situation? If I were to experience such a strange thing, what would be the first thing I would say?"

"So? what did he say?"

"He stammered and stuttered as he said, 'Hi, my name's Ok Myeong-guk.' Haha! He looked so ridiculous. It looked so unnatural, but it also looked quite fitting. After that, I stepped closer to him and gave him a hug. It felt right, like touching a part of your own body: comforting and warm."

"You didn't keep hugging like that in the middle of the market, did you?"

"Of course not. We stopped hugging and went to a nearby café. At the cashier, he ordered the exact same drink in the exact same way I do. 'One lip-burning espresso.'"

"Don't espressos usually burn your lips?"

"Yes, but he used that exact expression to order. 'One lip-burning espresso.'"

"And what about his life? Is it the same as yours?"

"Actually, quite similar. He's a chef."

"But aren't you an architect?"

"Those two aren't similar?"

"You think they are?"

"I do."

"Well, I guess you could say that. But since you have different jobs, you two must be leading lives that are at least a little different, no?"

"I'm not sure. Sometimes I imagine the roads I haven't taken and think about the other lives I could have had. But the more I talked to him, the more I realized that, despite the many ways our lives differed, there was no fundamental difference between us. He was working a different job and living a different life on the outside, but underneath that, we were leading basically the same life. Our hobbies were the same, our tastes in food were the same, we even do the same things after work... I can't explain in detail what that is exactly, but I think it's enough just to say they're the same."

"Did you feel disappointed that your lives were similar?"

"No, quite the opposite, actually. I'm not sure why, but it was somewhat comforting. Neither his life nor mine is that grand, but the more I learned about his life, the more I felt like my own wasn't such an utter failure after all. But I don't know why. Anyway, after we left the café, we went to a love hotel – where we made love, of course. It was at once both great and odd. It felt like I was being loved. It was the kind of sex in which you can understand why you're having sex with that person. Warm, natural, respectful sex. After that, I stopped going to public bathrooms. I'm even considering getting married now. It's possible. Seeing as he's married, I might be able to get married, too."

"Have you met since then?"

"No. I go to that haejang-guk restaurant every Saturday, but since then I haven't seen him there even once. I called the phone number on his business card and I even tried visiting the address he gave me, but neither of them existed. I doubt he was carrying around fake business cards. But I don't know what else it could be."

He showed me the business card. According to the card, the man was head chef at a Japanese restaurant. Looking at the card, I wondered to myself if this man really looked like a Japanese chef. To be honest, he didn't in the slightest. But perhaps that was because he looked just like the man sitting in front of me, a man whom I knew to be an architect.

"We fell asleep together in the same bed, but in the morning, it was I who woke up first. When I got up, I looked for quite some time at the sight of myself, no, the sight of him sleeping. To be honest, I don't really like how I look. I never stare at myself in a mirror for long. I look so small and ugly in the mirror. I guess I have a bit of an inferiority complex. Maybe that's why I don't get a lot of attention at gay bars. But the sight of him sleeping was – how should I say it – very lovable. I looked like the type of person you might not consider particularly attractive, but whom you would still consider acceptable. The type of face that looked harmlessly warm and friendly, despite not being terribly beautiful. I thought to myself that I should live my life to the fullest because someone else was out there doing their best to live part of my life for me. I thought to myself that my life wasn't that bad. I thought to myself: my sense of existence had become small – and that that sense of existence was enough. I started thinking all sorts of complicated thoughts."

As he paused, I didn't say anything.

"When he awoke, we kissed long and passionately, as if we were lovers. And before we each left for work, we exchanged contact information. But I haven't been able to see him even once since then. And you know what's weird? Even though I'm left-handed, he was right-handed."

"Is that really that strange?"

"Is it not? I'm left-handed; why would he be right-handed? All of our appearances and preferences were the same. So, sometimes I get the feeling that one of us is a fake. That is, one of us is an illusion. Worst of all, I'm afraid the fake might be me. I could be the left-handed image he sees in the mirror each morning."

"Why did this happen?"

"I'm not quite sure."

"Is this a blessing or a curse?"

"It's neither a blessing nor a curse. It's just something that exists in our lives. Like the wind and the trees."

PROFESSOR KWON

It was several years ago when I first met Professor Kwon. I arrived at work one day to see a memo posted on my desk. "Kong Deok-geun from Records, come to Room 311 at 11:00 am sharp! Don't be late." From the words "sharp" and "don't be late" the note had a stench of authority. Unsure what this strange message meant, I asked Department Head Song and Section Chief Kim about why an average administrative worker like me would be summoned to someone's lab. They both seemed uninterested and said they didn't know because something like this had never happened before. But when I mentioned it was Room 311, they both dropped their jaws and said simultaneously, "But that's Professor Kwon's office!"

"This doesn't look good for you," Mr Song said.

"You must have done something really bad," added Mr Kim.

"But I didn't do anything," I said defensively.

"Just think about it. Why else would someone like Professor Kwon summon you," Mr Song said.

"If you cross that geezer, he'll bust your head open. You know Department Head Kim, right? The one who got this job through connections? When he first arrived here, he went around 'inspecting the premises' and got his head busted open for acting flippantly in the professor's office. They say Professor Kwon hit him over the head with a cane. And not just once but three times. He had two V-shaped gashes in his head and had to get seventeen stitches," said Section Chief Kim, oddly excited.

"What exactly did he do?" I asked, quivering with unease.

"Nothing really. All he did was say hello and ask the professor how his research was going."

"He got his head busted open for that? And Department Head Kim just took it? Couldn't he get Professor Kwon fired with all his connections?"

"He said he was completely overwhelmed by the old man's cane. I heard he even went to Kwon's office to apologize and give him a present. Anyway, he's one eccentric old coot."

"He must be influential."

"There are a lot of stories and rumors about him. Some say he's the son of the CEO's second wife, a powerful woman who runs things from behind the scenes. Others say he's the illegitimate son of a chaebol family. But no one knows for sure. What's for certain is that he's one of the founding members of this research center," Mr Song said.

"There seems to be a theme of illegitimate births."

"That's because the old man doesn't have any family," said Mr Kim.

"But why do you think he wants to see me?"

"I really can't say. This has never happened before. Be careful. And wear a helmet if you want to keep your head on your shoulders," Mr Kim said flippantly.

Just before the clock hit eleven, I slowly went up to the third floor. Admittedly my legs were shaking a bit. Professor Kwon's room was at the very end of the hall. I stood in front of his office and carefully knocked on the door. From inside I could hear an irritated voice saying "Come in." The irritation in his voice made my muscles even tenser. I slowly opened the door. Sitting behind the desk was an old man with piercing eyes. He looked at me and motioned me over with his hand. Respectfully I followed his directions and approached his desk as humbly and politely as I could manage, making my body small like a cat. When I reached his desk, Professor Kwon looked toward the TV that was placed opposite his desk.

"Do you want to see something interesting?" Professor Kwon said in a calm voice.

As suggested, I turned to look at the TV and... My god. There on screen was footage of me squatting in front of a cabinet, chuckling to myself as I read files. A sudden hiccup came from my throat. I had never imagined that rundown file room would have a security camera. Professor Kwon spun the globe on his desk like a toy as he began speaking.

"Who sent you? I bet it was someone from the syndicate. Those guys have no honor."

"Syndicate?"

"So, you want to play dumb. You still don't understand what all this means, do you? It means both that you're going to jail and that you're going to go broke. Jail because you committed a criminal offence by giving away lab secrets, and broke because I'm going to sue you for the damages you caused when you gave away those lab secrets. You can't begin to imagine how much I'm going to sue you for."

At this moment, my vision started to blur. I was so flustered I couldn't understand what was happening to me. The only thing I could understand was the palpable taste of fear in my mouth. I started stammering and making incoherent excuses.

"I just... I had no intention of... I just... you see... I didn't have anything to do... and I was bored... that's what it was... I was so bored... That's all... Please believe me... I was bored, so I went to the sauna... and I tried to make model ships like Mr Song... but I've never been interested in model ships... I'm really sorry."

Professor Kwon looked wholly uninterested in my most sincere attempt at an apology.

"What were you trying to achieve by opening that cabinet? You spent an entire week on that lock. Normal people wouldn't obsess over a lock for a week unless they wanted what's inside.

And the way you picked the lock was just about the most foolish way I could imagine. Going through all ten thousand combinations one by one. What was your goal? Tell me now and maybe I won't call the police."

And so I confessed everything to the old man. Why I opened the cabinet; how bored I was at my job; how desolate a man's life could be made by boredom – I explained it all. I also explained that the reason for picking the lock was the same reason people did Rubik's Cubes: to overcome boredom. After listening to my story, Professor Kwon appeared deep in thought.

"How much did you read?" he finally asked.

"Very little... I only read–"

"I might look old, but I can still hurt you with this cane."

Hiccup!

"OK, I read it all. And I reread a few of the files. Several times."

"Which ones?"

"The one about the conjoined twin cremating her sibling, for example, and the one about the lizard lady."

"Why?"

"I'm not sure."

"Did you feel pity?"

"I'm not sure about pity, but I did feel a bit sad."

"You have access to all sorts of interesting things just by turning on your computer; so, why do you think you read those files locked away in a dusty cabinet?"

I wasn't able to answer this question. To be honest, I myself didn't know why it was that I read them or why it was that I had become so obsessed with a cabinet of files which ejected a flurry of dust every time you picked them up. It looked like Professor Kwon was thinking hard about something again. He might have been starting to think that what I was saying was believable. Feeling more confident, I continued:

"I might have read them, but I didn't tell anyone about them.

And I won't be telling anyone about them. I mean, why would I do such a strange thing like telling someone a ridiculous story about a woman with a lizard for a tongue. And even if I did try to tell someone, obviously no one would believe me. Yes, I'm just your average, hard-working young man. Besides, isn't it your fault for leaving such important documents in an unguarded file room?"

"Who said it was unguarded? You're the only person who has been able to get through my security system. Until now, it's had an untarnished record."

Professor Kwon spun the globe as he thought some more. After a few moments, he began again.

"How about this. I won't send you to jail. Besides, I get nothing out of sending you to jail, and squeezing money from a poor man like yourself won't be easy. In return, however, starting tomorrow morning, you'll come up here and do the chores I don't want to. I'll tell the director of the institute that I'm borrowing you."

"Excuse me?"

"Fuck, I hate people who make me repeat myself. Just come here every day starting tomorrow morning. Got it?"

"Like a research assistant?"

"You? A research assistant? Don't make me laugh. You'll be doing things like cleaning and answering the phone."

"What about my work?"

"You're joking right? Didn't you just say that you were bored because you didn't have any work to do downstairs? And everyone knows that people who work at this research institute have nothing to do. I bet you think you can sweet-talk your way out of this. You're saying to yourself, 'This old fool won't really send me to jail.' Maybe you're right. But since I don't like you, I could easily tell the director about all of this. If I do that, you'll be kicked out of here, at the very least. I may not look it, but I'm pretty influential. And if you get fired from here, you'll have to start looking for work again. That'll

be a shame. Jobs like this are hard to find. You know, ones that
are secure, well-paid, and relaxed because you don't have any
work."

"What in the world do you want from me?"

"You blockhead, haven't you been listening? All I want you
to do is to come up here every morning and empty my trash
bin, mop the floor, and dust the room. At least until you've had
enough time to think about what you've done. Besides, from
what I hear, you don't have anything better to do downstairs."

He wasn't wrong. I really didn't have anything better to do
downstairs. If I was stubborn and tried to refuse him, I might
get kicked out of the research institute. Even though I doubted
he would go through with it, I couldn't be sure. After all, this
was the guy who bashed in that Department Head Kim's head
and didn't even pay a penny toward his hospital bills. I thought
for a while about all the ways I could lie my way out of this,
but eventually, without any other way out, I said, "Ok, deal."

And that's how I came to work with Professor Kwon under
the condition that I would go up to his office and clean every
morning. Slowly the work I had to do increased. At first he
said that all I needed to do was clean and watch the office. So,
I cleaned and watched the office. But soon he got annoyed
with me and asked why I didn't answer the phone when
someone called. So, I started answering the phone too and had
ridiculous conversations with even more ridiculous people.
And with time, I even began recording phone calls, scheduling
appointments, organizing files, typing up conversations,
and following Professor Kwon on his way to meet potential
symptomers. And just like that, one year turned to another,
and before I knew it seven years had passed. I had spent seven
years with Professor Kwon. And yet I still had nothing to do at
my job downstairs.

But there was one question to which I could never find the
answer. Why was it that Professor Kwon needed an assistant
like me? For the last forty years he had never taken on a single

assistant or pupil. Nor had he formed a research team. He'd always been alone. So why me? Why take me as an assistant when I had absolutely no background in science? This was a mystery I could not solve, not matter how hard I tried.

Attached to the inside of Cabinet 13's door was this note:

Strong as an elephant that can obliterate an entire tree,
  Tenacious as a hyena that can drop a rhino,
  Patient as a crocodile that can fast for six months in a
swamp,
  Vigorous as a fur seal with a thousand mates
  Together with your passion for shedding light on the
world's darkness.
  – Professor Kwon

I see this note every time I open the cabinet. Each time I read it, my chest lurches and I mutter to myself, "Darkness of the world, my ass! What does he know about darkness?"

MEMORY MOSAICERS

In the beginning, it was just a few misspelled words in an old diary which needed editing – at least, that was what Susan Bring, who would later become a voodoo witch and the queen of all memory mosaicers, thought. Susan had no particular goal in mind. She was simply embarrassed by her past as it was recorded and thought it would be awful if someone were to read the diary after her death. She started with editing a few misspelled words in her diary. But, while she was at it, she would also erase entire embarrassing sentences about things she didn't want to remember. And in their place, she would write new sentences, new memories. And as time passed, she would forget that she had ever edited her diary. And because she often read old diary entries while making new diary entries, this process would repeat itself, again and again. Read, edit, forget; read, edit, forget – until the past itself was edited.

Such primitive forms of memory manipulation obviously have their limitations. They lack the ability to do anything about traumatic memories or influence the realm of the unconscious. But even memory manipulation of this level has the potential to change one's present life in dramatic fashion.

Susan Bring is the prototypical memory mosaicer. People who remember Susan when she was young would never have imagined she would live such a glamorous and peculiar life: graduating from Berkeley Law and becoming a successful lawyer; becoming a famously witty columnist for the *New York*

Times; suddenly leaving behind her life in Manhattan one day, when she was on top of the world, to live in Tibet for five years; and coming back from Tibet to become, of all things, a voodoo witch. They couldn't have imagined this because the young Susan Bring was an ungifted child, unable to even do the simplest arithmetic; who, until she was twelve, couldn't read what was in her textbooks or write what was on the chalkboard; an introverted Black girl with B.O. who was picked on by the other students.

It was Father Bryan who changed Susan's life. Objectively speaking, what Father Bryan did for her was nothing special. He merely taught the alphabet to a girl who at the time couldn't read or write, and preached to her about the importance of keeping a daily journal.

"There are two types of lives people can live," he said. "The kind of life in which one writes in a diary every day, and the kind of life in which one doesn't. They're as different as a country with a history and one without. So, Susan, what life will you choose?"

Susan Bring chose the former. But, unlike others, she also chose to edit her diary from time to time. Having been shown the magic of letters, she read furiously at the library, as though she were trying to make up for all the lost time as an illiterate. And as a result, she learned about herself and about the language of others. And the more secrets she uncovered from reading, the more she felt embarrassed about her past and how ignorant she had been. That embarrassment overshadowed her current life. She wanted to live boldly. She realized that a person's existence was defined by their past. So she changed her past. And it was effective. With each embarrassing memory she erased, her personality became more confident, more outgoing, more daring. Slowly, she began tampering more and more with her memories. Propelled by the will to forget and the natural human tendency for forgetfulness, Susan's edited diary little by little came to define what she remembered.

Through much trial and error, and with the help of chemistry and modern medicine, and by appropriating mystical secrets from Tibet and various secret drugs used in voodoo, Susan Bring created the very first prototype for a memory mosaicer.

For the next twenty to thirty years after Susan Bring, the techniques of memory mosaicers developed rapidly. The techniques used by second-generation memory mosaicers were varied and complex, but with that variety and complexity came danger. Modern mosaicers are not satisfied with just forgetting or modifying one or two small memories like their predecessors were. They treat memories like files on a computer, deleting, embellishing, modifying, and syncing them. Obviously, this is a dangerous game. And that's because for memory modification to be possible in such a short amount of time, a person has to attempt terribly risky procedures and experiments. Invasive surgery, taking chemicals, using the mystical arts – they've tried it all.

The drugs that mosaicers use when they delete or modify memories have not been explored scientifically and it is hard to know what side effects they might have. They started with drugs like LSD and cocaine, then moved on to making cocktails from drugs like those used to treat neurological disorders and depression (such as Janax, Penzolfen, and Syndrofoam), heart disease, and even colds. They also attempt recklessly risky experiments without any scientific evidence or reasoning. Some experimented with acupuncture to shut off parts of the mind, and others experimented with applying ultrasonic and electromagnetic waves to specific parts of the brain. Needless to say, all of their ridiculous experiments failed and many of the test subjects either died from brain hemorrhages or became paralyzed.

There's no way to confirm the effects of these secret techniques, which spread by word of mouth between mosaicers – and even if one could prove their efficacy, the question of whether they are safe would still remain. The only way to know is to try it for oneself. Even self-hypnosis, which is generally believed to be the safest of memory moasicer methods, lacks expert approval.

Because of all this, there have been many unfortunate incidents involving second-generation memory mosaicers. One Chilean immigrant, who was trying to rid herself of the memory of her abusive and alcoholic father, killed herself by punching a hole in her head with a mixer blade when she could no longer handle the migraines. A woman on the east coast of the United States, who wanted to erase the memory of being bullied as a child, caused a great tragedy when she pointed her machine gun at a nearby elementary school.

And in spite of all this, mosaicers say:

"Living with bad memories is far more fatal, far more dangerous than any potential side effect. And that's because living with bad memories is hell on earth."

Mosaicers manipulate the past and fool themselves. They erase specific memories and rehash the remaining ones. They manufacture the present with new memories, and with that present they reimagine their future. But mosaicers aren't escapists. On the contrary, they are conquerors. Much like how people use plastic surgery to erase their insecurities, mosaicers are merely modifying the memories that debilitate their reality. Some people might question whether what they are doing is any different from publishing textbooks with revised and distorted histories. And they might have a point. But mosaicers don't have the luxury to think about the ruin their own fabricated memories, which have nothing to do with the rest of the world, will bring to them.

Benefiting from the advanced research in neurology, the discovery of drugs that regulate hormones and the brain's emotional response centers, and the rapid development of the computer industry, third-generation memory mosaicers have evolved into safer creatures than their forebears. And this is the result of the relatively successful integration of brain nerve stimulation with computer programs, the increased effectiveness of chemotherapy, and the widespread realization that you can't solve everything at once by taking dangerous or destructive measures. Yet in spite of all this progress, there still remains one problem: addiction.

Memory mosaicers who succeed in obtaining happy memories become addicted to the act of fabricating those happy memories. This happens because their manifest present and future always seem unhappy in comparison to their glorified past. Whereas their past might be filled with glory and praise, their present and future are filled with uncertainty and fear. Simply put, they become unsatisfied with their present. And their future always seems downhill in comparison to the past. But because they are unable to do anything about their future or present, they throw their undetermined future to the wayside and turn to editing the past. They completely lose themselves in the past. And little by little, all for the sake of editing more of their past, they began to use again more destructive methods of memory manipulation – methods their predecessors had once used.

Quite a few memory mosaicers are known to live in South Korea. But no one knows the exact number. What is clear, however, is that the number of them who are experimenting with dangerous and reckless methods is continuing to grow.

Within the drawers of Cabinet 13, there are eight files of different memory mosaicers. All of those individuals are members of the Red Rose – a local group created for people suffering from the side effects of memory modifications that went wrong. Among its members is a pianist who accidentally erased all her memories relating to the piano, an automobile mechanic who thinks he's married to his ex-girlfriend from ten years ago, and the miserable priest who ruined his memory so badly that he can't even differentiate between his own memories and countless confessions he's heard over the years.

The group meets once a week on Friday night. I used to participate in the meetings from time to time when I didn't have any plans. The members of the Red Rose sit in a circle and talk for two hours. Some days they have a lot to say, other days they don't say anything, and everyone has to sit in awkward silence. But in all honesty, this isn't unique to the Red Rose. They usually talk about the past they remember, the past they can vaguely recall, and the past that has been modified. They also talk about the fuzzy and dark times that are stuck between one memory and the next. And when the meeting is over, people usually go back to their houses, but sometimes they go to a nearby bar and have a beer. It's not a particularly enjoyable atmosphere, but neither is it excruciatingly depressing.

P, the pianist, erased all her memories of the piano. And, because of this, she can no longer play. She forgot what her body remembers. It's truly very strange. Even when people have amnesia, they don't tend to forget how to drive a car or swim. So the fact that P, who played the piano since she was three, would one day suddenly lose the ability to play, is quite strange indeed. The way she describes it is that she feels like all of her memories are suspended in midair.

"None of my memories are connected to each other. There's a huge, black hole in my head, and all my memories of the piano have been sucked into that hole. The life that I can remember seems so short. It's probably because everything in my life was connected in some way or another to the piano. The school I attended, the people I met, and all the relationships I made were because of the piano. Aside from my family, I rarely met anyone who wasn't in some way related to the piano. I studied at a conservatory in the Czech Republic and spent the majority of my life practicing and playing the piano. So now, the majority of my memories are completely empty. A life filled with nothing but the piano... Can you imagine?"

Thinking that she might regain her memory if she struck a

few keys, we once sat her down in front of a piano. But all she did was sit and stare at the piano for an hour, never touching a single key. Finally she turned to us and said, "But I don't know how to play the piano."

Father L can't differentiate between his own memories and confessions he's heard. In other words, his memories have become mixed with the memories of all the people who've come to him through the years.

"Confessions are the stories of pained and disgraceful lives. It's rare for someone to come to me to confess a memory that's happy and beautiful. Since I've lost the ability to discern between my memories and others' confessions, everything's gone south. My head's about to explode with their pained memories. One day it's the all-too-real memory of a murderer who killed his father, and the next it's the memory of a prostitute. I even have memories like this one: I'm walking down a dark alleyway one night when three wicked teenage girls appear before me. The girls try to seduce me, saying they've always wanted to have sex with a priest. One girl licks my face, and another raises her skirt to reveal her underwear. She asks if I have an erection and begins grabbing at my crotch. I slap one of the girls, but they don't back off. At that moment, something inside me snaps and I give them what they want. Yes, I have sex with the three girls! O, forgive me Father! And they were minors, too. Did I mention I'm a priest? But I can't tell whether this is my memory or someone else's. My head's a mess and I can't tell this from that. What if I really did have sex with those girls? How can I be received by our Lord and Savior with such a body?"

There's Mr Han, a bachelor and automobile mechanic who thinks he's married to his ex-girlfriend from ten years ago. Not only does Mr Han think he hasn't broken up with the woman, he thinks they've been happily married for the last ten years.

"A while back I went to see her. But to my surprise she was living with another man. She even had a kid. Imagine my shock. Obviously, I told her to come back with me. But she got angry and looked like she had no idea what I was talking about. I'm positive we lived together for ten years in intimacy, but she pretended not to know of any such thing. The traces of her still remain all over my house and body. I can remember every detail of the last ten years. I can tell you what we ate, in what positions we had sex, and even the color of her underwear. We didn't have kids. She wasn't able to have them. So we raised a cat instead. It was a Siamese cat name Chestnut, and she loved him so much. I really liked him, too. So I asked her if she remembered the cat we raised together. And she said she was allergic to cat fur."

And then there's Madame Song, the proprietor of a once prosperous brothel in Gangnam who has forgotten everything about the year 1998. As an eventful year, the year 1997 conjures all sorts of memories for Madame Song – the good, the sad, the irritating, the money she lost, as well as the two apartments she bought and the countless bills. But when it comes to 1998, nothing comes to Madame Song's mind but a single carrot. Stunned by this, we all asked in unison, "A carrot?"

"Yes."

"But why a carrot?"

"That's the rub. It's clear to me that I modified my memory to make 1998 remind me of a carrot, but why I felt the need to do so I cannot remember. I always wonder, 'Why a carrot?' I've tried everything – cutting carrots, eating carrots, putting carrots on my face – but I can't remember anything. Why in the world is 1998 a carrot? Why a carrot and not a cucumber or bell pepper or onion? It's torture not knowing. I don't even like carrots that much."

The members of the Red Rose are tortured by the disappearance of their memories. They want to find their lost memories. But what they'll find there can never bring them happiness. They erased those memories because they were unhappy ones, because they couldn't live with those memories anymore. So why do they want to find those painful memories again, those memories they so fervently tried to erase? They want to only because they forgot the reason for their pain. If they did regain their memories, if they did find the origin of the pain they erased, they would probably regret it and try to rid themselves of it again.

It's still not well known how it is our brains work, or what thoughts and consciousness are. A single human brain has one hundred billion neurons, each of which is linked to ten thousand other neurons. The human brain generates nerve impulses and secretes chemical transmitters in nearly an infinite number of combinations. I sometimes wonder if we humans, as finite beings, will ever be able to tame the infinity that exists in our brains. Yet, many scientists say that in the not-so-distant future we will understand the inner workings of neurons and nerve cells and be able to directly connect human brains to computers. I don't believe that such a thing would be possible without side effects, but, if it were possible, I guess I would want to try to hook my brain up to a computer. What would appear on the monitor? I wonder. To be honest, if it does come to that, I hope my wife and children aren't with me. What if, god forbid, pornographic images were beamed from my head to the computer monitor?

Those who argue for the sanctity of humanity express grave concern over the fusion of man and machine. Some people even get ready to protest in front of the National Assembly, cutting red ribbons and buying red pens to write with on picket fences whenever such news is reported. "Machines and people should never be connected! Preserve the sanctity of humanity!" If people like this exist around you, I hope you tell them that the time for such things has yet to come. We still have a long time before we connect human brains to computers. After all, we still don't even fully understand how migraines are caused.

"If you had a time machine would you go back to the year 1998?"

"I would. Even though all I can remember from that year is a carrot."

"Aren't you scared?"

"I am. But when you think about it there's no time in our lives we haven't been able to endure. If there was such a time, we wouldn't have made it this far. We live with happy memories. But we also live with unhappy memories. That's the power of loss and ruin."

PINOCCHIO

Now I want to tell you a story about a toothpick. Yes, that lowly, insignificant item no one has shown interest in for thousands of years. A product that no CEO would ever be proud to admit their company makes. I'm going to tell you a story about a man who had no choice but to live a life full of toothpicks.

"More and more I'm starting to resemble a toothpick," he once said to me. "But I'm not worried. You'll see. By the year 2100, all machines will look like humans. And if that's not the case, all humans will look like machines. It's got to be one or the other."

From the times of the ancient Greeks when natural philosophy flourished, to the early Middle Ages when universities first emerged, not a single philosopher has ever taken interest in the existential essence of toothpicks. And who would? But of course, neither were they interested in the existential essence of things like chairs, bathtubs, pots, or mosquito nets. Most people don't think much at all (indeed, the people of antiquity and the Middle Ages had a hard enough time just thinking about how they were going to feed themselves each night); and for the type of people who did think – such as the well-fed Roman youth of aristocratic families who grew up with a dozen private tutors, or the monks who were so bored at their monasteries that they couldn't help but think about philosophy, or the people who worked in the then-new profession of professorship (new in that professors of universities had the unprecedented luxury of selling "knowledge" in fancy buildings without much need for aggressive business pursuits, as opposed to the sophists of ancient Greece who made their living running small academies or scouring flea markets in search of wealthy families with dim-witted sons in need of tutoring) – for people like this, there was time to ponder nobler, more metaphysical questions. Whether gods had internal organs, and if they did have organs, whether the gas produced in those organs made them fart – you know, the type of questions that had no relevance to daily life. Anyway, what I'm trying to say is that from antiquity to the Middle Ages, no one took serious interest in or tried to understand the things known as toothpicks.

And by the sixteenth century, people started to emerge who pondered questions more concrete, more realistic, and more substantial than those concerning the internal organs of gods – questions about things that could physically hurt someone if thrown. These people were the humanists who carried the Renaissance, and their research dealt with things like the Moon, Venus, and Mars; sailing vessels, trade winds, maps, and mountain ranges; gold and silver; mainsprings and compasses. Yet still no one cared about toothpicks.

It was an Arab butler named Allal Rashid who first attempted to capture the essence of the toothpicks. In his work *The Book of Lost Things*, he started inquiry and research into civilization's inventions and the things civilization has lost. He carefully worked to uncover the essence of those things that had been lost to time.

The story of the toothpick appears on page 7233 of *The Book of Lost Things*. According to this story, there once was a merchant by the name of Caspi who had elevated the status of toothpicks to a level hardly imaginable by today's standards. Caspi the merchant left Damascus for Rome with grand dreams. Back then, the Mediterranean Sea was still the center of all trade, the Pope was attempting to restore Rome's ancient buildings, and the renowned House of Medici was spending lavish amounts of money for the sake of artistic production.

However, while on the way to Rome from Damascus filled with ambitious dreams, Caspi was met with heavy seas that caused his ship to run aground on a coral reef. Caspi spent all night clinging to the reef as he watched the waves engulf his belongings. Caspi survived through the stormy night, and when day finally broke, he was saved by a Spanish merchant vessel passing by. With their help he arrived in Rome, but now he had nothing to sell. The only thing he had in his pockets was a lone knife. The homeless Caspi wandered the streets of Rome until one day when he had a bright idea that compelled him to start hacking away at a tree with his knife. He was making a toothpick. The toothpick he made was similar to ordinary toothpicks in that it was pointy, but unlike other toothpicks, it was the size of an erect penis – in fact, if you looked at the toothpick's handle, it looked particularly phallic.

Intrigued, people approached Caspi and asked him what the object was used for.

"This is a toothpick."

"Goodness, but why the odd appearance?"

"This is not just any toothpick. Cheap Roman merchants say that you should use toothpicks because not doing so is bad for your dental health and will lead to bad breath from the leftover food rotting between your teeth. But they've forgotten about the essence of toothpicks. What they are selling can't be called genuine toothpicks."

"Then what's a genuine toothpick?"

"Genuine toothpicks are a conduit for magic. They must force self-reflection upon the servants who use them to pick from their teeth the scraps of the food their masters filled their bellies with – reflection about how they got this food; how they can repay their master for this food; how noble and magnanimous the generosity of their master is; how they must eat this food to show their gratitude; how they must repay their master's generosity; how

much work they must do to please their master. When servants
use these toothpicks, they will repay the cost of their food and
then some by tilling the land and reaping its plentiful crops; and
when butlers use these toothpicks, they will never waste or steal
their master's money; and if you somehow were able to make
horses or oxen use these toothpicks, they would work for you
until they run themselves into the ground; and if your wife or a
nun used these toothpicks... Oh, look at me, I'm getting carried
away. This pagan almost said something inappropriate."

Once Caspi finished his pitch, there erupted a loud murmur.
All the landed aristocrats gathered there began to think to
themselves, "Ah ha, it wasn't a whip that my slaves needed,
but this man's toothpick!"

"Does it matter if several people use the same toothpick?"
one aristocrat asked.

"As long as the user doesn't reject the toothpick," answered
Caspi.

"Fantastic. Let's see – If I buy one toothpick for every twenty
slaves – I'll take thirty."

Despite the steep price, Caspi's phallic toothpicks sold
extremely well. Even after all the landed aristocrats purchased
enough toothpicks for their slaves, they kept selling. All the
noblewomen, widows, and tomboys were secretly buying
toothpicks, though I don't have the slightest idea why. There
were even rumors that a large order had come in from a
convent, but these rumors were never confirmed. After meals,
people would take these odd-looking toothpicks and think to
themselves, "Why in the world did I eat food? O, on such a
lonely night, what now is the most valuable thing I can do
with this toothpick?"

Of course, Caspi did not invent the toothpick. Since
inconvenience drives invention, there are thousands, maybe
tens of thousands of people who claim they invented the
toothpick. But even though Caspi wasn't the inventor of
the toothpick, he was the one who endowed it with valid

existential value. By imbuing toothpicks with fantasy and magic, he elevated the toothpick from its lowly position on the hierarchy of objects.

Now let me tell you about the boy who turned into a toothpick. There was once a boy who turned himself into a toothpick after thinking about toothpicks for too long – a boy who "evolved" into a toothpick, so to speak (for those who might say this was a devolution and not an evolution: no, it was definitely an evolution). A boy who was so satisfied with his new life as a toothpick that he had no intention of ever turning back into a complete human again.

The boy's connection to toothpicks traced back to his father, who ran a small cottage factory that manufactured them. Yes, a father that made toothpicks. But the son hated toothpicks. And – as anyone who knows the history between fathers and sons could tell you – such a combination was inevitably going to the lead to unhappiness for the boy.

The reason the boy loathed toothpicks so much was that everything about him – his nickname, his identity, his very existence – was derived from, and bound to, that despicable piece of wood. Indeed, because he was scrawny, it was only a matter of time before people started to call him toothpick. In fact, he had so many nicknames that were puns on the word toothpick that he was almost never called by his proper name. His friends always teased him with names like "Pick" or "Picky" or even "Pick Pick." And to the old people in the neighborhood, he was always "Pick's second son." Why it was that they said "Pick" and not "Toothpick" isn't hard to figure out if you just try pronouncing each ten times fast. Language always has the tendency of being contracted when pronunciations are cumbersome. Therefore, considering the unlucky fate of language to be repeatedly created, altered, and annihilated, it's important that one always follows the principle of "simple pronunciation" when giving an object or a theory a name. The nickname the boy hated most was that derogatory name which identified him with his toothpick-making father: "The Toothpick Bastard." He hated toothpicks. He hated his father. He hated his father's small toothpick factory. He hated the toothpick machines. He hated the factory workers who eyed his mother's ass as she worked. He hated the fact that, out of all the millions of objects in the world, it was toothpicks to which he was bound. And most of all, he hated the strange tradition his family had of always using toothpicks after eating, be it only some vegetable side dishes or a fried egg. He often wondered to himself whether it was really necessary to use a toothpick after every meal. As if his family were holding on to the 100,000 arrows that Zhuge Liang famously stole from Cao Cao, it was custom to have a million toothpicks just rolling around in the boy's house at any one time.

In his senior year of high school, the boy applied for the military academy. The reason for this was simple: he wanted to choose a career as far away from toothpicks as possible. And that for him was the military academy. However, on the application for the military academy, there was a line for his father's occupation. He was finally about to start a new life, but it seemed as though toothpicks had followed him there too. For days he anguished over what to write. Then finally he had a brilliant idea. For his father's occupation, he wrote "timber processor." But when he turned in the application at school, his homeroom teacher stared at the words "timber processor" with an incredulous look. The boy crossed his fingers in hopes that the teacher would let it pass, but as is often the case with life, things never go the way you want.

"What does your father make with the timber?" the teacher asked in a low, calm voice.

The boy said nothing. In all honesty, he didn't want to say one word about what his father did. But his teacher waited patiently for an answer. With no other choice and blushing up to his ears, the boy said in the smallest of voices:

"Toothpicks."

But the teacher neither laughed nor showed any hint of surprise. The teacher merely cocked his head slightly. His homeroom teacher was usually taciturn and didn't smile much.

"Then why did you write timber processor? You have to be clear when you fill out these forms."

The teacher lightly reprimanded the boy. Then after staring at the application for a while, he finally crossed out what the boy had written with two lines. Above it he wrote:

Master Wood Craftsman.

I think that teacher had at least some understanding of the essence of toothpicks. Anyway, that year the boy passed the entrance examinations and entered the military academy without a hitch.

From then on, his life continued to distance itself from toothpicks as he had hoped. And after he graduated from the military academy, it looked for a while like his life would continue down the road of a soldier. But that was not the case. The unit to which he was commanding officer was struck with several suicides and desertions He had been in line for a promotion, but now he suddenly found himself discharged from the military. After his discharge, he was able to get an administrative job at a munitions manufacturer with the recommendation of his superior. But, being used to life in the military, he often clashed with other employees and didn't get along with the researchers. So he quit and found work at an insurance company. But this time the former commander was met with the shining flower of capitalism: business.

"You lack what it takes to be a salesman. No customer on Earth likes a salesman who barks orders at them."

He quit in less than a month. Finally, with the severance pay he received from the military, he opened a fried chicken chain with his wife. Fortuitously, a large apartment complex had just finished construction nearby, and it seemed like he had finally gotten a break. His fried chicken chain saw a boom for two months. But by the third month, more than ten other fried chicken chains had set up shop in the neighborhood. All of the famous chains were present. There was even a place that gave away free pizza. What's more, a Chinese restaurant got in on the action; they even had a promotion for free jjajangmyeon or fried dumplings with every order of chicken. The former-commander sat for three months in that fly-infested fried chicken restaurant eating daikon radish before he forfeited his security deposit on the lease and sold the store. It was around that time that he started to lose it. He took all of his money and put it into stocks. The stock market wasn't doing badly, but for some reason he kept losing his money. Little by little he started taking bigger risks, and before even six months had passed, he had already lost all his assets. He began racking up debt. Once that started, he became obsessed with betting on horses. Everyday there was a new winning horse, but his horse was never "the horse." Soon his debt became too much for him to manage. So, he sold his apartment and his car and his piano, But he wasn't able to make a dent in the money he owed. He sold his kidney and one of his eyes, and still his debt didn't go away. When his wife demanded a divorce, he didn't even protest as he signed the papers.

He lost everything and became sick. He had nothing left. He didn't even have a place to sleep at night. All he had to lean on was the toothpick factory that his old man still ran in his spare time. Defeated, he went back to his father. When he arrived, he said to his father, "You win. I'll make toothpicks. I'll make these damn toothpicks."

The man started working at the toothpick factory. Yet it wasn't like his life made a remarkable turn for the better. He simply worked at the toothpick factory making toothpicks for many years, just as his father had done. Of course, the reason this man was included in Cabinet 13 was not because of his normal, unfortunate life. If that were the type of file Cabinet 13 accepted, then it would have burst from all the sad stories of this city's inhabitants long ago. No, the reason he's in the cabinet is because of his finger. While working, he had an accident in which he lost three fingers to a cutting machine. He said nonchalantly that such accidents were common in this line of work.

"Losing a couple fingers won't kill you, even if people do treat me like I'm a cripple. It doesn't bother me. The problem is I lost too many fingers. You need to have at least three fingers to make toothpicks. A thumb, an index finger, and one other finger to support them. I would have been fine if I had only lost two fingers, but it was just my luck that I lost three. So, I spoke to the local hospital and they told me they had a prosthetic finger. They really do have everything these days."

The man had a prosthetic finger where his middle finger had been. A pin attached the prosthetic finger to his hand. But the manufactured finger was cumbersome and hurt the man's productivity. Keeping only the pin, he threw away the prosthetic finger and replaced it with one he fashioned himself from wood. He made countless iterations until he had one that was just right for him.

"But then one day I took out the pin to wash my face, and the wooden finger wouldn't come off. I pulled my hardest but it was stuck to my hand like a real finger. I thought it amusing at first. Isn't it amusing? A wooden finger pretending to be a real finger."

The man now had three wooden fingers. Of course, those wooden fingers didn't bend at each joint like real fingers. But as if they were flesh that had grown from his palm, the wooden fingers were perfectly adhered to his hand. Stranger yet, at the point where the wood met the man's flesh, there was a type of carnification taking place in which it looked like the material was a mix of half-wood half-flesh. Underneath the surface of that wood-flesh mixture, you could even see a few veins. How could flesh fuse with the wood, I wondered.

"This is surprising, indeed. There have been instances of organisms growing on people's bodies, but this is a first."

"Things like that happen?" he asked with an intrigued expression on his face.

"People like that are called chimeras. People who have lizards for tongues, tales of gingko trees growing from people's bodies. But this is the first time I've seen a dead piece of wood fuse with human flesh. Can I touch it?"

He stuck out his hand without hesitation. I examined the three fingers for several moments. They were made from the same everyday wood he used for making toothpicks. They didn't have fingernails and there were tree rings in the place where normal fingers would have fingerprints. The middle finger was bent slightly into a hook shape, perhaps for better dexterity while working. And for some reason, his pinky finger was one segment too short.

"Why is the pinky finger so short? I can't believe you would have cut it this short by accident," I asked.

"I accidently snipped a part of it off with the cutting machine. I wasn't quite used to the finger back them."

"Thankfully it was your wooden finger this time. That could have really hurt."

"Oh no, it really hurt for a wooden finger," he said with a straight face.

"Does it feel uncomfortable or foreign?"

"Of course it does. After all, it wasn't my finger to begin with. But slowly that foreign-body feeling is going away. Little by little the finger is changing. It's getting less cumbersome and sometimes bends in the direction I want it to. Of course, sometimes it bends in the direction I don't want it to. At first when I would look at this wooden finger, it felt like I was a monster. I sold my eye to repay my debt, and now I have a fake one in its place. A wooden finger and a plastic eye. I felt so pathetic. But now it's not so bad. Just you wait. By the year 2100, all machines will look like humans. And if that's not the case, all humans will look like machines. It's got to be one or the other. I know this because I can see that humans and objects are starting to resemble one another."

"Do you still hate toothpicks?" I asked.

He didn't answer me at first. Finally, after several moments, he spoke.

"Well, I don't hate them as much as I used to, but neither do I have a newfound love for them. They're just ok. Sometimes I wonder if humans aren't meant to eventually return to the place they once loathed and live there in harmony."

When he finished talking, the man lit a cigarette between his index finger and his wooden finger. Then after taking a lengthy drag, he blew a long stream of smoke into the air.

The man told me that he was beginning to resemble a toothpick. What he meant by that exactly, I'm not sure. A future society in which humans and objects resemble each other – what does that mean? Does it mean that in the twenty-second century, tables, vases, and wine glasses will love, cry, and feel loneliness like humans? Or does it mean that in the twenty-second century, people will live empty lives like vases and tables, unable to feel love, pain, or loneliness?

One day after coming back from the market, Pinocchio made a worried face and asked Geppetto the woodcarver a question.

"Papa, am I a human or a wooden puppet?"

Geppetto the woodcarver looked at Pinocchio with sadness in his eyes.

"My child, don't be sad. If you have a kind heart, you can be whatever you desire. You can be a human or something much greater."

Then Pinocchio shouted with joy.

"Then I want to be the best wooden puppet ever!"

FRIDAY, CLOSE THE BLINDS

Darkness fell outside the window. I got up from my chair, closed the blinds, and glanced around the office. It was quiet. All the employees with families had gone home early; it was Friday, after all. Of course, all the unmarried employees had gone home, too. They had dates or were hanging out with their friends on Fridays. They had healthy bodies for partying and having fun, and their wallets were fat because they were single. What need would they have for staying late at the office on a Friday night? The only people who would look after the office on a Friday night were people like me: people without a spouse or a significant other, people who lived alone. Besides, even if I did go home, the only thing waiting for me would be a refrigerator filled with cold heaps of rice, a half-eaten can of mackerel, and a flat can of beer. I lived in this cursed city alone, without anyone to love.

Recently I hadn't been dating. It might sound strange, but for the last seven years I hadn't met a girl whom I would want to date, nor had I had the desire to meet such a girl. Thanks to that, I'd been less depressed and less lonely. On the weekends though, it got tough. It was impossible to go to restaurants alone to eat and drink on weekends. People gave you looks of pity. Worse yet, sometimes they would tell me they didn't have any tables when I said I needed a table for one. So I had no choice but to cook on the weekends. I went to a supermarket, bought a ridiculous amount of groceries (because the supermarkets, who didn't want to sell items individually, were detestable and subtly forced you to buy in bulk, damned if you didn't want to), checked out, then took my load of groceries home with me. And when I got home, I started cooking. As I did this, I often thought that cooking dinner for oneself was such a imprudent act. Not wasteful, but imprudent. Would prehistoric humans have hunted wild boar just to eat dinner alone? Well, considering the fact they didn't have butcher shops back then, they might have. But most likely there were no Cro-magnons who lived alone. And that's because they wouldn't last two days without their pack.

There was one other person besides myself who hadn't gone home yet. Son Jeong-eun from General Affairs. She always stayed late at the office. With her chubby body hunched over, she sat in the most isolated corner of the office as she worked on something before going home. But in this office where there was no real work to be done, what was it that she was so busy doing?

The other people at the office all said she was odd. I too thought she was a little odd. Even giving her the benefit of the doubt, it would be a stretch to call her normal. First of all, she never talked. Never engaging in small talk with anyone, she only spoke when her job required it of her. Sometimes it was as if she were a mute, or had vowed never to speak with another human. Or perhaps she had just forgotten how to talk. She also had never been to any company gatherings – be it a formal business party, team outing, office track meet, or just a casual drink after work. She always ignored our boss's intimidations when he said the office parties were mandatory, and simply skipped and went home. Everything she did she did alone – eating, working, and going home. In other words, she never did the most important thing for surviving in this city: being sociable. She was excessively reticent, excessively straight-faced, and excessively shy. She didn't want anyone coming near her. She didn't accept anyone. She was like an overgrown porcupine.

Friday night. She and I were the only ones left in the office. I should have been the only busy one at this office, held hostage again by Cabinet 13; so for what reason could she have been working so late?

It might have been because she took her time finishing all her work. As if her world was a slow-motion video, everything she did was excessively slow. Her walking speed, her movements, even her speech (when she did speak) was slow. Anything that entered her world, be it work or some other project, became slow and lethargic. All the other female employees got annoyed with her sluggish pace and complained about her. "I can't work with her. We're just not in sync." But, in all honesty, there was no work in this office with which to be "in sync." We all knew it, too, and it was embarrassing to ever imply otherwise. Not only was there nothing with which to be in sync, there was nothing with which to even kill time. All we had to do was finish our measly work alone. The real reason the female employees got annoyed with her was because they didn't like how quiet she was, how slow she was, and the fact her stoic behavior made her hard to read. That was the real and only reason they disliked her.

Another reason for her staying late at the office was because the tedious work that no one wanted to do was all dumped on her desk. It wasn't like everyone was conspiring against her (then again, maybe they were), it was just the way things were. If it was anyone's fault, it was hers because she never protested when someone assigned her any work. And that's not an exaggeration; she never complained. When something urgent was placed on her desk, she would just quietly sit there and begin working, albeit slowly. In that sense, perhaps it was not unexpected that she worked late. Not only did she get all the tedious work that no one wanted to do, but she also worked excruciatingly slowly.

Watching her sluggish movements, I often got frustrated with her, too. I couldn't understand why someone would choose to live in such a way. I got especially furious when Ms Chung, who talked about Jeong-eun behind her back the most, would come to Jeong-eun just before it was time to go home and tentatively hand Jeong-eun a file as she said, "Would you take care of this for me, honey? I've got sudden plans." This was the only time Ms Chung ever gave Jeong-eun a friendly smile. But behind her teeth Ms Chung was mocking Jeong-eun. *It's not like you have friends or a boyfriend anyway.* Each time this happened, I was overcome with the urge to slap Ms Chung. But what really got me angry was how Jeong-eun quietly took Ms Chung's file and sat down. Ms Chung said, "Thanks, honey," and Jeong-eun nodded her head as if to say she understood. It bothered me when she took that file. Why didn't she scream and say, "No!" Why didn't she show her temper? Why didn't she curse at Ms Chung and say, "Piss off, bitch. Do it yourself. Or, better yet, shove it up your loose hole or between the cleavage you like to show off so much!"

What a strange life she had. A life as a punching bag. A life with a note on one's forehead that said, "Punch me." A life with no regard for her own body. I had never once known someone like her. Is a life in which one never defends oneself even worth living? I always got angry watching her. It was like I was the one who was getting insulted. It felt like I was looking at my own battered face in the mirror. But I wasn't quite sure why it was I got overcome with that feeling when I looked at her.

I had been watching her for several years now. I watched how she walked; I peeked at her through the blinds as she left work; I even glanced furtively over at her hunched shoulders from time to time. For some reason, my eyes always wandered in her direction. Perhaps you think I empathized with her. Empathized is a funny word. With whom would someone like me empathize? Then, perhaps, I had a crush on her? I'm not

saying it wasn't true, but if I had, it would have been a surprise
to everyone. All the female employees would have thought I
was joking and laughingly said, "No way." Section Chief Kim
would have shaken his head in disapproval and said, "Kong,
you have odd taste in women." And my boss would have said,
"Are you out of your mind! What, did you send your brain
on a business trip? Pull yourself together, man." Honestly, not
even I knew what kind of feelings I had for her. Perhaps I
just never had the opportunity to confirm what those feelings
were. Or perhaps I never had the desire or the courage to. I
really can't say.

I had a friend who was known as the Count of Myeongdong.
This friend not only claimed that he had sex with more than five
hundred women before graduating college, but he also swore
that he loved every last one of them. Once while drinking, he
told me that love is like canned food. "Like all canned food,
love has an expiration date, a price tag, and a warning label. In
order to love, you need to check the price tag to see if you have
enough money in your wallet, observe the warnings given in
fine print, and finish matters before the expiration date. Only
then is it a smooth process for everyone."

Perhaps he was right, perhaps love in this city really is
like canned food. As long as you have the will to check your
money, the expiration date, and a can opener, you'll be able to
find love – mediocre, safe, and palatable love.

When the office clock hit 7:15 pm, Jeong-eun got up from
her seat. Whenever she got up, her chair would make a high-
pitched creaking sound. The office was completely empty as
all the other employees had gone home for the week. Even so,
she glanced once around the office. Then she picked up her
old leather bag, which she'd had since she first started working
here. Even back then it hadn't been new. It was a tattered
leather bag, one that she had to carry around on her bosom

because the strap had broken. The kind of tattered leather bag that carried some strange secret. I always wondered what was in that bag of hers.

She headed toward the door. As if she were walking on snow, the flat soles of her shoes made a crunching sound. As she turned the doorknob to leave, something came over me and I called out to her in a loud voice, "Ms Son, are you heading home?" Startled by my voice, her shoulders flinched. She then slowly turned around to face my direction. But instead of answering, she just bowed by dropping her head toward my desk (yes, I'm positive that it was not me but my desk to whom she was bowing). Her eyes were slightly crossed as if she was trying not to make eye contact by looking down the bridge of her nose. I often wanted to ask her why she never looked people in the eye. But I couldn't bring myself to. It would be as silly as asking why her shoes made a squishing sound when she walked. It might even be as rude as asking about her weight. I returned her bow by nodding my head slightly. It almost felt as if I was giving her permission to leave the office, which I wasn't. I'm sure she also knew that's not what I meant. As she began to turn around to leave, I called out to her again.

"Ms Son. Cheer up. Don't pay attention to what the others say."

This sudden outburst didn't match the situation. It was so random, it even surprised me. I guess subconsciously I did empathize with her and wanted to give her some encouragement. But it probably would have been more courageous if I had said, "Jeong-eun, you need to be careful. The boss is just waiting for you to give him an excuse to fire you. Everyone wants you out of this office. You should grab coffee with people sometimes, engage in chitchat, come to office parties. You know, come to karaoke to sing and clap and play the tambourine. You're not the only one who hates it, you know."

As if she also thought my sudden outburst was bizarre,

Jeong-eun cocked her head to the side slightly. And when she realized I was still looking at her, she started searching for a response. Scrunching her eyebrows together, she made an expression as if she were trying to give an evaluation of herself and the office. Her eyebrows, which were furiously twitching, were asking, "Am I OK? Is it OK that the people in this office treat another human being like this? Perhaps I am having a hard time…"

"Office life… is… fun," she said finally, with a quivering voice. It had been a long time since I heard her speak. Her small weak voice was child-like. She bowed her head once again toward my desk then slowly walked out of the office. I could hear the sound of her flat, rubber soles as she walked down the hallway. I had once wished that her shoes would tip-tap like the other female employees' heels. But she wasn't the kind of girl who would wear stilettoes. Perhaps she could at least find shoes that didn't make the sound of crunching snow. I clicked my pen several times as my eyes followed the sound of her footsteps as she reached the end of the hallway and began walking down the stairs. Office life is fun? What's so fun about life in this shithole office?

I sat at my desk and stuck a cigarette in my mouth. On the office wall were the words NO SMOKING written in red letters. Now that she was gone, there was no one in the office but me. But even so, that didn't mean I could smoke. No smoking meant no smoking, even if you were alone. I lit the cigarette in my mouth as I muttered to myself, "You really shouldn't be smoking in the office." I raised the blinds and opened the window slightly. A creaking sound came from the rusty blinds. How tedious. These wretched blinds. By the time I finished half the cigarette, she was exiting the front door of the office. Her body was even more hunched over than usual. She was probably holding on tightly to that old leather bag. What was in that bag she held so closely to her chest?

BECOMING A CAT

Have you ever imagined what it would be like to transform into a cat?

Cats are optimistic, curious, cute creatures that sleep on average sixteen hours a day. Look at their agile movements as they launch themselves up onto high ledges; the effortlessly elegant way they jump from rooftop to rooftop; their amazing balance which allows them to fall from a tree and plant a soft landing by making split-second adjustments in their center of mass. Just look at those bottomless eyes of infinite mystery.

Cats are truly marvelous creatures. While their friends the jaguar and cheetah are struggling to survive in the slowly dwindling savanna and tropical forests, domestic cats have adapted to the city in impressive ways. They understand the streetlight system and even know to avoid dangerous high-tension wires and electric fences. Cats know what day the compost is taken out in the city, and they know the color of compost bins. And because cats have such an eclectic palette, they can eat almost anything, from scraps of ham and canned mackerel to moldy bread and over-boiled anchovies. This junk food, so to speak, doesn't really suit the preferences of elegant and noble cats, but they can't be picky or complain. They silently accept the terms this world has given them.

Even though cats eat all sorts of urban trash, they still have the pride of a wild animal. They exist on a different plane from dogs, who receive food and shelter in exchange for cute wagging tails and warm hugs from their master. In fact, cats are not subservient to anyone, regardless of if they're strays or house cats. That is to say, cats have no masters. They only recognize friends and subordinates. You might *think* you're raising your cat as its master, but your cat doesn't think that. To your cat, you're probably closer to a maid or butler, maybe a friend at best. If you don't do your duties as a maid, you'll hear a warning from your cat in the form of a stern *meow. Meow!* It means "My bowl is empty."

Once cats have had their bellies filled, they freely roam about their jungle of parks, rooftops, telephone poles, and empty buildings. They jump, they run, they charge, they hide. They may be staying in the city, but they've never lost their jungle muscles. They're both wild and urban! Having the body of a cat – that is a truly marvelous feat.

Paulus Willems once said, "There's only one way for a human to be happy in this city. And that's by turning into a cat."

You're probably thinking to yourself, "Is life that much of a joke to you? Do you have that much time on your hands that you can daydream about turning into a cat?" I agree wholeheartedly. Life is not a joke. No matter how charming cats may be, people should never turn into cats. Why, you ask? Because life is not a joke, of course.

And despite this, I still met up with that tiresome lump of a man named Hwang Bong-gon. You remember, the guy who calls me every morning saying he wants to be a cat. But I had a good reason for meeting him. Not long ago, Mr Hwang attempted suicide. They found him (I don't know how or where) having consumed a whole bottle of sleeping pills. What was more impressive than his survival was the fact that he was able to push so many pills down his throat. Thankfully, it didn't take long for someone to discover him. He was quickly taken to the hospital and had the contents of his stomach pumped. I guess someone was looking out for him after all.

When I arrived at the restaurant, he was already on his fifth bottle of soju.

"I'm in love," he said as he looked at me with bloodshot eyes. "I said I'm in love! Do you even know what that means? What's the point of life if you can't be who your love wants you to be? It hurts so bad thinking about how I'm going to live my whole life in a form she cannot love."

Mr Hwang buried his face in his hands and began to sob. Hwang Bong-gon. He's a large man at 6'3" and 290 lbs. It was hard to believe this large man sitting in front of me could go on whining about love. All the people in the restaurant were staring at me. It was mortifying.

"You're making a lot of noise just for love. But really, turning into a cat for love – come on, man."

"She's a cat-lover."

"A lot of people love cats. They're pretty cute."

"She's not interested in me at all. I'm just a waste of space to her."

"Everyone has their type. So what if you're not hers?"

"Just look at me. Even I hate myself. There's not an inch of my body worthy of being loved."

"You're being too hard on yourself. You can be a little annoying at times, sure, but there's lots of girls out there with unique taste in men. Even some who like hefty guys. All you have to do is look."

"There's no one like her."

"If it were a matter of effort, maybe you could do something about it. But that's not how love works. Turning into a cat's the same business – probably more so. Maybe it's time you call it quits?"

"I can't love anyone but her."

"You might think that now, but it'll pass with time."

"No, I've loved her for seventeen years now. It only gets more intense with time. I was destined to love her."

I was getting tired of this game of verbal tennis. It felt like I was wandering through a maze with no exit. I felt bad thinking that he could have actually died, but I wasn't cut out for this kind of conversation.

"If you insist that she's the one, why not just lose some weight? Lose some weight and I bet you'll look like a new man. You're tall; you'd probably look dashing. Don't worry about looking like a balloon head; I heard you burn the fat in your face first. Go to the gym and jog a little... Yeah, they say cardio is the best for burning fat."

"You just don't get it, do you? As long as I'm a human, she'll never love me. She can't feel that kind of emotion toward other humans. Pity, empathy, love, even hatred – she doesn't feel any of them. She has no interest in humans. She once told me, 'I have no interest in people, just like you have no interest in pine trees or grass. I've tried a million times to love another person. But I just can't do it. I don't feel anything.'"

"What, does she have a disorder or something?"

"I'm not sure. The doctors say the part of her brain that controls emotions is broken. But what do they know! It's not like she can't feel any emotion. She loves cats. Cats make her feel happy and sad, too."

Mr Hwang took another sip of his drink, and I took a sip of mine, as I sat next to this stubborn, dense man who loved, and had loved for seventeen years, a woman who could feel no emotions toward humans. I didn't know what to tell him.

There are some people who can't feel love or fear because of a problem with the part of the brain that governs emotion.

These individuals – whose brains could have been damaged by anything from car accidents or disease to radiation poisoning or genetic disorders – can think perfectly logically and rationally; their only problem is when it comes to emotions. According to a recent article published in *Psychological Science*, such individuals tend to be better at finance, investing, and gambling. Because they can't feel the fear, they can make calm and rational investments or bets carrying risks that would scare away most people. The article also reported that there are a significant number of famous Wall Street investors who cannot feel such emotions.

Kim Yuri, the woman Mr Hwang loves, suffers from a similar disorder. But unlike others, she *can* still experience emotions – when it comes to cats, that is. Doctors don't have a good explanation for this. Kim Yuri's condition wasn't brought about by some traumatic accident. The disposition has developed slowly since she was a young girl.

"I grew up in an orphanage," Mr Hwang explained to me. "She was the headmaster's daughter. The headmaster was a remarkable man. He treated all the children like his own. Because of this, his daughter had to wear the same clothes and eat the same food as us. She even slept in the same quarters. Ironically, it was his own child who had to grow up like an orphan. But she was a sweet girl. She never abused the fact she was the headmaster's daughter and she never complained or asked for special treatment. She never acted jealous or envious of anyone else. In fact, she liked sharing her crayons and dolls with the orphans. She would always sit on top of the Zelkova branches and look down at the other children. I've loved her for seventeen years. I've always looked after her, and even now I stay by her side. When the headmaster passed away, his dying wish to me was to please look after his daughter. So, I've always stuck around her. And on the rare occasion she calls me first, I go running. She has a lot of cats, so it's hard for her to manage them all on her own. She appreciates my help. But it's purely platonic. She's tried to feel something for me. We even tried sex once. But it just didn't work. It was like if a human tried to have sex with a hippo. She simply couldn't do it with me."

According to what Mr Hwang tells me, Miss Kim showers her cats with love. In fact, she already has forty-nine of them. And raising forty-nine cats in a small place would take a lot of love because cats are very territorial animals. What's more, she owns almost every breed of cat there is, regardless of taste. Indeed, she doesn't care about breeds. Whether it's an expensive cat, a mixed breed, pretty or ugly, it's all the same to her.

"She takes care of all forty-nine cats by herself. She even puts out food in each alleyway for the strays. With this in mind, the real number of cats she looks after is much larger. Naturally, when she sees a cat that's been hit by a car with its leg broken or its intestines on the street, she can't just pass it by. Once she saw a cat that had been hit by a motorcycle, crawling around on the ground with its intestines trailing it; she almost lost her mind. She cried out about how evil and cruel humans could be. I had never seen her once cry while at the orphanage. That was the first time I had ever seen her cry. She wasn't the kind of girl who cried or smiled ever. But that day, she held that bloody cat in her arms as she ran to the vet hospital. The cat eventually died. Yuri didn't eat for three days. She has spent almost all her earnings on cats – buying cat food, cat litter, cat shampoo, cat toys. She's hand-built towers for her cats to play in. She nurses injured cats back to health and looks after stray cats. She sincerely feels empathy and love for cats. But she has no interest in humans. One day she asked me what love is. Here I am with my chest about to explode from love, and I couldn't tell her a thing about love. She once told me, 'If only you were a cat, I think we would be able to do that thing called love.' I can't forget those words. I want to teach her what love is. I want to teach her how tender love can be; it's warm; how noble the act of sharing love is. I want to show her that love is the only beautiful thing we humans are capable of."

Tears started to fall from Mr Hwang's now sober eyes. He wiped his tears with the back of his hand and took another shot of soju. Not knowing what to say, I also took another shot. The alcohol tasted like bitter medicine.

All afternoon I drank as I listened to him talk about love.

And, to be honest, I was moved by the innocence of a man wanting to change his entire being for the woman he loved. What's the point of life in this godforsaken city if you can't change everything about yourself for the one you love? We drank a lot that day. We were both drunk. Mr Hwang cried, and so did I. Finally, I made up my mind.

"All right. Let's turn this bastard into a cat!"

I learned that humans are a mirror of the world. After getting to know Mr Hwang, I started to doubt the symbols of the world I knew. The world I saw reflected in Mr Hwang's eyes had completely overturned my own world. Something was wrong. I didn't know if it was Mr Hwang or me or Miss Kim or this world, all I knew was something was wrong. And if something was wrong, what we needed was change.

I know, I can hear you saying, "But really? A cat?" You shouldn't be so quick to judge. I said it before. Sarcasm is no help and will never save us from the unhappiness of our lives. So, if you don't know a spell, or potion, or some special way of turning into a cat, please just be quiet. The only thing we need right now is the magic to turn Mr Hwang into a cat.

"Is there really someone who's turned into a cat?"

"There is. He was a Spanish-African named Paulus Willems. He's the legendary figure who successfully turned into a cat. He lived a respectable life as a human. He also lived a magnificent life as a cat. It took many lonely difficult years of practice. But eventually he was able to be reborn as a magnificent cat. He's an inspiration for millions of people dreaming of doing the same."

"What did he do after turning into a cat?"

"He was adopted by a good family. True cat lovers."

"Ah, of course–"

THE MAGICIAN

In his book *In Search of Lost Magic*, magician and esteemed student of the occult Callad de Lacras said this about magic:

> *You may never discover magic. But it won't be because magic doesn't exist. It'll be because you stopped dreaming. Magic exists all around us. In fact, magicians are quite common.*

I was on my way to meet a magician with Mr Hwang. I knew it was a fool's errand. The mere thought that it was possible to turn into a cat was foolish. But with what I knew from Cabinet 13, this was the only choice I had. And besides, it was the least I could do to help Mr Hwang, who was bent on dying by suicide if he couldn't turn into a cat. I just wanted to know if it was possible, for his sake. So please, don't laugh. It was embarrassing enough as it is.

The magician lived in a town called Giseok in the shadow of Mt Taebaek. It was once a bustling place, but now it was a dying coal town. Teams of bronze-faced miners were headed to the mines for their shifts. Each time the wind blew, a cloud of soot was ejected from the coal stacks in the open-air storage next to the tracks. Several people were hanging around in front of the way station, which only saw two trains a day. As there wasn't a single person who looked even remotely like a magician, we assumed he hadn't arrived yet. But then, a shabby-looking man emerged from the crowd outside the stations. As the man approached us, I secretly wished it weren't him.

"Hey! You work for the doc, right?"

I was slightly taken aback by his informal tone. After taking a moment to look us over, the first thing the magician asked us was, "You must be rich coming all the way out here." Taking my silence as an admission, he suggested we get a drink. The next thing I knew, I was sitting down with the magician and 290-pound Mr Hwang at a bar with some webfoot octopus, pork belly, and a menagerie of side dishes including cucumber, carrot, garlic, and peppers. Was I excited by this magical meeting? Yes, I was excited – so excited about having to catch a train at dawn headed for the middle of nowhere.

"You're kidding me, right? You got dumped by a girl and now you want to turn into a cat?"

It was only after six quick shots of soju that the magician finally spoke. He was drinking alcohol like a starving man eats bread, and seemed to be suffering from alcohol dependence. An awful stench was emanating from his body, as though he hadn't bathed in days. I knew that ascetics often made such sacrifices, but the man in front of me looked less like an ascetic and more like a bum.

"Dumped or not, that's not really the point," I interjected. "The problem is the girl doesn't feel emotions for people. She only has feelings for cats."

"Tomayto, tomahto. She likes cats, she doesn't like you – what's the difference?"

"I guess so," Mr Hwang said timidly, making his portly frame as small as he could.

"Can you really make it as a cat?" the magician asked.

"I'd rather live as a cat than a human. I mean it. I'll do my best. Please, just help me."

Mr Hwang pleaded to the magician as he poured him another obsequious glass of alcohol. The more Mr Hwang promised to "try hard," the more irritable and haughty the fake magician became.

The reason I came to see this magician was because he was the only bona fide magician inside Cabinet 13. All the other "magicians" Professor Kwon had met didn't make the cut. And that was because Professor Kwon thought them all fakes. Most of their files either found their way into the recycling bin or became footnotes. That's to say, this bum that was sitting in front of me was the only magician who was able to pass that hardnose's test and make it into the file cabinet as a magician. The problem was, there wasn't a single thing magical about him. Perhaps there was a mix-up in the files? The magician and Mr Hwang continued their ridiculous conversation.

"And tell me, what are you going to do when you become a cat? Did she say she'll marry you if you manage it?"

"I've never wanted something so improper as becoming that beautiful woman's husband, or having sex with her, or bearing a child with her. All I want is to be by her side."

The magician emptied his glass and chewed on still-raw webfoot octopus as he took a moment to think before speaking again.

"Just forget about her. You'll be better off."

After saying this, the magician shut up and only opened his mouth to drink or eat. I wanted to punch the bum in the mouth as I watched him gnaw on the octopus.

The magician sniffled frequently, as though he had a cold. And there was an indescribably awful smell coming from his shoes, which he had at some point taken off. His socks were so dirty that you couldn't tell what their original color had been. With eyes filled with incredulity, I stared at this charlatan.

"Can you show us a simple trick or something?" I said as I poured him another glass of soju.

"Why? What do you think I am? Some cheap peddler?"

It was all I could do to not say yes. To be completely honest, calling him a cheap peddler would be too generous. But thinking about Mr Hwang and how far he'd come to meet this magician, I decided instead to suck up a little.

"But I heard you're Korea's finest magician."

"Says who?"

"Professor Kwon."

"Don't be ridiculous."

"It's true."

"That old timer doesn't believe in magic for shit. Neither does he believe in magicians. When he came here to see me all those years ago, all we did was argue. Why come to meet a magician if you don't believe in magic? What a crazy old coot."

Visibly upset by the memory of Professor Kwon, the magician hastily downed another couple shots of soju. Next to me, Mr Hwang was sitting with a look of worry on his face. We had emptied the grill of all the octopus and pork belly. The magician picked up his chopsticks only to put them back down in disappointment. I ordered another three servings for him, despite the fact he had eaten all three servings of pork belly and undercooked octopus without sharing.

"Please, have some more," I said as I poured him another glass of soju.

"You know, this place has great clam soup."

The magician spoke in a somewhat bashful manner. I was starting to get really annoyed with him, but nevertheless I ordered some clam soup.

"Mr Magician, Mr Hwang isn't trying to turn into a cat for kicks. He's extremely serious and desperate. We're not asking you to turn him into a cat, we just want to know if it's even possible. In your opinion."

"What, you think turning into an animal is easy? You know the transformation spells they have in movies, right? The kind you only need memorize if you want to instantaneously turn into a toad. Hogwash! In all my fifty years of being a magician, I have never once heard of a wizard or witch so powerful. And besides, that's not how magic works. Magic takes time. In fact, if you think about it, life itself is magic. And nature, too. We're born as tiny little babies, become strong young men as large as this fellow, then become small again as hunched-over old men before finally turning to dust. It might not seem like much, but when you really think about it, it's nothing short of a miracle. Look at those trees over there. They bloom in the spring, becoming lusciously green in the summer, turn bright red in the fall, and drop their leaves and fruit in the winter – all without dying. Is there anything more marvelous? This is magic."

Nonsense was spewing from the magician's mouth. "We don't need your useless philosophical talk," I said, irritated. "Just give it to us straight. Is it possible or isn't it?"

"Of course it's possible."

"Really?" Mr Hwang and I said simultaneously in surprise.

"Why wouldn't it be? But even for the great ancient wizards, doing it would have taken ten, maybe twenty years. For someone like yourself, it'll probably require at least thirty years of hard work."

"Thirty years!" I said in shock.

"So it's possible if I can wait thirty years?" Mr Hwang said with glistening eyes.

Mr Hwang was a nice guy. But thirty years? By that time, she'd be an old woman.

"Thirty years at the least! But to make the transformation, you have to first change your mind and body. First you must expel all the bad energy from your body through disciplined fasting and dieting. Then you must train your mind with the same level of discipline. You need to have a mind and body that can harmonize with other beings. A mind and body that can harmonize with water, the trees, the wind – even the flowers."

"But I can become a cat in thirty years, right?" Mr Hwang asked again anxiously.

"Yes, but I've never heard of any Korean turning into a cat. It's more common and traditional to turn into a bear or tiger."

"What do you mean, 'more common and traditional?'" I asked.

"You've heard of the myth of Dangun, right? Back in the day, ancient Koreans all wanted to turn into bears and tigers. But now everyone wants to turn into celebrities."

"Where in the myth of Dangun does it say that? I've never heard of such a thing."

"Didn't you go to college?"

"I did."

"And yet you don't know about this? If you've ever stepped foot on a college campus, you should at least know that. Just imagine if you were alive during the Paleolithic period. As a human, you barely have enough hair to cover your head; you don't have any tough hide; you're weak; and to top it all off, you're too slow to outrun predators. Now you tell me, would you want to be born a human into such a cruel wilderness? Or would you want to be born a lion – with no natural predators, and easy prey like impala and zebra handed to you on a silver platter; able to eat when you want to eat, and sleep in wide-open plains without a care in the world?"

"I'd want to be born a lion."

"If you lived in a swamp, would you want to be born as a carp or frog? Or would you want to be born as a crocodile."

"A crocodile."

"And if you were born in the sea, would you want to be born an anchovy? Or would you want to be born a shark?"

"A shark."

"See. Even ten thousand years ago, there wasn't a single person who wanted to be born a human. Everyone wished they had been born an animal, and that's why they worshiped beasts. The problem is which animal to become. And in the mountainous regions of the Korean peninsula, there were no animals fiercer than the tiger and the bear. As such, the magic for turning into tigers and bears was quite advanced. There were all sorts of different methods; they even developed medical botany to treat the transformation side effects. But then one day, according to legend, a bear named Ungnyeo came to Hwanung, the Lord of Heaven, and asked to be turned into a human. All the humans were madly trying to become bears, but here was this bear who wanted to become a human. In the history of magic, this was the paradigm shift that changed the fate of magicians forever. In other words, Ungnyeo was the first beast to break free from the world of magic and live with the power of a human."

"Does that mean you've transformed into a bear or tiger before?" Mr Hwang asked.

"Why would I want to turn into a tiger in this day and age!" The magician suddenly lashed out in drunken anger. "There are firemen and police on every street. If I turned into a tiger, I'd be captured and sent to a zoo for breeding. And I don't even want to imagine what would happen if I turned into a bear. People these days catch bears to suck up their gall bladder with a straw. I've heard stories of bears having their feet cut off during hibernation just so people can make soup. Isn't that gruesome? Just imagine you're sleeping one day when suddenly someone sticks a straw into your chest and starts sucking on your gall bladder. What could you say in that situation? 'Um, excuse me, sir. I'm sorry to bother you while you're enjoying your meal. But I'm not actually a bear.' Is this what you'll say? Just thinking about it makes my skin crawl. The world is a cruel place. No, never. Not a bear, not a tiger. They're completely useless now. Completely, utterly useless."

As I sat there hoping this pathetic conversation would end, I wondered to myself how it was that I had got here. But considering the fact I'd already ordered three more servings of octopus, that I had already spent the better part of my day coming out here, and that the last train for the city had already left, I resolved to stay put until the magician had finished. It appeared that Mr Hwang was also disappointed with the magician. We drank all day.

"I'm not talking about your stupid philosophical talk; don't you have anything more concrete for us? Don't get me wrong, but everything you've said so far just sounds like hearsay to me. I find it hard to believe that any of it's true," I said a bit crookedly. Having had a few drinks myself, I figured I'd just go with it. He too had already drunk a lot; what was the worst that could happen?

"This guy! You're not gonna stop until I show you a cheap parlor trick, are ya?" the magician grumbled. With this, he took his hand and placed it over a glass. Suddenly, the alcohol in the glass started to bubble. It formed into a sphere the size of a billiard ball and started to float in midair. It was really floating in midair. About thirty centimeters above the table. The sphere of alcohol hovered above the magician's hand as it slowly revolved. Our jaws dropped as Mr Hwang and I stared at the sphere of alcohol floating above the magician's hand. I leaned in closer until my face was no more than three centimeters from the sphere, but I still couldn't believe my eyes. I took my chopsticks and swiped at the air above and beneath the sphere, but the alcohol stayed in place. Finally, the magician took the floating sphere of alcohol and poured it into Mr Hwang's glass.

"Fundamentally, we are all made of the same stuff. People, water, trees, the wind – we're all the same. And because we're the same, we can change into whatever we want."

Seeing the magician's one magic trick, Mr Hwang was already completely won over. Filled with awe, he lifted his glass and drank the shot of alcohol. He then made a face of further amazement.

"It's water!"

"And it's a damn shame, too. I can turn wine into water, but I can't turn water into wine. I'm a failure of a magician. All I want to learn how to do is how to make water into wine," the magician said, making an expression of sadness and regret.

"Do I need to go into the mountains?" Mr Hwang asked, suddenly making his tone serious.

"The mountains? What for?"

"To undergo spiritual training," Mr Hwang said, this time in more resolute tone.

"Spiritual training, sure. But why the mountains? You hoodlums always hike up mountains and make such a commotion. You can cultivate yourself spiritually at home or at the office if you want. You don't need to come to the mountains for that. And besides, what need do city folk have for spiritual training? You don't even care about littering! People like that lack the fundamentals. The fundamentals, I tell you."

"So why do you train out here in the mountains?" I asked.

"Hey, I live here because it's cheap. You think I live here because I want to?"

The clam soup came out as the magician started to go on a rant about the people who leave trash in the mountains. The magician paused his rant to wolf down the clam soup. Mr Hwang and I followed suit and tasted the soup which was shockingly good.

"This is amazing," Mr Hwang said as he marveled at the clam soup.

And it was. If I were on death row, I would request that clam soup for my last meal, without a second thought. We stopped all conversation and buried our heads in our bowls as if we were competitive eaters. Before long, we had finished the lot.

"Cooking, is it not itself a form of magic? It's a feast of fire, ingredients, potions, and spells. If it weren't magic, could it taste this good?"

We kept ordering until we had eaten five bowls each. We ate and ate, but we didn't become sick of the taste in the least. When the hunchedbacked old woman, who looked over 90, gave us the fifth bowl of clam soup, she said, "We're out of clams now, you bastards." By the time we licked the fifth bowl clean, the three of us were quite drunk.

The drunk magician started humming "A Song of Fire", a strange song that I had never heard before. The magician also gave a speech about Spain, the spiritual home of all magicians.

He also talked about the revolution in magical aviation during the seventeenth century, when the orientation of witch brooms reversed. Before then, witches flew with the handle pointing forward, but after that, they flew with the bristles pointing forward and even hung candles as a sort of fog lamp. He also told us about how his father and grandfather had both been magicians. He told us about the time his grandfather went to see his magician friend in North Korea. He was levitating over the DMZ when his clothes got caught on barbed wire. He was shot by border police and died. The magician also bragged about how the mark on his forehead was from running into a branch while practicing levitation as a young boy. He also said that he missed the time when humans worshipped bears and tigers. "People should worship bears and want to be bears; they shouldn't suck them up them with straws," he lamented. The magician said the decline of magic was all because of bear-turned-human Ungnyeo. He said he hated her. He said it was all downhill for magic after that, among other ridiculous things. Then Mr Hwang talked about Miss Kim and cried some more. He talked about how the only emotion Miss Kim felt toward humans was the hatred she felt toward people who harm cats. He talked about how he felt bad for that girl who must be living in hell. He cried and cried. Patting Mr Hwang on the back, the magician said not to worry because he would take it upon himself to turn Mr Hwang into a cat. Getting on all fours to bow to the magician, Mr Hwang vowed to try his hardest and that he would never forget the magician's grace.

Drunk and with heavy eyelids, I thought to myself this was the most pathetic drinking party I'd ever been a part of.

The magician wanted to keep drinking, but thankfully we were able to send him home. After that, Mr Hwang and I found a rundown inn in which to stay the night.

"Don't be too disappointed. There are other ways," I said.

"Disappointed? About what? I believe what the magician said. I feel really encouraged after today. Tomorrow I'm going to go jogging and do some hula hoop. The magician said I need to be able to accept other beings into my heart, and possess a mind and body that can harmonize with those other beings. Starting tomorrow, I'm going to live to the fullest."

Soon after this, Mr Hwang fell asleep. A dark inn room in a coal town named Giseok. Listening to Mr Hwang snore a snore worthy of a man his size, I thought to myself that he had indeed gained a lot of courage today. I believed in the power of imagination. I was the keeper of Cabinet 13, after all. There was nothing that couldn't happen when it came to Cabinet 13. With the help of a fake magician, it just might have been possible for a man to turn into a cat – a 290lb super cat.

A magician came up to me and said:

"You might not believe me, but magicians have, since long ago, engaged in inter-Korean relations. Magicians from North and South Korea have a summit once every four years. In fact, magicians have played an important role in opening up relations between the two countries. But these days, there are a lot of fakes trying to get in. So there's a test of sorts."

"What kind of test?"

"Jumping over the East Gate."

"You mean the one on Jongno 5-ga?"

"That's the one. If you can jump over the gate, you can participate in the summit."

"What do the ascetics of the North and South do when they meet?"

"You know, discuss separated families, unification, denuclearization, humanitarian aid – there are a lot of things to talk about."

A different magician approached me and said:

"You might not believe me, but magicians have, since long ago, engaged in inter-Korean relations–"

"I've heard."

"Then you must have heard that participants are required to jump over the South Gate to demonstrate their magical powers and prove they're not fakes, yes?"

"Wasn't it the East Gate?"

"No, the East Gate is where the fakes go," he said confidently.

"Ah, of course–"

HOSPITAL ROOM

"How are things at the center?" Professor Kwon asked as he put down the book he was reading.

"Same as always. Messy, disordered, unreasonable... not to mention the absurd phone calls."

"I heard you went to Mt Taebaek recently?"

What a peculiar old man. How did he know about that, lying here in his hospital bed? That stubbornness which means he doesn't believe in the people closest to him; that paranoia which causes him to have unbearable anxiety if he doesn't have his feelers out – that's what ruined Professor Kwon. Pretending not to have heard his question, I turned my head slightly to look out the window.

"Are you ignoring me?"

"If I hadn't gone to Mt Taebaek, Mr Hwang would be in a coffin by now. And a big one at that, seeing as he's a big man."

"Don't waste your time. And besides, that magician's a fake."

"I saw him levitate a sphere of alcohol."

"You fell for that trick? Even illusionists can do that. Tell me, after showing you his trick, did he start reminiscing about magic in the old days?"

"The important thing is not whether he's a fake or not. What's important is hope."

"So did that fat ass get hope? After being fooled by fake magic, does he believe he can turn into a cat?"

"He been jogging every morning and even bought a

membership at the gym. He also says he's going to go hiking on the weekends and learn yoga. He's healthier than he's ever been. Those are life changes he couldn't have imagined even in his wildest dreams."

"We're not miracle workers, Deok-geun. We can't do anything for them and nor should we try."

"Then why for the last thirty years have you obsessed over that old cabinet? If you can't give them even the smallest bit of hope? I didn't go all the way to Giseok on my precious weekend because I wanted to."

I was surprised at my sudden outburst. Professor Kwon also looked surprised. He looked like he was about to say something but then stopped, which was unlike him. He turned to look out the window and stayed silent for a while. The two of us just gazed outside without talking. The hospital room was quiet. The room, which Professor Kwon had all to himself, was so quiet that you could even hear the dripping of the IV fluid. Come to think of it, it was strange that Professor Kwon had chosen to upgrade himself to a single. I have never once seen him spend extra money on himself or for others. He even took the bus and train when going to the provinces for business trips. And because the strange people we dealt with often lived far from civilization, he sometimes would walk for the better part of a day just to get there. He always bought a banana and a castella for lunch. He liked castella. I hated it. Even so, we always ate castella. "There's not a cheaper nor a better way to eat lunch than castella," Professor Kwon once told me. I told him about a million other foods that were cheaper and better than castella. And yet we always ate castella. And this was the guy who chose to have a hospital room all to himself. It was an unusual extravagance.

After staring out the window for some time, Professor Kwon finally spoke:

"We look after the files, that's all we do. I wish we could do something for them, but we don't have that ability. And besides, when it comes to surviving in this cold world, futile hope does more harm than good. We're just custodians: people who put files into the cabinet and lock the drawer. Nothing more, nothing less. I hope you remember that."

His voice was low and lacking in vigor, which was also unusual for him. "If you do something like that again, I'll bash in your teeth with a hammer." This was what he would say normally. Saying in a low, feeble voice, "I hope you remember that," didn't sound like Professor Kwon at all. Perhaps thinking that I had got the message, Professor Kwon didn't say anything more about my taking Mr Hwang to see the magician. He turned again to look out the window and fell asleep watching the oak tree outside. I look at his face for some time.

Professor Kwon was dying. Cancer and cirrhosis were simultaneously taking over his liver. When Professor Kwon asked the doctor, who was also his friend from high school, if he would be OK, the doctor smiled bitterly as he said, "When it comes to livers, there are no miracles." It wouldn't have been so bad if the doctor had said, "Well, let's wait and see," but that's not what the doctor said. Livers never experience miracles. Professor Kwon should have looked after his health a little and not been so obsessed with research and organizing files. If only he'd eaten something healthier than cup ramen and castella.

As there weren't going to be any miracles, it was settled that Professor Kwon was going to die. Even he knew it. He wasn't married, and because he had no wife and was conservative when it came to relationships, he didn't have any children either. All he did his whole life was research. But even so, because he hadn't published a paper in forty years, no one was interested in his research.

Why in the world did he use me as an assistant? Over the last forty years, he never once had an assistant, nor did he have any students; so why did he entrust the management of all these monsters to me of all people, someone with no background in science? For the last seven years I'd been asking myself this question. And now that he had only a few months to live, that question was becoming even more nagging. No matter how I looked at it, there was no reason for me to be entrusted with Cabinet 13.

It was late in the evening when Professor Kwon finally awoke. I was just about to head home.

"You're still here?" Professor Kwon said.

"Not because I was worried about you, or anything like that. I just wanted to avoid rush hour on the train."

"You don't have to lie."

Professor Kwon stared at the ceiling and let out a sigh. It was a warning. He was about to evoke my sympathy and make some sort of great request. But I wasn't going to be tricked this time. As expected, Professor Kwon turned his head toward me and looked at me with sad, vulnerable eyes. Secretly I wanted to say, "Haven't you asked enough of me? Just with answering your phone my head feels like it's about to explode." But whatever it was that Professor Kwon was going to say, I wasn't prepared for it. Being prepared. Professor Kwon would know better than me that it's impossible ever to be prepared.

"You know, right? I don't have much longer to live. When I die, what will happen to the poor people of Cabinet 13?"

"Why are you asking? Professor, people should have a sense of shame. And they should feel guilty making someone work so hard. And what's more, I don't know the first thing about biology, genetics, anthropology, archaeology, or psychopathology. And there's one other thing you should know; I majored in Korean Literature in college. Perhaps you, as a STEM major, don't know what that means, but Korean literature majors research useless things like features of vowels and consonants; there's nothing I'm qualified to talk about in those files except for the fact they're written in Hangul."

"No, you're perfect. You're perfect because you're outlandish and stupid. And you're terribly sincere. I can tell that just from seeing how you fell for that stupid parlor trick and how you've worked for seven years without any compensation."

"I didn't do it because I'm stupid; I did it because I pitied you."

"Even better. You're not just stupid, you're sympathetic, too. Must be hard living in this cruel world."

"Do you really intend on making me your successor?"

"My successor? I'm just a failed scientist and a loser. Someone like me doesn't have any need for a successor. I just need someone to look after those poor people when I'm gone. Someone like you."

"I can't do anything."

"You're just like me, then. For the last forty years, I haven't been able to use the power of worthless science to help those people. In fact, you're much better than me. You're stronger and nicer. I'm not asking you to do everything I did. I just want you to record and safekeep. And in such a way that people understand symptomers are not dangerous or dirty monsters, but our new descendants, and eventually, the new destiny we must come to accept."

"Isn't there anyone more suited for the job? Like another researcher in the field?"

"They don't understand. Science is stuck in a hole it created for itself."

Professor Kwon grabbed my hand with his, a hand that was now just skin and bones because of a liver that couldn't detoxify anything anymore, a thin hand that was black and brown from all the needles. The hand was cold despite having come from underneath his blankets.

"I'm begging you."

I didn't know what to do. And the fact I didn't know what to do was obvious to Professor Kwon because I lacked any skills or talent that would allow me to do anything. But I couldn't say no to a dying man; I had to at least lie. And yet, it felt like I was going to regret it if I said even a single word. Professor Kwon was reaching the end of the road, which was sad, but no one lives forever. Couldn't I say something humanitarian and encouraging at least? Then I remembered how much I resented him for having done nothing for me over the last seven years. How could he think of asking this of me? But then again, wouldn't it be too cold to say no to a dying man? I was afraid, too; taking over Cabinet 13 wasn't your everyday request. But here was Professor Kwon, batting his big, sad eyes at me.

So I hesitated. Why did I have to take over that headache of a cabinet? Professor Kwon had devoted forty years of his life to it; what more could I do? Wouldn't I first need to read some books on genetic engineering, molecular biology, and Mesopotamian hieroglyphs? These questions seem like they might have been smart things to consider in the moment, but actually, at the time, I wasn't thinking much. There was no way I was smart enough to consider all of this on the spot.

I was probably thinking instead about the bathroom on the fourth floor of the office. In that bathroom there's a large steel fan that spins round and round, and as it spins it slices and devours the smoke from my cigarette. I sit there with some coffee, a newspaper, and a cigarette as I take a satisfying shit, and as I sit there I always imagine absurd things, like my soul floating away with the smoke, up to the fan, where it is cut into tiny pieces before dissipating through the grates.

My tongue started to move on its own as the last remaining logical thoughts in my head were sliced up and dispersed by the memory of this fan blade, unable to reform into definite shapes.

"Professor Kwon, Cabinet 13 scares me."

Professor Kwon stared at me for a moment with a look of regret. Even so, he didn't press me any further. After saying goodbye to Professor Kwon, I took my bag and left the hospital room.

"Was I being too selfish?" I asked myself on the way home.

"You've always been selfish," I replied.

DRINKING CANNED BEER

Everyone has times they want to forget. 1997 was such a time for me. Nothing compares to how bad of a year 1997 was. My banker friend once said this to me:

"Unhappiness never comes in installments. It always comes in one big lump sum. That's why it's always so tough to deal with unhappiness."

It was January of that year. My mother had collapsed. By the time we got her to the hospital, it was too late. At the emergency room, the resident was useless and flustered, and the nurse seemed to be having difficulty understanding my explanation of what had happened. Back in the ambulance, my mother had been holding my hand like she knew she was going to die. "Son, get a stable job. One that's good."

I guess these were what my mom thought were the most important words with which to part her pitiful son.

My bum of a father – who may be still alive, I'm not sure – left when I was just a baby; after that, it was just my mother and me. Because the only relative we had was my uncle, my mother's funeral was as lonesome as her life was miserable. After they put my mother into the incinerator at the crematorium, I said this to my uncle:

"I guess I'm an orphan now."

My uncle stomped out his cigarette on the floor before saying:

"Don't sweat it, kid. We all end up orphans, in the end."

I graduated from college that spring and was cast out into the world. Needless to say, I wasn't the least bit prepared for it. Since the fall semester of my senior year in 1996, I had applied to a total of 126 companies and failed to get a single offer. As though to say they were uninterested in meeting someone like me, seventy of them outright passed on my resumé. Another fifty rejected me after I took their test. I did get six interviews, but I failed all of them. One salt-and-pepper-haired interviewer asked me if I could bring anything special to the company. Being seated in the middle of the board of interviewers, he looked like the CEO. I was terribly nervous as I said, "I don't have any special skills, but I'm confident I can do whatever work comes my way." A smirk formed on the corners of the interviewer's mouth as he said, "And when I was your age, I was confident I could conquer the world. But now look at me, sitting here talking to some naïve kid fresh out of college." He was right. Now that I thought about it, my answer was naïve. Confidence wasn't enough in the twenty-first century. It wasn't the Wild West anymore. What I needed were certificates that vouched for my skills, not confidence.

That summer, I broke up with my girlfriend of 8 years and 7 months. Well, to be more accurate, it wasn't that we broke up, it was more like I realized she had already left me. As high school sweethearts, we had always been by each other's side, so when she left it felt strange. I wasn't sure exactly at what moment she and I broke up. Neither of us questioned what had happened, and because no one questioned, no one answered. I called one day only to find out she was already married. This might sound too crazy to be true, but it's not. I called her after a long time of not talking and said, "Sorry I haven't been able to call lately. I've been busy with studying for tests. Anyhow, do you want to meet this weekend and see a movie or something?" And she said in a stuttering voice, "Deok-geun... I'm married." At that moment, I didn't have anything to say. What could I say in such a situation? Not surprisingly, she also didn't have much to say to me. We just held our phones in our hands and didn't speak for what felt like hours. I could hear from the other end of the line the sound of a soap opera. Past the sound of the TV, I also heard the faint sound of a man's baritone voice saying, "Honey, there's no toothpaste in the bathroom!" After the long silence, she finally asked in a concerned tone, "Are you OK?" I said yes. I thought I really was. That was the last time I talked to my girlfriend of 8 years and 7 months. We were together for 8 years and 7 months when suddenly one day she was married to a baritone looking for toothpaste. It is what it is.

Did I love her? Of course I loved her. She was a sweet girl and beautiful; too good for me, really. But I let her go. Back then, helplessness and dread lingered around my life like a thick fog. The word employment sounded like a distant dream; I had no talent, no experience to offer. One of my friends once complained to me about preparing his CV: "How do they expect us to summarize our entire life in just ten lines?" Hearing him say this made me feel miserable. How nice it must be to agonize over how to summarize all your experiences and achievements. When my friends asked me if I planned on getting married, inside my head I would say, "Married? I don't have any money to get married." Indeed, I would hate to cast a shadow over her future by combining it with my poor future.

The dog that my mother and I had raised for the previous ten years also died in the summer of that wretched year. He was a Labrador – laidback, quiet, and understanding. He never yelped in pain or cried for long. And true to character, he passed away quietly. He might have been trying to send me a message, but if he had I didn't notice. If you've raised a dog before, you'll know the pain of losing a cherished companion. It's hard to explain the sadness of losing your dog. I still don't understand how this was possible, but on the day my dog died, I held him in my arms and cried harder than I had at my mother's funeral.

The day after he died, I wrapped my dog in a black garbage

bag, put that bag in a shopping bag, then rode the bus out of the city. I was going to bury him on top of a small mountain. On my way up the mountain, I passed a man who suspiciously eyed the shopping bag in my hand as he asked where I was headed. I told him I was on my way to bury my dog. The man frowned as he told me, "That's illegal, you know." I just scoffed and went my way.

It was hot on the summer mountain trail, and my dog's carcass was heavy. I had wanted to bury my dog on a mountain top overlooking the area, but I gave up halfway up the mountain and simply buried him where it was easiest. Needless to say, this too was illegal. I sprinkled alcohol on my dog's grave and took a sip for myself. As I smoked a cigarette, I spoke to my old friend.

"We had some good times, didn't we?"

I'm not sure what I was thinking, but on my way home from burying my dog I took all the money out of my bank account, which contained the inheritance left to me by my mother. Aside from my rented apartment, that money was my only possession. And then I used all that money to buy hundreds of cans of beer. It was about four hundred and fifty boxes of beer, which came out to more than twelve thousand cans. The cashier at the large discount store said she wasn't allowed to sell this many boxes of beer all at once. What happened to unbridled capitalism? I couldn't understand why I couldn't buy whatever I wanted as long as I had the money – after all, it wasn't like I was buying chemicals or guns, just cans of beer. So, I made a scene. "What do you mean I can't buy these!" Not long after I started screaming, someone with more authority came out and told the cashier that it was all right as long as she took down my phone number and address. So, the cashier asked me for my contact information, and I gave it to her. I had the beer delivered to my apartment.

I still don't quite understand why I did something so stupid. It's not like I wanted to do anything as dramatic as drinking myself into the grave. No, I just didn't want to see anyone; didn't want to talk with anyone; didn't want to have to make any more lame excuses to anyone. I just wanted to dig myself a hole and stay there.

That summer I locked myself in my apartment and began drinking my cans of beer. I literally did nothing but stay in my apartment and drink beer. I stacked the boxes of beer I had purchased with all my money in the main bedroom, living room, kitchen, balcony, and even in the bathroom, and chugged beer for the next 178 days. I started drinking as soon as I woke up and kept drinking until I fell asleep from exhaustion. During those days, I consumed nothing but beer, peanuts, and the occasional glass of water.

But it wasn't as hard as I thought it would be. All I had to do was open the fridge, take out a can of beer, break the seal, drink it, crumple it up, and toss it in whichever corner I fancied. When my throat was sore or I felt hungry, I ate peanuts. Then I would open another can of beer and repeat the process. Each time I finished a beer, I made sure to crumple up the can. It might sound like a small detail, but it was absolutely essential to the process. Oddly, the moment I crumpled the can, I got a destructive, devil-may-care feeling and that destructive, devil-may-care feeling is what gave me the strength to take another can of beer from the fridge.

As long as you don't ask yourself why you keep doing something, you can keep doing it until the day you die. You might experience a bit of mouth vomit at first, doing what I did. You might even feel, after sticking your face in the toilet and puking several times, that you'll never be able to taste another can of beer again. But that feeling's only temporary. Give it a few more days and you won't puke anymore. Eventually you'll get over the torture and nausea; you might even think you're not doing something that extreme. You won't even feel hungry, despite only consuming beer, peanuts, and water. You'll probably have the same ridiculous idea that I had that beer, peanuts, and water might contain all the necessary nutrients to sustain human life. And when that happens, you've achieved stable orbit. When that happens, you can really focus on opening cans of beer, drinking cans of beer, and crumpling cans of beer. When that happens, reality with all its envy, fear, and anxiety disappears, and all that you'll be left with is the unreality that enters your head. When that happens, the mere thought of ever stopping will frighten you.

For 178 days, I repeatedly woke up, opened a can of beer, drank the beer, crumpled the beer can, and cracked peanuts until I collapsed from exhaustion. Sometimes I would pee into the toilet and watch the urine stream out of my body with a blank stare. Sometimes the sun outside my window would glare like a tropical blaze before tripping on the powerlines over the sunset, and the hazy sound of car horns would soar into the sky faster than a speeding bullet. But just like the laundry hanging from the townhouse balconies opposite my apartment meant nothing to me, these things also meant nothing to me. The wind would rustle the laundry on the opposite balcony, the sun would dry it, then someone would come out and air out the clothes before folding them. What was it they were trying to air out? I would ask myself while watching a woman from the townhouses air out grains of sunlight. Perhaps she was trying to get rid of her husband's sundried sperm – those desiccated spermatozoa that were beyond resurrection. But I wasn't really that interested in what the woman was trying to air out. The only reason I was merely imagining such fanciful things was because it was what was in front of my eyes.

Sometimes I would get a call from utilities pressing me to pay my bills, but I would just half listen to them or say I didn't have any money. I also got a couple calls from what I think was the tax office. I found it laughable that buying four hundred and fifty boxes of canned beer was grounds for getting an audit.

"We're aware that you've recently purchased a large amount of beer. Such a large purchase of alcohol needs to be reported. We've had instance of undocumented illegal distribution before. So, was the beer for some event? If so, could you give me the name of the event. We need it for documentation."

"There's no event, nothing like that. I'm just drinking it by myself."

"Come again? You mean to say you're drinking four hundred and fifty boxes of beer by yourself? That's impossible."

Click!

I drank those cans of beer for 178 days straight. To be honest, I might have been more interested in crumpling the cans than I was in drinking the beer. Inside me, there was a silent churning riverbed of violent despair and helplessness that could not mend itself. Or at least I thought there was. Come to think of it, I'm starting to wonder if it was ever there at all. Can people really die from a broken heart? Probably not. Humans can't die from love – at least, not me, apparently.

I stopped on day 178, even though there was still some remaining beer and peanuts. There was no reason for my stopping, just as there was no reason for my starting. You either keep doing something or you stop doing something, that's life. Anyway, by then, strewn about my apartment were enough beer cans to make my apartment an aluminum deposit. On the last day, I threw away all the cans and said to myself:

"I guess I have nowhere else to run. Maybe it's time to get some fresh air."

I'll never forget the taste of the seolleongtang I ate that day after leaving my house for the first time in 178 days. I cried to myself over that bowl of seolleongtang, but it wasn't in reflection or regret. I realize now they were tears of joy – joy brought about by those delicious hot mouthfuls of soup.

PART 2
City of Heaven

TIME SKIPPERS

June 14, 1999. Kim Yun-mi went missing in a subway on her way to meet her boyfriend B at Jongno-3. Her family and the police searched for two years and even offered a reward, but not one single piece of useful information ever surfaced. Kim Yun-mi had disappeared into thin air. But then, exactly three years later on June 14, 2002 at 5:00 pm, she was discovered in Jongno-3 in front of the KumKang building. That day was the last day of the round of sixteen for the World Cup, and Jongno was bustling with all the street supporters in Gwanghwamun Plaza. The good Samaritans who took her to the hospital said they were stunned she didn't know what day it was.

No one knew where Kim Yun-mi had been for those three years or what she had been doing. No one claimed to have seen her, and there were no traces of her whereabouts. In fact, she was discovered wearing the exact same clothes and shoes she had been wearing when she left her house that day. There was nothing she remembered about the three years she had been missing. She even looked exactly as she had on the day of her disappearance.

But this wasn't a first for Kim Yun-mi. When she was a sophomore in high school, she had disappeared for three months before being discovered in a clothes factory. She also disappeared for six months while studying to retake the College Scholastic Ability Test. When Kim Yun-mi told her parents that it felt like her time had just disappeared, they simply laughed at her.

"We get it. When she was in high school, she was picked on by the other kids. And retaking the CSATs must have been incredibly stressful. She's always wanted to run away from her problems. I'm not sure if she prostituted herself or lived with some bum. I'm just glad she came back in good health."

The fourth time Kim Yun-mi's time disappeared was in June 2004. But this time, the disappearance didn't surprise her much. At just two months, it was relatively short too. She didn't make excuses to her parents about her disappearance, nor did she act hysterical, as was common for time-skippers to do. She came back as if it were nothing and returned to her daily life quietly. When I interviewed her, she joked that "It doesn't seem that bad." She then added with a wry laugh, "I've got experience under my belt now." A week later, she hanged herself in her room.

"I know what death is," she once said to me. "Death is when the balance in your bank account of time reaches zero. You've either used up all your time, or someone has taken it from you. That's all it is. You simply have no money to revive your bankrupt life."

Because pain isn't quantifiable, I cannot understand how much pain she was in by losing time. So it would be rash of me to say it was rash of her to choose suicide. Yet I can't help but think there must have been a fair amount of time left in her bank account. A balance large enough to restore her life from bankruptcy. I've always regretted not being able to tell her that. Although I doubt if anything I said would have helped much.

There are people whose time disappears. On the subway, flipping through the pages of a book, rushing to an engagement, or even simply staring at the clock – at any moment, these people can lose time ranging from as little as a few minutes or hours to as long as several days or years. They think only a few seconds have passed, but in reality, an absurd amount of time has elapsed. Well, disappeared to be exact. And during that time, there exists no events nor any memories of any events. They have no memory of that time, and the world has no memory of them.

Missing time and disappearing. People who experience this phenomenon experience greater trauma than we can ever imagine. When I asked what it felt like to lose so much time, Sua Lee, an accountant, said this:

"It felt like my whole life had been taken from me."

Ironically, time skippers are thorough when it comes to managing the time they do have control over. They prefer regulated and punctual lives and are thorough with their time almost to the point of being compulsive.

"I feel uneasy if I don't have plans or rules. I feel like I need to plan out my life. I try my best to not waste time. I remove uncontrollable variables as best as I can, take advantage of my spare time as best as I can, consider the amount of exercise and sleep I need for the next day, and am meticulous when meeting people so that I don't have any gaps in my schedule. I even make time on the weekend to relax. But for some reason people act like I have OCD. Doesn't the media always go on about how keeping a regular schedule is good for your heath?"

They had a point. I don't know what's wrong with that, either. But in modern theoretical physics, time can disappear. Despite what we generally think, time is neither continuous nor regular. It can be added and subtracted, expanded and contracted. Time can be distorted, warped; can appear, and disappear.

Perhaps time skippers appearing in random places and times is a result of large twists in the fabric of spacetime. Ship engineer Gu Dong-jin disappeared from Yeoksam subway station and woke up three years later on a small island in the South Pacific.

"I had experienced instances of losing anywhere from ten to thirty minutes at a time before that. But losing three years at

once was a first. Once I came to, I was on some island. The
local children were catching crayfish. Beautiful women with
bare chests and brown skin were laughing at me. The sun
was beaming, and the seawater was clear. It's what I imagined
heaven to look like. I just stared out into the ocean. I thought
for sure I was dreaming. Only a minute before I was like an
ant on the subway headed for work, and now I was suddenly
on a coral island in the South Pacific. I just sat there with a
blank expression on my face. The children kindly gave me some
grilled crayfish and boiled bananas. It was good. Obviously, I
couldn't communicate with them, and my phone didn't have
any service. I couldn't use my credit card, and I didn't have my
passport on me. What could I do in such a place? At first I just
resigned myself to staying for a few days, but as time passed, I
didn't want to think about anything. It felt like my head had
been emptied dry, and all that was left was an honest body. So I
just stayed. I learned how to catch crayfish from the children and
how to fish with a spear. I swam in the ocean; dived under the
water; peeled bananas and coconuts; took naps in a hammock.
I even got married to a local girl so beautiful she could be on a
calendar. Her name is Buba. Isn't that a beautiful name?"

"Didn't you want to return to Korea?"

"No."

"Why not? It's your home, after all."

"Home is such a funny word. We make the decision to live
somewhere and then it's called 'home.' We eat there, work
there, get married there, buy a house there. We root for the
home team and become friends with people solely because
they're from the same part of the world. But I've had a lot
of bad times in Korea. Something was just off – spatially,
temporally. I know now what a happy life is. I've been on a
long journey. I don't think 'home' is that important. To really
know yourself, you sometimes have to become a nomad and
forget about home." He spoke with a definitive tone.

* * *

The problem for time skippers is returning to their daily lives after coming back. While on the surface the world appears as though it hasn't changed, for them everything feels strange and unfamiliar. Like a piece of film that has been cut and taped back together, something feels off. Like they've woken up from a long dream. But the world runs at its own pace. In their absence, their cactuses grow large; their subordinates at work become their superiors; their babies become bratty six-year-olds; their puppies become old dogs. Their lives, which stopped of their own accord, feel desolate, like a life abandoned in the desert. So was the case with Park Jung-gu, who lost time and became a cripple.

"They called me a workhorse. Once I started something, I saw it through till the end. I thought nothing was done correctly if it wasn't done by me. And it wasn't just me. 'If it weren't for you, Vice President Park, our company would have already closed shop.' That was what the board of directors said at one of our office parties. It felt good hearing that. I liked working, too. So I worked myself into the ground, not even thinking about how tired I was. All the important projects were mine to oversee. But then suddenly six months of my time just disappeared. I had only blinked once, but in that time, six months of my life had become empty. I was so utterly dumbfounded by the whole thing, but I had no one to complain to. No one was going to believe me. Anyway, so I came back to my company. I had thought the company would be in shambles without me, but nothing much had happened. My team was doing well under the supervision of another, and the company was sailing smoothly. I should have felt relieved that the important projects hadn't failed, but somewhere in my heart I felt miserable. 'Well, shit, I guess the world doesn't need Park Jung-gu after all,' I thought to myself. I was despondent. I had thought the machine would have come tumbling down without its main engine – after all, that's why I trotted like a workhorse. But in the end, I guess

I wasn't that important a piece after all. I was an expendable part. I turned in my letter of resignation not long after that, and now I stay at home and get drunk. The missus tells me to go out and earn money, but I don't have the appetite to work again. We still have some money in our savings, and I have my severance package, so I think it's OK if I rest a bit more. I can think about how we're going to get by once the money runs out."

Then there are some who have changed their life for the better. A designer and diagnosed workaholic, Hwang Miok changed her life completely after experiencing an extended skip. After a two-year time skip she became a little lazy, a little slow, and a little incompetent. But because of her laziness she had also become a little bit happier.

"I couldn't stop working. I worked like a crazy person. Even after work, I would go to a language school to learn Spanish or take night classes at a graduate program for business management. And when that was over, I would head back to my office to work. I wouldn't go home until two or three in the morning. And in the morning, I would leave for work again without being late. That's what it's like working as a designer. Once you get started, there's always more work to be done. Back then, I never gave myself a moment to rest. It was the age of endless competition. Then suddenly two years of my time just disappeared. I was so shell-shocked I had to receive therapy, though nothing the doctor said was of much help. Anyway, I returned to my company. I had always been a good and organized worker, and my uncle on my mother's side was on the board of directors, so it wasn't difficult getting my job back. But something was off. Nothing had changed, per se. The people were all the same, and the work was just as I remembered it. But after the incident, I started doing a mediocre job. I was fine with 'just good enough,' and when it was time to go home, even if I still had some work to do, I would go home anyway. I used to have a habit of being mean and berating the younger designers, but now I said things like, 'That'll do. The world's not going to end just because their clothes are a little less pretty.' And after leaving the office I would relax or party. After all, I had already wasted two years without any recollection or experiences, what was three or four more hours? So I would either drink beer or go to nightclubs with friends who had hot bodies and with whom I got along. I don't have particularly painful periods, but even so, I always demand menstrual leave now. It's my right after all – I don't know why I must feel ashamed in front of my boss. And, despite everything, it's not like my life has fallen to pieces. I think it'd be more accurate to say that it's become a bit loose. Or maybe it's that I've finally achieved some balance. But I want to ask your opinion on something. What should I do if one day while working really hard, I time skip again and turn up as a grandma? Should I start going to cabarets instead of nightclubs?"

We regulate our lives because of anxiety. We make detailed plans and adjust our lives to follow those plans. Because we make our lives move in repeatable and regular ways, the most efficient system rules our lives. In other words, we attempt to live life through the power of habit and rules. But really, an efficient life? Can such a thing really exist in this world? Sounds like a life in which you do the same thing every day – a life that ends without having ever experienced more than a couple of memorable days.

Lim Yuna, a time skipper with six episodes under her belt, once said this to me:

"I wonder if my lost time is rolling around somewhere. The thought of that makes my heart ache. I could have loved someone with that time – I could have done something beautiful for someone. But I've nothing to show for that lost time. No waste, no ruin, no regrets, no pain. No feeling of having been alive."

The following is a piece taken from the Center for a Leisurely Life:

Statistically, there are probably 800 times as many time skippers as there are normal people. So don't work so hard. Don't make so many plans. Don't struggle so hard just to be more successful than others. Otherwise, you'll lose so much time. And wouldn't that be unfair? Like dying-in-a-car-accident-the-day-you-paid-off-your-house-loan kind of unfair?

The only way to save up time is to take it easy. Take menstrual leave. Take it every month. Miss a deadline once in a while! And if your boss asks you if you're going to take a bonus in exchange for less holiday, just say, "Fuck you." And on days you feel down, why not just take an absence without calling in?

THE CLOCK OF BABEL

The first thing the Clock of Babel does each morning is raise the shutters at the city's subway stations. And with that, the city is open for business again. Subway operators yawn; power is sent to the turnstiles; the subway trains begin to chug. Soon people rush inside. Trains move, streetlights turn on, and traffic signals change all according to the hands of Clock of Babel. The clock also manages all the city's alarms.

"Hey, wake up! You're one step away from being fired, and you're thinking about being late?"

But because our biological clocks are slow and irregular, they're always behind the Clock of Babel. Our bodies demand sleep, but the Clock of Babel demands we wake up and go to work. The Clock of Babel doesn't care if we're not hungry: it's time for lunch; it's time to eat. The Clock of Babel doesn't care if we don't want to talk: it's meeting time – time to flick our tongues rapidly and come up with new ideas.

The monolithic Clock of Babel governs everything in this city – the police stations, the fire stations, the traffic lights, the sewers, the telephone lines, and all the electricity racing along at the speed of light. If its spring were to suddenly break, this city would instantly fall into chaos.

"You slowpokes. Pick it up, will ya? It's the twenty-first century!"

The Clock of Babel pushes me to move faster. Whenever this happens, I feel myself groping for the rusty lever that will allow me to move my clanky metal suit of armor a few more inches. The colossal Clock of Babel shouts out to the city, "We're on Modern Time!"

I must confess, I think we're in different time zones.

And yet in spite of this, I have lived an honest life under the Clock of Babel, timid man that I am. I stand in line when everyone else stands in line; I eat when everyone else eats; I run when everyone else runs, despite not knowing what for. So in my freshman physics class when I first learned of Einstein's theory of relativity – which says there is no such thing as absolute time and that time runs differently for each person – I wasn't able to wrap my head around it. According to Einstein, inside every object, inside every being in the universe, there exists a unique clock. Objects that move fast have slow clocks, and objects that move slow have fast clocks. In other words, because people on Earth are moving slower than people in orbit around the Earth, people on Earth age more quickly than those in space. Not understanding how that could be, one student in the class raised their hand. "Wait, you mean to say the faster you go, the slower time ticks? How can that be?" To this the professor said, "Not even Einstein knew *why*. That's just how the universe works."

Damn. Not even Einstein knew why time moves on its own.

Regardless, time moves differently for everyone. And this means that nowhere in the universe can there exist a Clock of Babel that decides when and how to march. Because the Moon, the hare, and the Flash each have their own clocks, if one said to gather on November 11 at 9am at the Martian Public Stadium for a galactic track and field meet, on November 11 at 9am the stadium would be completely empty. And that's because the Moon, hare, and the Flash each have clocks that move at their own pace, making the date and time of November 11, 9am as chaotic and meaningless as a table of random numbers. At the very least, the bunny, whose physical environment is similar to ours, would arrive closest to 9am, and then the Moon. But as for the Flash, for whom there is no time because he can travel at the speed of light, he might never arrive at the stadium. And in the end, the hare and the Moon would be left in the empty stadium with the flags of nations waving pitifully as they waited till the end of time for the Flash to arrive. They might even sing a song and title it "The Eternal Traitor, the Flash."

A track meet in which that traitor the Flash never comes. The hare and the Moon are about to race in the 100-meter dash.

"Are you ready?" asks the hare to the Moon.

"Just a second! I need to warm up before running."

"Warm up all you want – you're not beating this hare. Haven't you heard of the story of the tortoise and the hare?"

"What's that?"

"What a shame. That story, that's me. I'm the hare of legend."

"Congratulations on becoming a legend. You keep doing that. I need to warm up."

But the Moon who went to warm up didn't return for an entire month. Enraged, the hare went looking for the Moon.

"What in heaven's name are you doing? If you're afraid of losing, just say it. You can't keep a busy bunny waiting forever."

"Hey," said the Moon as it languidly moved its body, "I've only just finished stretching my left hip. Wait for a minute, will you? I just need to do the right side now."

It wasn't a misunderstanding. The problem was time. The problem was they exist in a universe in which time is fundamentally different for everyone. This cosmic order shows us an important lesson: no one can erect a Clock of Babel and demand others follow its fascist ticking. This isn't because freedom-seeking humans will always rebel against fascism (of course, if that were the case, it would mean that fascism would never return; sadly, I don't think humans are such infallible beings). No, it's because everyone has their own clock. Existing complacently beneath a Clock of Babel, our bodies start to itch: something doesn't fit, something feels off; you make frequent stupid mistakes. It's not because we're fundamentally stupid; it's because our clocks don't match. Fascist order can never be kept, no matter how hard we try to follow it. As long as everyone possesses their own clock, we will never know true order.

"Man-made, forced orders don't work," the universe tells us. "Just go on silently enduring the inner order that was given to you. I gave each of you a uniquely tuned clock. Why don't any of you use it?"

According to this cosmic teaching, the only time an individual can perceive is its own. It is less that we lack empathy and more that we never could understand each other in the first place. The Flash can't understand the Moon, and the Moon can't understand the hare, and the hare can't understand the Flash.

The fact that some of us age faster; that some of us get hungry faster; that some of us fall in and out of love faster; and that some of us can cry all night after a breakup with a dearly loved partner and wake up the very next day to fall in love with yet another man is a fact that we cannot ever hope to understand. All we can ever say are things like "Why don't you love me like I love you?" "How can you not love me anymore?" and "I didn't do this to you, so how can you do this to me?"

Not long ago I gave counsel to a man who received his PhD in economics in the U.S. only to come back to Korea to sit in front of a 486 PC for ten years playing FreeCell. He told me he played FreeCell for twelve hours every day for ten years. While everyone else was getting hired and promoted, buying apartments, getting married and sending their children to their first day at school, he had shut himself in his house to play games all day. And, of all things, he chose a game that only involves matching numbers and suits. You might think he was stupid. But he was actually highly intelligent. He did, after all, receive a PhD in economics from a prestigious American university with top marks.

"But why?"

Indeed, this is the usual order in which people ask questions. But there is no why. He was just that way. While for other people it was time to chase promotions, perhaps for him it was time to play FreeCell. After graduating top in his class with a PhD from a prestigious university, he simply shoved that diploma in his closet and played FreeCell for the next ten years. Nothing more, nothing less.

But we can't accept that people can have different lifestyles than our own. We can't understand that they created that order, despite its apparent absurdity and foolishness, because it was the only way they could make it in this world. Not only can we not understand it, but we also don't even try to accept it. So, we look at them with pity and warn them:

"How about not playing FreeCell anymore and focusing on something a little more productive?"

When I tell people he would probably kill himself if you took his FreeCell away from him, people scoff at me as if I were joking. But it's true. Because he knows no other way outside of FreeCell to bear this tedious and overwhelming world, he really might take his life without it.

To be honest, before rummaging through the files in Cabinet 13 and coming to know these strange individuals, even I had not fully grasped the number of different ways to live life. I had never tried to understand it, and I lived just fine not understanding, too. But there are people who live lives that I could never have understood with what I knew then, with the world view I had. "So what? What do you want me to do about it? The world's a big place. Of course, there can be all sorts of strange and incomprehensible people living in places like the Congo or Gabon or the Amazon. Who cares about them? I have enough to worry about as it is."

But sometimes things of no concern to us show up in our

living rooms to stare us straight in the face. Whether we want it or not, we are stalked by foreign things. We mix with these people inside the chaotic Erlenmeyer flask that is the world. I'm not preaching beautiful solidarity, or anything like that. I'm just talking about the human condition.

There is a fascinating story contained in the 1998 annals of the Brooklyn Police.

On a subway train bound for Brooklyn, a kid was counting hundred-dollar bills from his wallet. This naïve kid had just received his first ever paycheck. But counting money on the New York subway is an extremely dangerous thing to do. Suddenly an old woman approached the kid. The woman, who had illegally immigrated to the US from Mexico, said that her granddaughter was dying in the hospital because couldn't pay the 750-dollar hospital bill. To prove that she was telling the truth, the old woman took out a hospital bill for 750 dollars and said, "If I don't pay, they'll stop giving her treatment." The kid cocked his head to the side as he listened to the old lady.

"Let's say what you tell me is true, lady. I have 800 dollars, just enough to pay your bills. But why do *I* have to give *you* my money?"

"You'll get hundreds of paychecks, hundreds throughout your life, but my granddaughter only has one chance. Please think about her precious life."

"Lady," the kid said as he scoffed, "we just met on this train by chance."

The kid was stabbed to death in a back alley in Brooklyn not far from the subway station. And all for only 800 dollars. He was murdered by a group of thugs who saw him take out his wallet on the train.

"Today's my lucky day," said one of the thugs as he wiped

the blood off his knife. "You picked the wrong train to count your money."

Those gang members were apprehended by police thanks to the old woman's descriptions. What she said to the police was simple: "I saw those thugs on the subway."

I was curious about what happened to the woman's dying granddaughter, but the report ends there. So, what's the moral of the story? Don't take out your wallet on the subway? Criminals must be punished? Don't turn your back on a neighbor in need?

To be completely honest, I agree with the kid. In a colossal city of more than ten million residents, it was only coincidence that he and she would meet on the subway train during rush hour. Asking for someone's hard-earned paycheck to save your granddaughter, whom they've never met, is a bit much to request of a stranger. I'm just an average citizen of this city, and the feeling of solidarity with its ten million other average citizens is weaker than I thought. All I need to do is ignore you once to keep my wallet fat for a month. And the probability that I'll bump into you next month is one in a million. Besides, a month's wages are barely enough to survive in this city. How long could I last here if I up and quit my job today? There is no moral to the story. We always look for the moral of a story or some nice adage, but morals and adages never changed anyone's life. That there is no moral of the story – that's the moral of the story.

"We're all riding the same subway train!"

ALIEN RADCOM

The group Alien RADCOM sent radio communications to exoplanets. Its members included law clerks, janitors, truck drivers, pianists, plumbers – people with no relation to each other socially or occupationally. For six to twelve hours every day, these individuals would send out radio signals to exoplanets using large antennas and high-powered amplifiers that they set up in their yards or on their roofs. Did they get replies from aliens? Do you even need to ask? I think it's safe to say there's no way they got replies. But they thought the replies were on their way.

Alien RADCOM was slightly different from your average radio club. First, the members of Alien RADCOM never exchanged messages with people on Earth. If someone else started using one of their frequencies, they would quickly change channels. And they never exchanged messages with each other. Ironically, even though radios were made for human communication, they refused to communicate with other humans. They found their own unique frequencies and busied themselves with sending radio signals to the far reaches of the universe, where there might have been no one listening. In my opinion, they would have gotten the same results if, instead of expensive radio equipment, they took empty cans of tuna and whispered into those.

It takes a lot of money to send something into space. Be it satellites, missiles, or even a screw or a crumpled beer can, sending things into space is never a simple task. There isn't a single person or object that could easily free itself from the stubborn pull of this planet's gravity. Radio waves are no exception. In order to transmit radio waves outside of the Earth, you need expensive equipment – in fact, the farther you wanted to send them, the more money you need. The cost of the parts of the radio equipment I found in Ko Du-shik's room alone totaled 400 million won. But because he assembled it himself he was able to save a lot on the cost. For the last twenty years Mr Ko had worked driving a refrigerated truck for twelve hours a day, every day. Then he would take his salary and send most of it to the aliens, so to speak.

Why did they waste their time and money on such foolish things? They didn't make money from sending signals to exoplanets, nor did they ever get replies. I asked Mr Ko this question. He leaned in close to my ear and whispered in a quivering voice, "Don't tell anyone. We're not from Earth. We're the descendants of aliens."

I was so surprised by this answer that I accidently exclaimed, "Oh!"

According to Mr Ko, the members of Alien RADCOM may have looked like Earthlings, but they weren't. They were descendants of aliens from planets outside the Milky Way who were long ago banished to Earth. What did I think? Sounds ridiculous, doesn't it? They received appendectomies; they completed their compulsory military service; and they had babies just like the rest of us. An alien who has their appendix removed? I didn't think such a thing was possible. No matter how you looked at it, they were human. My conclusion was that Alien RADCOM was nothing more than a group of humans who lived with the *delusion* that they were the descendants of aliens.

The members of Alien RADCOM got up every morning and went to work in the big city. Ostensibly, they needed to work because they had little to no remaining inheritance from their alien spaceship. Their workplaces included accounting offices,

trucking companies, piano stores, and the like. They faithfully
did the work the city had allotted them. They tuned piano
strings; removed underwear and stockings from drains; and
they transported frozen tuna caught while chasing a school of
Pacific saury near the Tropic of Cancer. Work that anyone might
do in the city. If there was one difference between the members
of Alien RADCOM and the rest of the citizens of this city, it was
that, instead of paying back the loans on their apartments, they
spent their hard-earned money on high-powered antennas,
modulators, and other expensive radio equipment.

They worked in fields that didn't require them to have
complicated personal relationships or talk much. As such, the
members of Alien RADCOM almost never went to karaoke or
office parties or to drink with old friends at school reunions.
Unsurprisingly, neither were there ever events for the members
of Alien RADCOM to get to know each other. They only ever
talked to each other about technical problems concerning
radio communications – and even then, only through online
forums. I asked Mr Ko: if they weren't going to be friends with
Earthlings, didn't they at least want to be friends with each
other?

"We all come from different home planets."

Indeed, that would make it difficult. Being from different
planets, they were themselves aliens to one another. Just like
asteroid B612 and the lamplighter's planet from *The Little Prince*
were alien worlds to one another.

The members of Alien RADCOM worked quietly but
diligently at their workplaces. They waited for the complicated
daily events in this chaotic and incomprehensible city to pass.
And when night silently fell, leaving them in solitude, they
would eat a simple meal, shower, then sit in front of their
radios. They turned on the power and increased the output.
They sent radio signals outside the Earth for as long as time
allowed. They were sending radio messages to their home
planets somewhere in the Milky Way.

One member would lean into the radio and sing their anthem; another member would rant about the most annoying customer they met that day. One would talk about how planet Earth was the by far the worst planet of all the planets harboring life and that it was cruel punishment for their ancestors to send them and their descendants to live here. They would go on and on about the difficulty of such a theatrical life in which they needed to pretend to be Earthlings, and sometimes they would even tell their radios embarrassing secrets. And yet they never forgot to say Merry Christmas on December 25. One member would mutter incomprehensible gobbledygook into his radio. According to another member, the language was from his home planet.

The members of Alien RADCOM all had issues with communicating and maintaining personal relationships, big or small. Even during mundane daily conversations, they would feel at a great disadvantage. They stuttered and sweated. Sometimes, they even panicked or had seizures while talking to people. Conversations made them frightened, and when the conversations were over, they would feel terribly ashamed and depressed. And some even felt the fear of death. So, they protected themselves with silence and rejected all the pretense and fake friendships that approached them disguised as courteous yet insincere language.

"Earthlings are strong. We could never win in a fist fight. Humans come toward us acting friendly, but deep in their bellies they are hiding wicked intent. I am frightened by this. I can never guess what will happen. So every night I send radio signals to my home planet begging them to rescue me from this hellish penal colony."

There were members who could carry on basic conversation easily, and there were members who felt great difficulty in carrying on basic conversations. They spoke as little as possible, avoided people when they could, and looked for work they could do alone and in peace – they didn't care about low pay.

They lived in this city talking with a stutter, like immigrants speaking a foreign language.

The members of Alien RADCOM didn't break their backs to achieve success on Earth. This place was neither their home nor where they wanted to build a life. Earth was nothing more than an alien planet to them. Just like we humans would never waste our time trying to become famous among a group of monkeys, they felt no need to do so here on Earth.

A life of exile on Earth. A life without a home. They tried their best just to survive on this penal colony named Earth. Every day they dreamed of escaping this planet. Perhaps that's why they bought powerful radios capable of sending radio signals to the edges of the universe.

Even tonight, their lonely radio signals which they sent to their home planets somewhere far away, are racing past the dark side of the Moon toward the edges of the universe at the speed of light.

Why couldn't they live as human beings? Why couldn't they identify with *Homo sapiens*? They diligently paid for health insurance, they paid all their taxes, followed traffic lights – so why did they believe so ardently that they weren't human?

I really can't say. But when I think about this tedious and trite world in which it's impossible to find even one human soul I can talk to, it's not like I am totally unable to understand what they meant. If I had a radio that could send signals beyond Earth, I would probably say something into the radio, too. But all I would say is that the only aliens I know are E.T. and the Teletubbies.

"Frankly, I'm sick of this world too. What's it like talking with more aliens than humans?" I asked.

"Lonely," said Mr Ko.

THE GIRL WHO EATS
BENEATH A DUSTY FAN

There was a company cafeteria beneath the research center. Today we were going there for lunch. As we walked to the cafeteria, I wondered to myself why it was that we were eating at this frustratingly poor company cafeteria when the world was filled with so many good restaurants. Why was it that we were eating at this cafeteria, with its single-item menu where they treated customers like homeless people, when out there were countless restaurants with long splendid menus where they treated patrons like kings. I wanted to think it was because this cafeteria was much closer than other restaurants; because this cafeteria was so much cheaper than other restaurants; because we didn't have to worry about who was going to pay or how we were going to nudge absent-minded Department Head Song toward the register because we all had our own meal ticket. Indeed, every time we left a restaurant, every time we had an office party, we would always furtively push poor Department Head Song toward the counter as he tied his shoes and looked for a toothpick. But Department Head Song had three children dependent on him, the oldest of whom was going to college this year. So I wanted to think that it was because our conscience had finally got the better of us. I wanted to think that we were eating at the company cafeteria for humanitarian reasons.

But obviously I wasn't being honest with myself. The real reason we were miserably going down to the cafeteria was because there had been an official announcement to "Use the company cafeteria as much as possible!" I guess the manager of the company cafeteria, a well-connected fellow, had complained to the higher-ups that business was slow. But even considering this, it was low of them to make it seem like we had any choice in the matter by adding the deceptive phrase "as much as possible." As much as possible was as good as all the time. Really, it was a cowardly way to word a mandate.

But that's what being a salaryman was all about. If there was an order from upstairs, you had to make adjustments. You had to at least refrain from complaining about how the cafeteria tasted like cement or dog food. The rebellious nature of humans was, of course, charming and good. And humans should resist and rebel against the injustices of the world. But men had to choose their fights carefully. It wasn't becoming of a man to get worked up over something as silly as cafeteria side dishes. It seemed a bit cheap, too. And unjustified. So we had to let little things like that go and save ourselves for bigger, more important issues. All we had to do was shut our eyes and bite the bullet, so to speak. Shut them tight.

So here I was. Sitting in the cafeteria. Sitting in the cafeteria with the same side dishes that they miraculously served all week, as if consistency were the only virtue in cooking – all the while giving intermittent applause to the lectures and jokes of my boss, the mere sight of whom never failed to give me indigestion. I'm meticulously chewing on rice and swallowing hard. How's the rice, you ask? Well, it tastes sort of like it had been mixed with raw hairtail.

"Hey, look over there, at that girl."

The vice president pointed toward one corner of the cafeteria as he clicked his tongue. There in the corner, was Jeong-eun from General Affairs, eating by herself. No one ever sat in that corner because it was occupied by a large refrigerator, messy trash cans, and the incessant whir of a rotating fan. Seeing her at lunchtime, even I felt slightly annoyed, and wondered why she chose to eat alone in such a place.

"Why does she do that to herself. Why does she always eat in that smelly, bacteria-infested corner? And boy, can she eat! No wonder she looks like that. Honestly, there should be a limit on how fat someone can get and still be considered a woman. Doesn't she think about the deep culture shock she gives society by walking around with that body? But then again, she is uncultured. No?"

The vice president looked at us as he asked this question but everyone just ignored him. What else could we do but ignore him? We definitely couldn't say, "Yes, sir. She is shockingly fat." And the vice president's assumption that she ate a lot was only a prejudice he formed against her because she was fat. If he had actually looked at her tray, he would have discovered an unbelievably small amount of food. With no one answering him, the vice president began spouting off again.

"Well, fat or not, why gorge yourself in the corner with that fan blowing dust all over you? It's much more fun to eat together and be chummy with your colleagues, isn't it? Is that the only way she can enjoy a meal? What an odd creature. An odd creature indeed. Just looking at that woman annoys me. Isn't that right, Mr Park?"

This time, instead of asking the unspecified masses, the vice president called out Mr Park.

"Yes, sir!" Mr Park answered with enthusiasm.

I wasn't sure to what Mr Park was saying yes. He probably hadn't even been listening to the vice president. But then again, when someone asks you the question "Isn't that right?" chances are, the correct answer is "Yes, sir!" I guess being positive was a good way to go through life. And Mr Park seemed to be doing well. But the real reason Mr Park answered so enthusiastically was not because of his positive personality. It was because Mr Park never had an opinion on anything.

Even as the vice president was talking shit about her, Jeong-eun simply ignored him and stared down at her plate as she methodically ate her lunch. At the table across from us were a group of female employees from General Affairs cackling about something. They might have even been talking about Jeong-eun as well. The most entertaining conversation at this research institute was always gossip about Son Jeong-eun. People talking about everything from her weight and her ridiculously dated sense of fashion to her old shoes, dogged silence, and what she might be thinking. But I can't understand why people gossiped so passionately about a quiet girl whom you wouldn't even have known existed if you weren't looking.

"You know that Korean saying, 'You can live with a fox, but you can't live with a bear'? As in, smart women are the best to marry. But why a fox and a bear? Well, when I look at Ms Son, I think I finally understand why. She looks like she could be the bear-woman from the legend of Dangun. Just lock her in a cave for a hundred days with some garlic and mugwort, and I bet she'd turn back into a bear. Department Head Song, what's it like working with Ms Son?"

This time, the vice president made a serious face as he looked at Department Head Song. Not expecting to be asked such a question, Department Head Song swallowed the kernels of rice he had been chewing on and took a sip of anchovy seaweed soup. Yes, anchovy seaweed soup. This was today's daily special. Something you can't find anywhere else. If you're curious how it tastes, simply put, it tastes like shit. If that's too abstract of a description for you, just imagine seaweed and anchovies cooked in water that was used for boiling dishrags.

"Well, since she's not in our department–" said Department Head Song in a calm voice.

"Yes, but you work in the same office."

The vice president always asked twice. He was that sort of person. The type of person who had to hear the answer he wanted, whatever the situation. To survive working under such a person, you needed to answer every question they asked. But what did Department Head Song know outside of making model sailboats? Besides, answering such a question would require our company giving its workers more than the most meager scraps of work at least, something by which to assess individual skill.

"I heard she completes the work given to her in an orderly fashion." Department Head Song's response was unsurprisingly well-mannered.

"Orderly fashion? That half-bear, half-pig woman? Does she even know the meaning of the phrase 'in an orderly fashion'?" the vice president suddenly screamed. "Fine, let's say that she does do things in an orderly fashion, like you say," he continued. "But there's more to living in society than just that. Completing your work – that's a given for a paycheck-earning worker; there's got to be something more. Women office workers – they're the flowers of the office! They liven up the workspace, make working together fun, give you someone nice to talk to – you know, things like that." The vice president lowered his voice as he leaned in close to us. I could smell the strong odor of dead skin and blackheads. Thankfully, I wasn't eating the anchovy seaweed soup, otherwise I would have thrown up.

"You guys wouldn't know because you're young. But it's hard to get it up as you get older. But you know what? Just looking at that pig is enough to get rid of any hard-earned boner. And I hate that feeling; it's the worst! There's no other way to describe it. At my age, there's nothing more depressing than losing a boner you worked so hard to get. Anyway, what I'm trying to say is, that bitch makes me depressed. Hahaha!"

And this was the punch line of his longwinded diatribe? Realizing that he had been trying to tell a joke, everyone started laughing awkwardly. Haha, hoho, hehe. But, shit, it was hard to laugh together. Laughing always had to be done in unison, but it was too obvious that our laughs were forced. Everyone felt terribly uncomfortable. It was impossible not to feel embarrassed after such a bout of forced laughter. As the fragile respect we held for one another crumbled, it felt like we were all saying, "What can we do? Enduring awkward moments together like this is what it takes to survive."

In the meantime, the vice president had finished the food on his tray. Seeing how he finished even the boiled-dishrag-water anchovy seaweed soup, I guess he must have an amazing appetite. But then again, is there anything a man like him can't eat? There's not a bribe he wouldn't take; he'd take anything – money, goods, gift cards, assorted gift sets, even a six-month IOU. All you had to do was put it in front of him, and he'd find some way to get you something in return. Indeed, he had a bad record taking bribes and being involved in scandals, and after traveling up and down the ladder for many years, he had finally transferred here. After a few years of lying low, he would leave again when the world had forgotten. People always said the vice president's connections had landed him here, but the only landing he had made was an emergency one.

The vice president got up with his tray. Mr Park and I quickly rose and offered to take his tray for him.

"I'll take that, sir," we both said simultaneously with embarrassed hands outstretched.

"Why thank you."

The vice president's eyes went back and forth between the two of us until he finally gave the tray to me. Then he took another glance at Jeong-eun sitting in the corner of the cafeteria.

"And look at what she's eating. That stuff tastes horrible. You know, I've never once seen her offer her opinion during a meeting. All she does is shut her mouth and say nothing. She hasn't once gone to an office party or said hi to me on the way to work. And she looks so shabby. And fat, too. Who would marry a personality or waist like that? Not a chance. Not even a dying man would take that cow for a bride. But even so, I can't stop staring."

The vice president was talking to himself but as if he wanted everyone to hear him. Indeed, this time, he spoke quite loudly. Definitely loud enough for Jeong-eun to hear. Even though she continued to hunch over her food as she ate, you could see her ears flush and her shoulders begin to shake slightly, either from the anger or the tears.

In the book *Blue Lizard*, Édouard Manet said that when he was fourteen, all he wanted to do was "destroy the world with dynamite." That's the only passage I remember from that book. Thinking about it now, I was exactly the same at fourteen. Back then, I would have blown up my school if I'd had a stick of dynamite. I was always so angry at everything that surrounded me.

For example, I disliked the school rule that I had to button up my school uniform all the way to my neck. I felt like I would suffocate when I buttoned my shirt up like that. It was the same with the rule that said we had to think about our aspirations for a few seconds at least every day when we passed the bronze statue of the headmaster, on which was written the words "Boys must aspire to do." All boys aspire to become doctors, go to law school, or get into some college, but as for me, unfortunately I had no aspirations whatsoever. I couldn't even understand how becoming a doctor or lawyer was a natural thing for a boy to want to do.

I hated everything about school. Whenever I was hit with an eraser or had to stand outside in the hallway just because I had dozed off a bit during class, I would often wonder to myself how it was that students didn't revolt. I just couldn't understand it. Children were too nice. I wasn't smart, nor was I any good at sports. It was common for me to fumble over my words even when the teacher asked me about something

I knew, and because I wasn't good at fighting, the bigger kids always stole my lunch money. I was just your average kid. That's what my teens were like for me. But what's so bad about being average? This world is full of average things.

It was October, if I remember correctly. I was looking outside the window during class at the sports field. A large whirlwind was spinning the October gingko leaves round and round, sending them high into the sky. Following the shape of the twister, the gingko leaves spun as they soared up past the flagpole. The image of gingko tree leaves being whirled as if they were pieces of ice in Saturn's rings was beautiful and wonderous to behold. I had never seen such a beautiful gust of wind. Without realizing it, I let out a gasp in admiration. At that moment, my ethics teacher – whose nickname was "Silica Gel" because of his skeleton-like thin face and skin so dry you couldn't find an ounce of moisture on it – called me over to his desk. "What were you staring at?" Thinking that such a beautiful scene only occurred a few times in a young boy's life, I thought my teacher would understand how I felt. So, I told the truth. "I was gazing at a beautiful gust of wind as it spun round and round a pile of gingko tree leaves." All the children began laughing. Silica Gel gave me a dry stare. He then said, "The boy's gone mad." Silica Gel took out his watch and began slapping me. One, two, three, four. But it wasn't my cheeks that he hit; it was my heart. Pale, sad things that had been deep in my chest came up through my throat. I began screaming like a madman. "Ahh, ahh, ahh!"

Silica Gel was so shocked that he had to take several steps back. He stared at me in awe. The children also stared at me in silence. It felt like the entire classroom had paused for a moment. Finally, I stormed out of the classroom.

So why the ridiculous story about a whirlwind? Well, despite being an average fourteen-year-old boy, I knew what beauty and anger were. Just look at this lunchtime. It was as unreal as something from Cabinet 13. I mean, how can someone think it's OK to call someone a pig in the presence of other people, just because he's the boss? I wouldn't feel right even saying that to a real pig.

But no one was enraged by those words. It even felt natural that no one was enraged. Where did it go? Where did all that anger from when I was fourteen go? Looking for my missing rage, I rummaged through my pocket with one hand as I placed the vice president's lunch tray through the hole at the tray return station with the other. Looking through the hole I yelled, "Hey, do something else tomorrow. I'm sick of the anchovy seaweed soup!"

I'M OVER HERE, TOO.

I dream the same dream once or twice a month. The dream is about a traumatic experience that happened when I was in the military. In the dream, I am aware that I am dreaming. But knowing that I am dreaming doesn't help me escape the horror I feel. All around me is fire, and as I stand in the smoke, I am waiting desperately for something. But what I am waiting for? I am probably waiting for an order, any order.

It's a fire drill. My old sergeant is tilting his head.

"I've been in the military for thirty years, and I've never seen such a stupid training exercise."

The drill situation is this: Our troops are retreating. The barracks have been bombed and are on fire. Our objective is to evacuate the barracks in order of most strategic importance. Getting the order correct is essential.

A blue tag is attached to things that need to be evacuated immediately; a red tag on things that can be lost to the fire. I adhere to my chest a blue tag and stand inside the warehouse with all sorts of objects – tables, entrenching shovels, gas masks, televisions. I'm playing the role of the injured soldier. Thankfully, I'm not on the list of expendables. Looking at the blue tag on my chest, I think to myself I am lucky. After all, I'm not expendable.

The training exercise starts, and someone lights the inside of the warehouse on fire to make it more realistic. Another person sets off a smoke bomb. In seconds, the smoke fills the barracks. (Ah yes, realistic combat training. Whatever floats their boat. Personally, I thought it was natural to keep training just training and leave realistic battles for the actual battlefield. But in the military, they had this stupid phrase, "Train like it's a real fight. Fight like it's training" – whatever that meant.) The platoon leader enters the warehouse wearing a mask, followed by the cadets. The soldiers hastily start trying to put out the fire with something that looks like a blanket.

"What are you guys doing?" asks the platoon leader.

"Aren't we supposed to put out the fire?" replies one cadet.

"You idiot. We're at war. It's raining bullets and you want to put out a fire?"

The platoon leader is furious. (Cough, cough. But he's right. Who would try to put out a fire when it's raining bullets?)

"Failing to follow orders will get you killed. Quick! Evacuate all things in order of strategic importance," cries the platoon leader.

First on the list is documents. Classified documents, top secret documents, secret documents, confidential material, maps, battle plans, codes, and ciphers (Cough, cough. I guess those things are pretty important). Fourth on the list is recon dogs (Cough, cough. Well, German Shepherds are worth 30,000,000 won). Seventh on the list are LAWs and Stingers (Cough, cough. I'm still hanging in there. And besides, light anti-tank weapons and anti-helicopter weapons are a luxury. They're a lot more valuable than Private Kong). Eighth, ammunition and grenades (Cough, cough. Now this is getting a bit ridiculous. They should have taken those out first! They'd explode if the fire got to them). Ninth, training guns and locks (Cough, cough. What? Locks? I can understand the guns, but what did they need locks for in a situation like this? Are they joking? I'm starting to suffocate from the smoke). Tenth, file cabinets (Cough, cough. Cabinets! I can't believe this).

And then it strikes me. Do people even know I'm here? What if the fact that an injured private is inside the barracks with all the dustpans and TVs has been omitted from the training plan? Suddenly I am struck by anxiety. So, I quietly raise my hand.

"Platoon leader, I'm over here, too."

When I say this, the platoon leader, who is in a gas mask, turns to the corporal standing next to him.

"What'd the fucker say?"

"He said he's over there, too, sir."

"I'm not deaf, you dumb shit. What does he *mean*?"

"I think he's asking when he can leave."

"Tell him to wait his turn. We haven't gotten to him yet. Number eleven is biochemical tarps."

The kind corporal comes over to me as I continue to cough.

"Hang in there, Private Kong. It's not yet your turn. Sorry about this."

"It's fine, Corporal Park. I can hold out a bit longer." (Cough, cough.)

There's nothing for the corporal to be sorry about. After all, it's not his fault that my turn hasn't come yet. But it feels like my lungs are going to collapse from all the smoke. The other soldiers are taking their time transporting the goods. My eyes, nose, and mouth are all oozing with bodily fluids. In fact, I'm now finding it difficult to even cough. In my hazy state of consciousness, I think to myself, "When will it be my turn?" I grab my chest and tear at my hair. Perhaps my role in this drill isn't to be a solider, but a corpse. There's no way a living soldier in a fire would be evacuated after the cabinets. The corporal turns to the platoon leader again, unable to bear it any longer.

"Sir, if we leave him any longer, he's going to pass out. The smoke is getting really thick. When is Private Kong going to be able to leave?"

"Didn't I say to wait? Let's see, wool blankets are seventeenth. Lockers can be left behind. We don't need to worry about canteens and soap cases. Wheat snacks and Shin Ramyun. Fuck, who put wheat snacks on here? The people at headquarters put anything on the list. Anyway, not that either.

Wool blankets are seventeenth. I said that already. Ah, here it is. Injured soldiers! Sixteenth. That means he can leave after the gas masks."

Yes, in other words, I am after the gas masks. After the German Shepherds, after the biochemical tarps, after the cabinets, and after the gas masks. Thank goodness, I am before the wool blankets. Thank goodness. I would hate it if the wool blankets left before me. They would strut out of the barracks saying, "Oh? A bit later than I thought. Anyway, good job, everyone. Now you know my place in the army. Now when you sleep, don't bunch me up and drool all over me."

Oozing snot and tears and coughing, I'm finally dragged out together with the gas masks. I wanted to run out of there with my arms outstretched like the guy from *Shawshank Redemption*, but my jelly-like legs quite frankly didn't have the energy to stand on their own.

That training drill changed me. It's hard to describe, but I started to look at objects differently after that. I was kinder to the cabinets, courteous to the gas masks, and when I put my gun away after standing guard, I would be sincerely polite to the safety lock. After all, they were of more strategic importance than me.

There were times when I felt my sense of existence shrink to an infinitesimally small size. It felt like no one would remember me, like my turn would never come. There were times when I was afraid that the person I loved most might value me less than a stapler or vacuum cleaner. I had finally become aware of the value and shape of my existence in this world. "Look, don't be disappointed," I once said to someone. "Being human is like taking a number. You just need to wait your turn quietly. There's nothing else you can do."

THE SPY, THE PROPOSITION, AND THE SHE-CAT IN FRONT OF THE CABINET

"Professor Kwon was so stubborn. Nothing I said could ever change his mind. But you seem more flexible."

As he spoke, the man, who was wearing a black suit, gave me his business card. Gilded on the black card were a lone "K" and a phone number. The card looked as expensive as the man's silk suit, but it didn't seem to accomplish all the responsibilities a normal business card should.

"For a man with such exquisite tastes," I said, "this is a terribly simple business card."

"Business cards don't need to be complicated," the man said with a smirk.

"So, you provide services, right? Like a private investigator?" I asked.

"Something like that, yes. But 'private investigator' sounds so very crude. We prefer 'consultants.'" The man furrowed his brows slightly as though he had been offended by my choice of words. I had frankly been shocked when the man opened the door to the office and walked toward my desk with his loud dress shoes. I had known of him for a long time. He spied on this research center and on Professor Kwon and me. Professor Kwon had told me that the man and the others like him were hired by the syndicate. They would spy on us, disappear for a while, then show up again later. However, this was the first time any one of them had approached me to talk.

"I have a proposition for you," the man said in a polite tone as we sat down at a café.

"Let's hear it. It had better be good."

"A man I can reason with – I like it. Then I'll skip the pointless prelude and get right to the point. How does a billion sound for the documents?"

A billion won. The number gave me an odd feeling. Such a large amount of money had never graced my life before. There was something surreal about it. Even stranger was the man's pointed face, which looked like it belonged to one of those samurai in Japanese historical dramas, and his narrow eyes, which reminded me of the anime *Ōgon Bat* every time I looked at them. The combination was enough to make me feel like I was in a dream.

"That's less than I thought it would be. I assumed you'd start your bargaining a little higher than that." I spoke in a sarcastic tone. To my surprise, the man gave me a wide smile.

"I'm glad you said that; I can be frank with you, then. Now, I've been instructed by the syndicate to offer no more than two billion won. And since the money is only for negotiating, it's not like I can take the remainder. So, let's not play this push-and-pull game like a couple of peddlers. I'll give you the lot if you hand over the documents without any funny games. You'll get all two billion."

"But can you tell me what documents you're looking for specifically?"

"We know our fair share about the symptomers Professor Kwon has studied. The syndicate has its own research division."

"Then what do you need more documents for? Why don't you just tell your people to continue their research?"

"The problem is most symptomers have no value. Take torporers and time skippers, for example. Information and data on symptomers like that has no commercial value. It's impossible to get an inventor's attention with stuff like that."

"Well, if that's the case, then there's no reason to drag this conversation on any longer. That's all I have. To be honest, I would sell you anything for two billion won. It's not like I'm some activist. I don't even know why someone would want to keep those documents a secret. I'd give them to you just to clean out the damn cabinet. It's not difficult. But I think there's something more to it that you're not telling me. Every document in that cabinet is either a third-rate novel or tabloid gossip: worthless stuff. If you wanted that, you could just flip through an old *Sunday Seoul*. All I've seen is stuff like that."

"We think Professor Kwon has some special files."

"Can you be more specific?"

"What we're looking for are files on chimeras."

"Chimeras? You mean people with gingko trees growing from their fingers and tails protruding from their behinds and lizards for tongues? Those chimeras?"

"Yes, something like that. You could call it a new epoch in bioengineering. They might hold the secret to hybrid species. The medical and military ramifications would be astronomical. I've heard even NASA is interested in chimeras to create humans that can adapt to life in space."

"I'm a little surprised, to be honest. You think Professor Kwon has created such a monster?"

The man let out a weak sigh as he reached into his coat pocket for a pack of cigarettes. He then offered me one. I took one from him and lit it. It was an imported brand unknown to me, with thick tarry smoke. The man blew a stream of smoke into the air before beginning again.

"I had thought you would be easy to talk with, but alas I'm back where I started. Here's a friendly warning. People like me aren't allowed wholesome lives. Work gets messy when things turn out this way, despite our best efforts. We always try to take care of business as gently of possible, of course. But when people treat me like some sort of thug, it doesn't make my job easy for me. And if my job isn't easy for me, it's not going to be easy for you, either."

"This sounds like a threat."

"A threat? No, I'm just asking for a little respect, that's all. And in return, I'll show you the respect you deserve." The man took another deep drag on his cigarette. He had the uncanny air of a man who moved in the shadows. "You know Mr Kim Woo-sang, right? He visited you guys in '98. The man with a gingko tree in his body."

"It wasn't *in* his body; it was on his finger."

"So you do know him! Then by any chance do you know his current whereabouts?"

"No, and if I did I wouldn't be able to tell you."

"Mr Kim is dead. We found him two years ago on Mt Chiri. When we got to him, his body was so shriveled up we could barely identify him. He was hanging from a gingko branch, you know. Dehydrated like a sundried pepper. It was ghastly, I wouldn't even call it human. Our guys almost missed him completely."

"So, what are you trying to say?"

"Mr Kim had a painful death. Deep in the mountains, where no one could help him, having the life sucked out of him by a parasitic tree. A bag of skin – that's all that was left of him. Just thinking about it makes me shudder. And you know what? The ginkgo eventually died, too. It couldn't get the nutrients it needed from the ground. Tell me, Mr Kong. Do you think Mr Kim's gingko tree was a naturally occurring phenomenon? A random mutation or something like that?"

"I do."

"You've never thought that it might be another one of Professor Kwon's experiments?"

At that moment, a thunderous bronze bell began to ring

in my head. Why had I never thought about that? Why had I never thought that the reason Professor Kwon thought that he couldn't and shouldn't do anything for symptomers was because of something bad he had done in the past?

"Professor Kwon's doctor says that he has less than three months to live," the man continued. "For almost forty years, he always conducted his research alone. He never took a successor, a disciple, not even a research assistant. And then one day he made you his assistant. You! Why do you think he did that?"

"You should know; you've obviously done your homework on me and Professor Kwon. But anyway, I'm not as capable as you think. All I do is clean and organize documents. And if what you tell me is true, if those files really are worth at least two billion won, then the Professor Kwon I know would never entrust such documents to someone like me."

"The chimera data isn't worth two billion. It's worth hundreds of billions, maybe even trillions. In other words, it must still exist. No one would throw away such valuable data so easily. And Professor Kwon risked his life to collect that data. There's no way he got rid of it. Presently, I would say you are the closest to those files. In that sense, you have an unusual opportunity in front of you, Mr Kong. There's no need for you to have any moral reservations. If there *are* chimera files, sooner or later they will end up in the hands of the syndicate. The syndicate is powerful and not easily deterred. We follow profit wherever it may lead us. The syndicate never gives up. What I'm trying to get at is this: Those files are eventually going to end up in our hands. It's just a matter of when and how. There's nothing you can do to stop it. My proposition is that we finish this in the easiest way possible. Take some time to think about it. Two billion for the chimera files. And if there's anything else of interest, it can be handed over in a separate deal. When you've made your decision, call the number on my card."

"But who is the syndicate?"

"I'm not at liberty to say. I'm sure you understand."

When he finished speaking, the man stood up from his seat. He gave me a slight bow and left the café. His movements were swift and decisive. After the man left, I sat in the café for a while. I called over the waiter and ordered a beer. I tried to think, but my head wasn't working. As I looked outside the window and sipped on my beer, I suddenly muttered to myself, "So Mr Kim is dead. That fat, shy man is dead."

It was past 11 in the evening when I returned to the research center. There was something I needed to check in the file room. My head was whirring. Was Mr Kim really the product of one of Professor Kwon's experiments? Mr Kim died alone, deep in the mountains where no one could help him. If it was true that he was unable to escape from that gingko tree, then he died an even slower and more painful death than we had imagined he would. I had never really thought of Professor Kwon as a moral person. But I had never really thought of him has an immoral person either. Then again, maybe this was never a matter of morality.

I knew going through Professor Kwon's desk and the cabinet in the file room was going to be a fool's errand. Professor Kwon was too meticulous of a person to put such files, if they existed, in a place where I could find them. But I still had to check for myself. If there were such chimera files, where would they be? Could there be a secret safe in Professor Kwon's office that I didn't know about? Or perhaps at his home? What about inside that black leather bag that he always carried around? Inside a bank vault, perhaps? But even if I could get my hands on those files, would I really sell them to the syndicate?

Who am I kidding? Of course I would. There was little doubt in the matter.

The lights were on in the security office at the front entrance to the research institute. But there were no guards to be seen.

They had probably left to go drinking like they always did. That's how things were at this place. I got through the front entrance with my access card and briskly walked to the file room on the fourth floor.

When I opened the door to the file room, something startled me. Someone was looking through Cabinet 13 with a flashlight. As soon as they heard the door, they quickly turned off their flashlight. My head was exploding with foreboding thoughts. Struck with fear, I yelled out "Who's there?" as I switched on the light. I was dumbstruck to see that it was Jeong-eun who was squatting in front of Cabinet 13. She also looked stunned by my sudden appearance.

"What are you doing here?" I asked.

Jeong-eun didn't respond. In her hands were several files, and a blue notebook in which it appeared she had been writing. I snatched the files and notebook from her hands. Written in the blue notebook were neatly organized notes about symptomers. I was such an idiot. It was clear she had been sneaking peeks of the files in Cabinet 13 for some time now. How could I have been so completely unaware of it?

"I said, what are you doing here!"

My voice burned with anger. Even I was shocked by my shouting. But she remained silent.

"Do you understand what I'm saying? Ms Son, whether you like talking with other people or not is of no concern to me. I'm not going to blame you for being a quiet person. Everyone has the freedom to live in whichever way floats their boat. But let me be clear, now is not the time to be silent."

And yet still she said nothing. Her shoulders were shaking slightly and large tears were beginning to form in her terrified eyes. Fuck, why did Jeong-eun have to show up out of nowhere and get mixed up in all of this? Today was not my day.

I sat down with Jeong-eun at the foot volleyball court. Today er a cigarette out of habit. She took the cigarette, lit it, and took a long drag in silence.

"I didn't know you smoked," I said.

"I don't often smoke around other people."

"How long have you been reading those files?"

"For a while."

"Can you be more precise?"

"About two years."

"And does Professor Kwon know?"

"…"

There's no way he wouldn't know. Nothing can happen around here without his knowing it. After all, his default mode is to not trust humans. But then again, maybe he didn't know. Maybe Jeong-eun was giving information to the syndicate right under our noses. I flipped through her blue notebook. She had organized nearly all the file's contents. This was on a whole other level from when I had read the files just for kicks back in the day.

"Did you make a deal with the syndicate?" I asked.

She raised her head to look at me. Her eyes were telling me that she had no idea what I meant.

"Then I guess Professor Kwon told you to do it."

She didn't answer. I pressed her again.

"Then why are you reading those files?"

"Someone has to look after the files if Professor Kwon dies."

So that was it. Unsurprisingly, Professor Kwon was a crafty bastard. His thoroughness was starting to get on my nerves. It didn't matter if it wasn't me. She might be insurance, and I might be insurance. But what difference did it make to me now? I couldn't care less what happened to that damn cabinet.

The weather was chilly and Jeong-eun was shivering slightly. And yet she wasn't betraying any emotion. Finally, I spoke.

"Let's go home. We can talk about the rest next time. It's almost morning anyway. We both need some shuteye if we're going to come to work tomorrow, even if just for a few hours."

EMBARRASSED OF THE HUMAN SPECIES

"So, how much did those bastards offer you? 500 million? A billion?"

As if he had been waiting for me, Professor Kwon launched into his attack as soon as I opened the door to the hospital room. His eyes were shaking with dread. Who could have told him? Was someone watching me? The agent? After all, I didn't know his true identity. Or perhaps Jeong-eun? Yes, it was probably her.

"Two billion. And a bonus if circumstances allow," I answered in a matter-of-fact tone.

Something close to relief appeared in Professor Kwon's eyes.

"I see the price has gone up..."

"Oh, stop your worrying."

Professor Kwon looked as though he was embarrassed of himself as he avoided my eyes and turned toward the window. I had come today to ask Professor Kwon some questions. I wanted to know the truth about the gingko tree man Mr Kim, about his back-up plan, Jeong-eun, and about those chimera files. But perhaps today wasn't the right day to ask these questions. According to Professor Kwon's doctor, whom I ran into before arriving at the hospital room, he had a week or two at the most.

"So?" Professor Kwon asked as he turned to look my way

again. "Are you going to betray me and hand over those files for two billion won?" His tone sounded both serious and sarcastic at the same time.

"Do you even need to ask? What favor have you done for me that's worth two billion won? I'll give them the files as quickly as I can find them."

"And what will you do with all that money?"

"Is there anything I *can't* do with all that money?"

"So, you have no intention of continuing to look after Cabinet 13? I'll keep giving you paychecks."

"How much?"

"A million won a month. And I'll increase your pay to match inflation."

"A million won?"

"Is that too little?"

"You're joking, right? That's even less than my current paycheck. I'd rather get paid for twiddling my thumbs at my desk."

"What could you possibly want working at that damned desk job? Bumming around, playing go, and telling bad jokes at a research institute where there's nothing to do – is that your idea of a job? That's a life for parasites with nowhere to go because they're too afraid, a life for people who dig their grave in the same place they take a shit. The only thing people like that can ever own is a 100-square-foot apartment."

He seemed angry, and the sight of him angry was ridiculous. I wanted to say, "Hey, what about me? I'm the one who should be shouting!"

"I caught Jeong-eun looking through the contents of Cabinet 13. I guess she's been reading symptomer files for the last two years. She even took notes. Perhaps she's just a meticulous person, but she organized things better than I had."

Professor Kwon didn't show any surprise at what should have been news to him.

"Is that why you're hurt?" he asked.

"No. Actually I felt somewhat relieved that you had a back-up plan."

Professor Kwon repeated the words "somewhat relieved" under his breath, then turned to me.

"What does Cabinet 13 mean to you?" he asked.

"I've been too busy to think about 'meaning.'"

"You could always have stopped."

"I felt bad for you, so I pretended to be fooled. Besides, I didn't have any work to do."

"It's my wish that you keep looking after Cabinet 13. It's an important task and not just anyone can do it. With a few exceptions, you're the right man for the job."

The right man! Is that so? For this job? I'd never thought that. I thought I was the *least* suited to looking after Cabinet 13. I wasn't calm or composed; I was clumsy, the first to get worked up and irritated during consultations, and intolerant toward foreign things and people. Was this the kind of man he wished would look after Cabinet 13 when he was gone? That was terrifying.

"Don't you mean Jeong-eun is the right person for the job?" I asked.

Professor Kwon stared into space for a moment as though he were thinking about the meaning of my question. At that moment I was reminded of a highway rest stop. Why was I reminded of something like a highway rest stop at a time like that? Gas stations, fish cakes, udon, kimbap, and truck drivers taking a siesta. I remember sitting with Professor Kwon at a rest stop like that. A highway rest stop. The weather was nice, and people were in good spirits having gotten out of the big city. I was happy to have an excuse to be outside. And it was nice to escape the city. On days like that, I always felt like I was going on a picnic. To think about it, Professor Kwon could have gone without me. He'd done fine without me up to that point, and it wasn't like I was much help anyway. So why did he bring me along? Was it all for the sake of leaving Cabinet 13 to me?

"But why Jeong-eun of all people? She can barely look after herself let alone important files," I said, showing my irritation.

"That girl is a bit of an odd one. A bit frustrating at times, too. But I think you two will do well working together."

"By any chance, is she a symptomer?"

Professor cocked his head at an angle as he looked at me. He suddenly changed the topic to the chimera files.

"Tell me, do you think I have the chimera files they're looking for?"

Suddenly, my face flushed with embarrassment. It felt like a shameful part of myself had just been exposed.

"Do you want me to speak honestly?"

"It doesn't matter how you speak. It's not easy fooling an old man like me; I've been around the block too many times. Especially not for a simpleminded youth like yourself."

"Yesterday I spent all day thinking about where you could have hidden them. Of course, I was also thinking about all the fantastic things I could do with that kind of money."

"I've spent the last forty years on this research. I'm not married, and I have no friends. Why do you think that is? Why do you think I've engrossed myself in my research like a madman? Is it because of some beautiful conviction that I could find something for the betterment of humankind? Don't make me laugh. I'm not such a magnanimous person. The reason I started this research was because of my youthful vanity. I wanted to show the world a masterpiece only a genius like myself could possibly conceive. My research was the product of vanity. Nothing more than selfishness. And through my research I have brought about so much pain. I bear that pain in my chest every day. I realize now that humans shouldn't tamper in the coming of a new species. Humankind has no say in the matter. It wouldn't matter even if we tried. The life of a human is too short to do anything about the future of the universe. That's why nature always does the choosing. New humans will be born on their own. All we have to do is wait.

I destroyed all my research. It was rubbish, anyway. It was so worthless it was dangerous. There are no chimera files. Don't even try looking for them."

After Professor Kwon fell asleep, I checked his IV fluids and left the hospital. I hadn't been able to ask him about the gingko tree man, Mr Kim. I wanted to ask if Mr Kim was also one of the sources of pain for Professor Kwon, one of the people he had hurt. But I didn't. There are moments in our life that pass by with just a murmur, and sometimes we need to pretend we didn't notice them. Instead, I looked at Professor Kwon's face as he slept and said to myself, "They told me Mr Kim died. That balding man with big puppy eyes is dead."

Thinking about it, I realized Professor Kwon was only ever exceedingly selfish toward me. Conversely, he was only ever selfless when it came to those people he defined as symptomers. He emptied his wallet for some of those symptomers. But he never even opened his wallet for me. Perhaps he never felt the need to be altruistic toward me. But he should have at least tossed me a look of pity once in a while.

Professor Kwon firmly believed that symptomers were a new species, different from humans. But I had a different opinion. I once said to him:

"I think symptomers are still human. They belong to the same species as us. The only difference is they're a bit sick. They've contracted some unknown disease."

"Possible. But I hope not."

"You hope not?"

"Tell me, do you think there's any hope for the human species?"

"Yes. I don't think they are perfect beings, but they are at least capable of reflection."

"Reflection! Don't make me laugh. The Korean War broke out when I was nineteen. People born in the same village, who fished and laughed together by the stream, were split into two groups by ideology. There was so much carnage and vengeance.

One day I saw one group stabbed to death by another with bamboo spears. They had lined them up to be stabbed one by one. And then they dug a ditch behind the elementary school to dispose of the bodies. An elementary school, where children laughed and played. Tell me, do you think *that* was because of ideology?"

"..."

"For the last fifty years, has there been any record of people 'reflecting' on that period of history? We've never stopped fighting. And for stupid reasons like maintaining the same square-footage of our apartment. I hate the human species. They're a disgrace. And we're still capable of much worse."

"And symptomers will be different?"

"No one knows. But I can't help but wish for a more beautiful species. I wish this planet was populated by a kind-hearted and more altruistic species that thinks about others as often as they think about themselves."

As Professor Kwon said this, I thought about that elementary school playground and wondered which group Professor Kwon had chosen. As a survivor, he must have been on the side holding the bamboo spears. If he hadn't been, he would have been buried in that ditch behind the elementary school with everyone else.

I'm not a scientist. I'm just a chronicler. Everything gets recorded. Whether it is by words or by fossils, by memories or by stories. All things in existence leave records. And as such, the files here are recorded because they exist, and because they have been recorded, they are preserved – whether we want it or not, whether we believe it or not. Regardless of our hate and our prejudice. These things are recorded simply because they just are. Not because they are magnificent or beautiful, but because they exist beside us. I have kept these records. That is what I do.

CONJOINED TWINS

The two women were born joined at the head. Their names were An and Chi, Chinese for eyes and teeth. Odd names, to be honest. I had never seen An's younger sister, Chi. She died at the age of seven from complications after a surgery to separating them. Chi died, and An survived. On An's face are the marks left from the parting with her sister.

While talking with An, she often covered her hands, which were remarkably small, like a doll's.

"After graduating from high school, I worked for a long time at a factory that made ship radios. My job was attaching parts to the radio boxes on the assembly line. Have you ever seen a 2mm diameter screw? They're terribly tiny – hard to pick up if you're new to the job. It takes some time, but eventually they stick to your fingers like magnets. Actually, stick would be the wrong word; it was more like they embedded themselves into the calluses on my fingers. I screwed on all sorts of parts to radios with those 2mm screws. Nine hours a day. Thirteen hours when I had to work overtime. Doing the same thing over and over: it was very monotonous work. I'd work from 8am to 10am, take a fifteen-minute break, then work again until 12:10, our lunchtime. After lunch, we'd work from 1 to 3, take another fifteen-minute break, then work again until dinner at 5:30. We were only given forty minutes for dinner. And then it was back to work again until 8:30. We had no time to rest outside official breaks. And that was because the conveyor belt could never stop. If one person went to the bathroom, all the remaining workers would have to work that much faster. The radios on the conveyor belt were like a never-ending wave. I would tightly grip my 2mm screws and parts as I stared at the radio chassis marching toward me."

"Everything is automated these days, isn't it?"

"Ship radios are all custom orders, so each radio has to be made to specification. Each ship's a bit different. Some want sets of 200, others want sets of 500. You know, stuff like that. So I guess you can't automate it."

"Tell me about your first experience being split in two."

"We weren't allowed to listen to the radio at the factory. Listening to the radio of course would lead to music, chatting, and, in general, fun. But as far as the factory manager saw it, listening to radios only increased the probability of defective products. Because of this I always had to work listening to the sound of running motors and metal on metal. Some people are sensitive to the sound of metal on metal. I think I'm one of those people. I tried plugging my ears with this and that, but the sound of metal still seeped through. And now it sounded even louder than before because it was the only sound that I could hear. I worked there doing the same job for eight years. And only four times did I skip overtime."

"Was overtime mandatory?"

"No, it wasn't mandatory. I just didn't really have anything else to do."

She took a sip of her water. Her hands looked so small as they gripped the cup. They looked like the hands of a seven-year-old. I couldn't believe those hands could have calluses.

"Not being allowed to listen to the radio, I spent all day daydreaming. I was dreaming about different places. The playground I used to play at as a child; the sidewalks I used to walk while holding my mother's hand; the alleyways where I used to jump rope with my friends; the art room where I used to hear the praise of my teachers. If you think about it, there are so many places held fondly in our memories. But on that day, what I was thinking about was the flower bed at the end of the factory. There was a flower I would give water and Yakult to during my breaks. Oh, I wish I knew the name of the flower; it would be so much easier to explain. But I'm not very good with flower names. Anyway, it was a tiny little flower with yellow petals. Smaller even than a fingertip. So small, you might not even think it was a flower."

"So, a flower like yourself."

Looking somewhat embarrassed, she gave a sheepish laugh.

"But the male workers liked to play foot volleyball around that flower bed. Naturally, it worried me. That day I was terribly sick. So, I went to the employee lounge during lunch to take a nap. But all the while I could hear the male workers kicking the ball; I was so worried about what might happen if their ball landed on the flower. I wanted to open the window and yell at them to not play foot volleyball there. I wanted to admonish them for being so inconsiderate. But I'm not the kind of person to do that. Besides, foot volleyball was the only thing that gave the male workers enjoyment. When the bell rang, I tried getting up, but my limbs felt so heavy. I needed to go back to the conveyor belt, but I was worried. What if they had killed the flower? I kept having an ominous feeling. So, I quickly ran to the flower bed in the back of the factory. Just for a quick look. I could hear the sound of the conveyor belt revving up, even from outside the factory. I ran faster toward the flowerbed. Thankfully, those yellow petals were safe and sound. But when I went back into the factory, there I was, sitting in what should have been an empty seat, screwing 2mm screws like always. It was so strange."

"What were you feeling?"

"I didn't have much time to think. I looked at myself for a second, marveling at how strange it was to see myself working, but then I was startled by the head technician who passed me and yelled, 'Why aren't you working!'"

"Do you think it was an astral projection?" I asked.

"I'm not good with big words. But if what you're referring to is like those scenes in movies where your spirit leaves your body, I think it was a little different from that. I was able to leave the factory and eat ice cream and gukbap. And it wasn't for free, either. I liked watching movies, and it would have been nice if I were a spirit and could enter the movies without buying a ticket."

"Was your consciousness in both bodies or just one?"

"For the first few minutes, my consciousness was only present in the separated body, but later it was in both."

"How do you think that's possible? I mean, the bodies were in two different places at once."

She let out a slight laugh at my question.

"It doesn't require much focus to use a screwdriver. The screws basically turn themselves. So, even though my consciousness was in two places at once, I could focus on the body outside the factory. The body inside the factory was really just moving by muscle memory."

"But wasn't it a little strange? Watching a movie in one body and looking at radios in the other?"

"No, it wasn't strange at all. No different from daydreaming about the playground from childhood while screwing together radios."

"What happened to the separated body after that?"

"My hometown is in Namhae. It's a beautiful place. Anyway, not long after being separated from my body, I took a bus and went down to Namhae. Of course, my other self was going to work every morning as if nothing had changed. I guess this sounds strange. But that's what happened. Anyway, I got off the bus and walked to the sports field of my old elementary school. I always used to imagine it while working at the factory. Seeing no students, I figured the school had been closed. I looked around the premises. I went inside the art room; plucked on the reed organ which was missing a few keys; went inside an empty classroom and wrote on the board with a piece of broken chalk as I pretended to be a teacher scolding children, "You there, stop talking!" When I was young, I wanted to be a teacher when I grew up. After that, I wiped down the dusty windows as I remembered the way I used to have fun cleaning the classroom with my friends. Swinging on the creaking playground swings, I looked at the leaves on the persimmon tree as I thought to myself how I hadn't felt this happy in a long time. I had spent the last eight years of my life turning 2mm screws. I just sat there for a long time. Then suddenly, the thought that I was going to die soon came to me. It's hard to explain, but I just knew I was going to die soon. I quickly left the playground. It would be bad to leave a corpse in a school. Children coming to play would be frightened by the corpse, and people would become suspicious. I thought for a second about where I should go next. Then I ran to where my mother and father's graves were located. I plucked the overgrown grass surrounding their graves and apologized for not coming more often. Then, lying down, I looked up at the sky and died."

"You died?"

"Yes, literally. So each weekend, I would go to Namhae to dispose of my dead body. At first I just buried it in the mountains out of fear. But now I go to the hermitage of a Buddhist monk to have it secretly cremated."

"You mean to say this is a recurring happening?"

"Yes."

"How many times has this happened to you?"

"I've died a total of seven times. And each time I've had to dispose of my dead body. The Buddhist monk lays a pile of firewood to burn me, just like a Buddhist cremation. As the body catches fire and the smoke rises, you can smell the scent of burning flesh. I can see the sight of my body shriveling in the flames. And once the flames have subsided, white bones emerge from the ashes. The monk grinds my bones into a fine

powder with a mortar and gives it to me. They're still hot to
the touch. Feeling the hot bones, I think to myself, 'So many
beautiful and happy selves have died, but that self which turns
2mm screws all day survives in utter monotony.'"

Seeing her cry as she finished talking, I quietly hugged her.
She had a slight frame, no taller than 4'11", no heavier than 90
lbs. She cried for a long time, so I held her for a long time – that
small-handed girl who looked like baby's breath.

People who see their own grave are rare. But I think that, before people build their houses, they should first make their graves. That's because people who have seen their grave know how to cherish life.

BLUFFER

There was once a patient who swore a crocodile was hiding under his bed. The doctor convinced the patient the crocodile was nothing more than a manufactured fabrication and sent the patient home. But, after going home, the patient never returned to see the doctor. The doctor called the patient's friend and asked if the patient's condition had improved. The friend responded, "Oh! You mean the guy who was eaten by a crocodile under the bed? That friend?" This is Jacques Lacan's famous tale of the crocodile.

There is a similar tale contained in the French short story "Bella B.'s Fantasy."

There once was a woman named Bella B who believed a spider was living inside her ear. A doctor and a professor told her that sexual repression and neurosis had caused her to develop arachnophobia. They also told her not to worry, as arachnophobia was a common phobia. At the advice of the professor, the woman went to a salon to have her hair cut. The doctor was hoping a change in physical appearance might be a nice distraction for the woman. However, while cutting Bella B's hair, the hairstylist accidently cut her ear with a razor blade. And from the cut crawled hundreds of baby spiders.

So I want you to ask yourself this. Did the patient really see a crocodile? Did spiders really come out of the girl's ear? Obviously, people will laugh at you if you answer yes. "Don't be ridiculous," they'll say. "It's just a made-up story." And yet there are twenty thousand people around the world who claim to have a crocodile hiding under their bed or in their closet, and forty people die every year from krokodeilophobia. Sometimes they even have bite marks and wounds on them that resemble those from a crocodile attack. Crocodiles have a bite force of nearly a ton, and tear at their food; there's no way another human could produce a wound like that. And there's also no way someone could commit suicide and make it look like that. Now, ask yourself again: Was the crocodile hiding under their bed really fake?

Doctors Canes and Musta, experts in reptiles and psychiatry, respectively, work together researching krokodeilophobia at Cambridge University.

"We still don't know why this phenomenon occurs, but stories about people seeing crocodiles under their bed are common and should not be a surprise. These stories are not unlike those about monsters in wells and bathrooms. Obviously, there is no way a swamp crocodile could end up in a person's apartment. Most doctors send their patients home after convincing them that there is no crocodile under their bed and that the crocodile will disappear if only they believe it is not real. It's common practice. But every once in a while, something dreadful happens. One patient I went to see was lucky just to keep his leg. The police and firemen searched every inch of a 10-kilometer radius, but there was not a crocodile or snake to be found. Mind you, it was Moscow in December."

Angela, a woman from Venezuela who has extreme acrophobia, always walks by shuffling her shoes so that she won't fall through the ground. If even one foot leaves the safety of the ground, she becomes paralyzed by fear. She can't even be ten centimeters off the ground. Obviously, riding an elevator up a skyscraper is out of the question; she can't even live in an apartment or two-story house because she's afraid of the stairs. She can live in a single-story house, but that's only after all the tall shelves and ledges have been removed or emptied.

"I was once invited to my friend's place for a birthday party. I didn't want to go, but I had no other choice; I had known her since elementary school and she had always been good to me. I had to drag my feet all thirty kilometers to her house. But when I arrived there and was about to step onto her lawn, I discovered a fifteen-centimeter ledge. I'd never been able to scale such a tall ledge before. I yelled out toward my friend's house, but everyone was inside, chatting noisily. Not being able to lift even one foot from the ground, I felt so pathetic and began to cry. I cried for an hour, then went back home. All the while, dragging my feet on the ground."

The first therapist Angela visited was inexperienced. That therapist told Angela that her phobia was just a figment of her imagination; that phobias could be overcome with a wave of the hand; that they were going to cure her of her phobia in no time. And such nonsense was probably written in the textbook the therapist had studied, too. In an attempt to convince Angela that stairs were completely safe, the therapist took her out to a sandpit with some play stairs for preschoolers and lifted Angela onto the stairs, against her protests.

"See, Angela. Even three-year-olds can play on stairs without any accidents. Stairs are completely safe. Can you imagine a world without stairs? That would be a dreadful place to live. Stairs are one of the safest things there are. Try stepping down; I'll hold your hand."

Stricken with fear, Angela yelled in further protest. And yet the therapist stubbornly continued his treatment. The therapist thought that Angela would be cured of her phobia if only she made up her mind to jump down from the step.

"Don't worry, Angela. Nothing bad will happen."

Then the therapist gave Angela a slight push from behind. Angela fell from the plastic steps onto the sand below.

When Angela landed, she ruptured her spleen, broke six ribs, and fractured her hip and spine. The ambulance came and took Angela to the emergency room. Her doctors said her injuries looked as though she had been struck by a car going at forty miles per hour. But the step she had jumped from was only a playground toy, no taller than thirty centimeters.

There are some people for whom the border between reality and fiction has dissolved. These people meet their fears, or perhaps the illusion of their fears, in the physical world. These people are killed by illusory crocodiles, break bones in falls from thirty-centimeter-high steps. These people shouldn't imagine crocodiles. Because when they do, the imaginary crocodile will turn into a real crocodile and attack them. And once this happens, these people become locked in a vicious feedback loop. Having finally met the crocodile from their hallucinations, these patients begin to imagine even scarier crocodiles. When this happens, their next attacker is an even larger crocodile with sharper teeth. The first crocodile laps at the patient's flesh; the second gnaws at the feet; the third takes the entire foot; and finally, the crocodile becomes so large, it swallows the person whole.

Now, let me ask you the same question again. Do you still think the crocodile hiding under their bed was fake?

"Of course it's there. It's a crocodile. The thing under my bed is most certainly a crocodile. I have to be careful of crocodiles. Of course I have to be careful. Each night as I wait to fall asleep, I see a crocodile that has slowly ballooned into a giant monster, crawling up my bed toward me. It has taken its time maturing, feeding on the prey in my imagination. With sharp teeth and thick leather armor, it slowly crawls toward me, swaying its gigantic tail back and forth with immense power. He's there, all right. I see the bastard every night."

"How can I tell whether this is real or not?"

"Try smelling it. Dreams don't have scent."

HAVING DINNER WITH HER

Jeong-eun and I met at a sushi restaurant. At the center of the restaurant was a large horseshoe-shaped bar, inside which were eight chefs busily making sushi. Most of them seemed quite old. I had thought the place was going to be a bit pricey, but nothing could have prepared me for the moment I saw the menu. 80,000 won for a regular. 120,000 won for a large. And 250,000 won for the special king size.

Yes, this was the restaurant she had brought me to. There were things we needed to meet about, and things we needed to discuss. But to be honest, I didn't know what to talk about. Surely not the future of Cabinet 13? That'd be ridiculous. But whatever it was, we needed to speak. The problem was, however, she felt uncomfortable talking with people. And likewise, I felt uncomfortable sitting in silence. I had tried to hint that if she wasn't going to talk today like last time, it would be better if we didn't get dinner together. On the other hand, if she was sincerely ready to talk, I said I would buy her a nice dinner. In a weak voice, she told me she would try. But had I known she would pick a restaurant like this... A place that sold sushi at 250,000 a plate. My mother once told me, "You never really know a woman until you've had a meal with her." My mother was always right.

Apparently Jeong-eun was a regular here. A paunchy chef came over to greet her, asking why she hadn't been in lately. She responded by saying "Oh, this and that." She must have been crazy to visit a restaurant like this on a regular basis.

226

Despite looking over sixty, the chef looked like he could make easy work of a couple of younger men.

"Today's eel is delicious. So is the red snapper. Have a taste and tell me what you think."

The chef wiped his hands with a towel as he spoke. His pronunciation had a bit of a foreign hint to it. When he left to go prepare sushi, I turned to Jeong-eun.

"He's a big man, isn't he?"

"Apparently he used to be a sumo wrestler."

"A sumo wrestler? Is he Japanese?"

"Zainichi. People say he would have become a yokozuna if it weren't for his injuries."

"Wow, I never would have guessed."

It wasn't that I didn't believe what she was saying. Rather, I couldn't believe that a sumo wrestler would become a sushi chef. To show me, she pointed to a picture hanging on the wall of a sumo wrestler shouting with both hands held high. The picture was in black and white, but the face of the handsome, strong man was clear as day. In that moment of victory with both hands held high, the man's face looked full of confidence, as though he feared nothing.

"All sumo wrestlers who started from a young age are said to be good cooks. They had to make meals for their senpai. People tend to think that sumo wrestlers can eat anything just because they're fat, but they're actually snobby food connoisseurs." Jeong-eun let out a small sigh as she finished. This was probably the longest sentence I had heard from her up till that point.

"Interesting," I said.

The assistant chef placed in front of us dainty plates with two pieces of eel and red snapper each. Not long after that, the almost-yokozuna-sumo-wrestler-turned-chef came out with a bottle of sake he had warmed up for us.

"This sake is made in-house. The first two bottles are on us, anything more and you'll have to pay. It's high proof, so it doesn't take much to get tipsy."

The chef let out a jolly laugh. Jeong-eun bowed her head slightly as she accepted the bottle. After handing over the bottle, the chef stared at me like a father meeting his daughter's boyfriend for the first time. Feeling awkward, I followed Jeong-eun by bowing my head slightly. We poured ourselves a cup of sake and drank it. The taste was deep and smooth.

"Not bad," I said.

"Right? Most of the food and drink at this restaurant is good."

I tried the sushi on my plate, but Jeong-eun didn't touch her sushi and only stared at it. The chef came over to Jeong-eun and asked, "So what'll it be tonight?" He looked as though he didn't give a rat's ass about what I wanted. Jeong-eun then turned to me.

"Mr Kong, what do you like?" she asked.

"You should order. Order what you usually like," I said.

I was secretly hoping she would order the (relatively) frugal 80,000-won sushi. After explaining the type of sushi she wanted in exquisite detail, she ended by saying, "And make it special king-sized." Special king-sized! In other words, she was ordering not the 80,000-won sushi, not the 120,000-won sushi, but the 250,000-won sushi.

"Are you fine with the menu, sir?" the chef asked me.

"250,000 won for a single plate of sushi? No, that's not fine with me!" I wanted to scream. The chef's tone of voice also bothered me. I couldn't tell if he was really asking me if the menu was to my liking, or if he was implying that a poor man like me wouldn't have money to cover such an order. I wanted to cry thinking about my soon-to-be empty wallet, but, with no way out of the situation, I turned to the chef and pretended to be cheery.

"Absolutely. It's Ms Son's day, after all."

The chef gave me a satisfied look, and Jeong-eun betrayed a bit of happiness by smiling slightly. I thought to myself that it was the first time I had seen her make even a suggestion of a smile.

The plate of sushi that came out next was not becoming of the title "special king size." Placed atop the square piece of china were a mere 10 pieces of sushi. How could they call this special king-sized? Not only did it not have any decorations, but it was also exceedingly average-looking. It was just ten pieces of sushi, some ginger, and rakkyo arranged on a square plate. Even if they sprinkled gold dust on the thing, I doubted it would be worth anywhere close to 250,000 won. But I soon realized why it was called special king size. Special king size meant they would refill your sushi as you ate. It was like a bottomless pot of gold.

I took a bite of the sushi. I couldn't tell what fish it was, but it was awfully good. Well, for 250,000 won, it had better be good. I took a shot of sake. Jeong-eun, on the other hand, still hadn't touched her sushi and was only staring at the plate.

"Are you not going to eat?" I asked.

"I'm taking my time," she said.

With her gaze fixed downward, she stared blankly at the plate of sushi for some time. As always, her silence made me feel awkward. It was awkward sitting with her, too. I thought it fortunate that we weren't sitting facing each other.

After about an hour had passed, I had eaten roughly thirty pieces of sushi, and drunk fourteen shots of sake. Jeong-eun had only eaten three pieces of sushi. On the other hand, she had taken ten shots of sake. I was full. Despite the quality of the sushi, at 250,000 won I still felt it left a lot to be desired, and each time I was reminded of this, my mood turned sour. Jeong-eun's cheeks were somewhat flushed from the sake.

"Did you find the contents of Cabinet 13 interesting?" I asked out of nowhere.

"I would say they were more comforting than interesting."

"Comforting? Have you had a hard life?"

"Yes, I have. Very hard, in fact. I wish I were something else. And I don't mean that I want to change or become a better person. No, I wish I were something else completely. I don't care if it's a blade of grass or a butterfly or a..." Before finishing, she bit her lip.

"You wouldn't mind if it's a cat?"

"You act like that's a bad thing. I'd love to become a cat."

Odd. Why do I know so many people who want to become cats?

"Why are you doing this work, Mr Kong?" she asked.

"Well, long story short, it wasn't my choice. I fell for that old man's trap."

While talking, the sumo-wrestler-turned-chef took our plates without asking and threw the remaining six pieces of sushi in the trash. I looked at him with a confused expression. He looked back at my confused face and gave me a smile.

"I know it's a waste, but I had to throw them away. Cooking is all about temperature, especially so with sushi. But I don't recognize you today, Ms Son. You haven't even touched your sushi. If there's something else I can get you, just let me know."

Jeong-eun's face flushed.

"Yeah, you barely ate anything. Order something you'll eat," I chimed in.

She hesitated for a moment before saying she would like some salmon. It didn't take long for the chef to come back out with a new plate stacked with salmon. She seemed to like salmon. Putting a piece of salmon into her mouth, she made a satisfied look and slowly began to chew. She took another shot of sake.

"Why do symptomers exist?" she asked.

"I'm not sure. It's probably because this city is no longer able to maintain our humanity. After all, species don't evolve when their environment is safe. If in fact the city isn't an environment where humans can maintain their humanity, and if that will continue to be the case in the future, then humans have no choice but to change. I guess it's less an issue of evolution and more an issue of survival."

"Then are symptomers monsters?"

"It doesn't matter whether you call them monsters or

not. Even monsters are gentle beings when their masks are removed."

She carefully lifted her glass and took a sip of sake. Having already finished the two complimentary bottles of sake, we had to order a third. When the new bottle came out, she poured herself some and took another shot. The rate at which she was taking shots seemed to be increasing.

"So, you want to become a symptomer?" I asked.

She didn't offer any answer to my question. Instead, she just took another shot of sake.

"Well, symptomers aren't able to choose whether or not they become symptomers. That's up to nature," I said.

"Then perhaps I already am one. And perhaps I'm not just a useless monster; maybe I'm also a drain on society."

With this, she took another shot of sake. She then called out to the chef for another bottle. From what I could see, she was already a bit drunk. And now that she was drunk, she started eating her sushi in earnest. Once she cleaned her plate of the salmon, the sumo-wrestler-turn-chef, who had been talking with a colleague, came over to her and started making some more sushi.

She didn't say a word as she continued to eat. Watching her eat like that, the chef wore a pleased expression. But something seemed wrong. She kept eating sushi and he kept making more sushi for her. When she finished her eightieth piece of sushi, the chef said with a laugh, "That's number eighty." It appeared like the chef enjoyed watching her eat. I also ate a few more pieces of sushi, but because I was so full, I eventually just stuck to sake. But the sake was bland. "Sake is a silly drink. You can drink five hundred bottles and still not get drunk," I thought to myself.

"If you've had your fill of Korean-style sushi, how about some Japanese-style sushi?" the chef asked me.

I nodded. A few moments later the chef came out with some raw blowfish. Jeong-eun had already eaten eighty pieces of sushi, but it didn't seem like she had any intention of stopping. Rather, the rate at which she was eating seemed to be accelerating. Now she was eating faster than the chef could prepare the fish, and whenever more sushi came out, she would wolf it down as if she had been waiting a long time. I watched her doing this with a blank stare. Noticing my staring she turned to me.

"Sorry, I can't stop myself once I start eating. It must look disgusting."

"It's OK. It's not disgusting."

I said this with a laugh. I really wasn't disgusted by her eating. What was so bad about a little excess eating? Now that the sake had finally hit her, she seemed to be in a much better mood. Actually, to be more precise, it might have been the hundred-plus pieces of sushi that she had eaten. She gave her cup to the chef and poured him some sake, and the two of them talked about things that had happened since their last meeting. I had never seen or imagined her being so social. And it was nice to see. It felt like we were having a nice drink.

"The chef says he's seen a sumo wrestler eat 1,800 pieces of sushi in one sitting. The man weighed more than 500 pounds," she said, rather excited.

She kept eating as she talked. I wondered how much she had eaten by this point. 120? 130? And yet she still seemed like she had no intention of stopping. In fact, she was eating even faster than she had been earlier. Before she even finished chewing, she was shoving the next piece of sushi into her mouth. Suddenly, as if something had gotten stuck in her throat, she covered her mouth with her hand and began gagging. I offered her some water. She waved her hand.

"Do you still think it's not disgusting?

"I like the way you look right now – better than any other time I've seen you. I mean it."

And I did mean it.

"That was great," she said. "I don't know why, but there

was a time when I spent all of my paycheck and savings on sushi. I went to all sorts of sushi restaurants, and this place was the most comfortable. They don't give you looks if you eat too much, and the chef is such a nice man. So, I made this my place. Although I haven't visited much lately."

"You're so well-spoken; why are so quiet at the office?" I asked in a joking manner.

She lifted her glass and took a sip of sake. Her face turned suddenly somber.

"I know that everyone at the office hates me. I'd hate me too if there was another me at the office."

"People don't hate you," I said. However, my attempt at comforting her didn't seem to be helping much.

"Eating sushi alone at this restaurant, I used to feel so miserable. As I ate the sushi, I would think about how this sushi was bought with the money I so painstakingly earned while enduring the hate of everyone at the office. Thinking like that, I feel so hopelessly miserable."

She lifted her shot glass again. Seeing that it was empty, I poured her some more. Quietly, she emptied the glass. She then put another piece of sushi in her mouth. How many was she at now? 150?

She extended her glass toward me. I picked up my glass and we toasted. It was our first time clinking glasses. Using sushi as a chaser, she ate two more pieces in quick succession.

"You can really hold your liquor," I said.

"Not really. But occasionally I drink my fair share."

We poured each other another glass of sake.

"Have you ever seen someone eat so much in a single sitting?" she asked.

"No, but I sometimes do it myself. Very seldomly, though."

"How much can you eat?" she asked with eyes full of curiosity.

"There were seven months when I only drank canned beer. I probably consumed twelve thousand cans of beer," I said.

She gave me a look of astonishment.

"That's amazing," she said, smiling.

She was very drunk. But in my opinion, she looked much better drunk than she did sober. She picked up her glass again to toast. I met her glass with mine, and then emptied it.

"I would eat until the food was literally coming back up through my throat. You need to stretch your stomach to its limit and stuff as much food down your throat as your body can handle – only then does food come back up through your throat."

"And what would happen then?"

I asked because I was truly curious what would happen. She finished her glass of sake. Our bottle had gone dry, so I ordered another one. What number were we on? Was it the ninth or tenth?

"I would throw up, then fast for several days. Then again I would… I couldn't stop myself. It's an embarrassing part of my life. I tried seeing a doctor about it, but there was nothing they could do for me." When the sake came out, she poured herself another glass and downed it in a flash. Then she poured herself another glass and finished that one too. As she reached out for the bottle once more, I put a hand on her arm.

"Slow down a bit."

She brushed my hand away. She then poured herself another glass and drank it. And then another. As she continued to guzzle down glass after glass without any breaks, the old sumo-wrestler-turned-chef came over and gave her a stern look as if to say she had had enough to drink.

"Ms Son, I think it's about time you were on your way."

I got up from my seat. But Jeong-eun didn't seem like she wanted to get up. She lifted the bottle again and poured herself another glass. She drank the sake, and poured again. This time, however, the bottle only filled up half the glass before running dry. She drank the half-full glass. She then shook the bottle and asked for more. I left her behind for a minute as I went to the counter to pay the bill. I asked the waitress at the counter

how much the bill was for, and at this moment, Jeong-eun
let out an embarrassingly loud scream as she ran toward the
counter.

"No, Mr Kong! I'll get the check. I'll get the check. I'm the
one who ate like a pig today. I'll get the check. I'm obviously
the one who should pay."

She was screaming so loud that everyone in the restaurant
began staring at her. Clumsily running toward the counter, she
bumped into another customer's table. A bottle of alcohol came
crashing to the ground. If anyone hadn't been staring already,
they were now. The sumo-wrestler-turned-chef quickly came
over and sat Jeong-eun down. He then apologized to the
customers whose table she had bumped into and gave a look
to another chef to clean up the mess. Jeong-eun was writhing
furiously, trying to make her way to the counter, but the chef
was holding onto her tightly, making it impossible to leave her
seat. It didn't take long before she began sobbing.

"Please, let me get the check, sir. I beg you," she said to the
chef. The chef finally nodded his head and let Jeong-eun walk
to the counter.

I went over to Jeong-eun and told her that she didn't need
to pay and that I had genuinely enjoyed the food and drink.
But she ignored me and took out her wallet from her old
leather bag to pay. She then ran to the restroom. Because the
restrooms were next to the counter, the sound of her vomiting
into the toilet could be heard from outside.

"She's actually a good girl," the chef said to me in a whisper.
"Yeah, I know," I said.

When she came out of the bathroom, she seemed to have
sobered up a bit. I helped her outside and into a taxi. Jeong-
eun mumbled her address to the driver, then looked out the
window. She was crying. I couldn't say anything. When we
arrived at her apartment complex, I asked, "Are you OK?" She
dropped her head and gave me a polite bow as if to say yes.
She then began staggering toward her apartment.

"Ms Son, are you really OK?" I asked again to her back.

She didn't answer. She continued to stagger away. I lit a cigarette and anxiously watched her from behind. Instead of going into her apartment, she went inside the next-door supermarket. By the time I finished my second cigarette, she was leaving the supermarket with a large plastic bag brimming with groceries in each hand. Holding those plastic bags, which looked as though they were about to burst, she staggered toward the front entrance to her apartment building. She lost her balance as she climbed the stairs and fell over. I was still watching her when this happened and ran toward her. She stared at me for a moment as though she was amazed that I still hadn't left, then said, "I'm fine. I trip easily." Inside the two plastic bags that had dropped to the ground were biscuits, ham, milk, cheese, bread, chocolate, ice cream, apples, honey, pears, and the like. With both bags in one hand, I helped her up with the other.

She continued to lose her balance in the elevator. But she wouldn't grab me or rest her head on my shoulder. Propping herself up in one corner of the elevator, she tried her best to keep her balance. Her room was on the eleventh floor. She took a key from her old bag and tried opening the door. But because she was still drunk, she couldn't quite find the keyhole. Unable to watch her suffer anymore, I opened the door for her. At the entrance was a giant dog. The dog was so huge that I thought it was a bear cub at first. It was an Alaskan Malamute sled dog, and it was too big to be raised in an apartment. The dog came over to Jeong-eun and nuzzled her with its face. She petted its head. As she hadn't exactly invited me into her apartment, I decided to stand at the door holding the two plastic bags. The Malamute was staring at me. Jeong-eun began walking toward the living room but fell again. Worse yet, she wasn't getting up this time. Taking off my shoes and entering her apartment, I helped her up then laid her on the sofa. I covered her with a blanket I found in the closet. I then retrieved the groceries from the front entrance and placed them on the kitchen table. I stared at the contents of the bags for a moment before taking the things that shouldn't be left out, like ice cream, milk, and fruit, and putting them on the table.

I opened her refrigerator to discovered it completely empty. There wasn't a single crumb of food to be found, only a lonely bottle of water. I stood there for several minutes just staring at her empty refrigerator. Occasionally I could hear the rattle of the motor behind the refrigerator spinning. I was somewhat suspicious of that mechanical sound which was so furiously cooling the inside of an empty refrigerator. I placed the ice cream, milk, and fruit in the refrigerator and closed the door. Then I gave the Malamute obediently sitting by her side a pat on the head and left her apartment.

"Perhaps you feel lonely among people, or like no one understands you."

"I am a little prone to loneliness."

"And do you feel like no one understands you?"

"No, actually I feel the opposite."

"What do you mean 'the opposite'?"

"People actually understand each other quite well. But it doesn't matter. People know you're lonely. In fact, they're just as lonely as you. But there's nothing they can do for you, right? That's why we become lonely. In the end, it means the same thing."

AM I A SYMPTOMER?

I love to collect tickets. Concerts, exhibitions, movies –
wherever I go, I simply must collect the ticket and some
pamphlets. Going on vacation or visiting somewhere new is no
different. Anything will do, so long as it reminds me that I was
there. Even something as simple as a souvenir or a ballpoint
pen. And I never forget to take the business card of someone
I'm meeting for the first time. If I don't do these things, life
in the city loses its meaning. Sometimes I ask myself, "Gosh,
what did I do this last year?" I get worried when I feel like I
can't answer that simple question. That's why I collect tickets.
And I can't throw them away. My house is filled with useless
stuff. In fact, when I run out of space, I end up throwing away
the necessary things instead. It's a shame because eventually
I'll have to buy new ones.

I job hop. They're usually unpopular, low-paying jobs that
anyone can do. When quitting, it often takes less than ten
minutes to hand everything over to my replacement. In fact,
the process is over so quickly that I often think to myself,
"Huh, is that all my job entailed?" When I start a new job, I
try hard for the first few months to get settled in. I act kind to
people and always smile, but then after a few months I think
to myself, "What am I doing here?" Just when the work gets
easier and I've established good relationships with everyone,

suddenly I fall into a state of panic. So I quit. Sometimes I try to give good reasons first before quitting, but when my circumstances don't allow for it, I just act irresponsibly and don't show up for work one day. Then I lay curled up in my room for a time before finally going on a trip. I feel much better after traveling for a while. And when I come back from my trip, I start a new job. This cycle repeats itself over and over. But it can't be helped; contrary to popular belief, locking yourself in your room and doing nothing isn't free. Anyway, when I do eventually go job hunting again, I look for a place that is as far away from my old job as possible; that way, I won't bump into my old colleagues by accident. It's not like I've done something wrong or am on bad terms with them, I just don't want to see them. And because of this, I've been having a tough time finding a route to work these days. Looking at a map of Seoul, it feels like there are fewer and fewer neighborhoods I can go to. Three years from now, I'll need to work in Gyeonggi Province or move to some small city. Of course, it's impossible to ever be completely satisfied. I'm not complaining. In fact, in some ways, I'm very satisfied with my life.

I'm an insurance salesman, and I cannot bear to ride the subway. Riding a city subway makes me feel like I've become excrement spewed out by the city. Yes, that excrement, the one in the toilet that is swept away with the push of a button. The people in the afternoon rush hour crowd are either dozing off, their faces tired and desolate, or blankly staring at advertisements. Sometimes they have no other choice but to stare at each other's faces awkwardly. But staring too long at another person's face is rude in the city. So I try to avoid other people's faces and eyes, but doing this makes me feel like I'm a corpse trapped in a cramped coffin. It's so hard to move around in the subway car. Rush hour frightens me. I always recite these words to myself, "Don't worry. Don't worry. Only ten stops left."

When I finish that stifling journey home and finally arrive at my place, there's a brief moment of sublime peace as I collapse on the sofa like a piece of dirty laundry and fall asleep. But when I wake up from my nap, I become filled with dread thinking about how tomorrow morning I must enter that giant city sewer again. Just seeing the subway car is enough to make me puke these days. I once threw up three times in a subway car and fainted. If you include its satellite cities, Seoul is a colossal metropolis where more than 25 million people live. Indeed, this is a very big city. But how can you live in a place like this without taking the subway?

I keep hearing the sound of a bell. I open my cellphone, but no one's called me. In fact, for the last several months, I haven't received a single phone call from anyone I know. After a while, I started to wonder if everyone in my life had forgotten about me. I've waited so patiently for them, but I guess everyone has forgotten I exist. It's frightening. Obviously, I can't call them first. Every day I would swap out my cellphone battery as I thought to myself, "What if I get a call from someone who remembers me today. I'll have to buy them a nice dinner. And get them a present that'll knock their socks off." But still no phone call. As weeks have turned to months, I've began to despise the people who should have known my phone number. How could they forget me when I was in so much pain and so lonely? Several days ago, I was eating by myself when I suddenly yelled, "They can all go to hell!"

I can't stop working. If schedules and weekly agendas aren't neatly printed and placed on my desk, I become so overwhelmed with anxiety that I can't do anything. Because of this, I tend to work late. It's not that I am bogged down with work, nor is it that my boss is a nitpicker. It's just because of anxiety. When I mindlessly watch TV at home, I often start thinking about the next morning's meeting or about things that I might have forgotten to do; sometimes I even drive my car into work at three in the morning. I can't think about or do anything outside of work. Did I mention I don't have any hobbies or social life?

I'm in debt. My father made the mistake of underwriting a relative's debt, and now that he's gone, our family has inherited his mistake. It is an inheritance, so to speak. And depending on how you looked at it, the debt could be large or small. If I had made monthly payments with half of my first job's paycheck, I could have probably paid the debt off in about fourteen years. In that sense, it wasn't even the cost of a 700-square-foot apartment in downtown Seoul. Alas, if only I had sucked it up and been diligent with my payments, things wouldn't have turned out this way. Not only would I have accrued less interest, but my ever-increasing paychecks would have helped me chip away at the principal faster. It probably wouldn't have even taken all fourteen years if I had invested a bit, too. But who thinks like that when they're young? Anyway, by the time my kid was born, I had new things to worry about. On top of paying off the debt with my monthly paychecks, I also had to raise a kid and save up money to buy a house. But I didn't have enough money to cover everything. It started to become too much. I tried my hand at stocks and even opened a business I had no experience in. And with each failure, the debt grew like a snowball. Some people get lucky with the lottery. But there's nothing I can do to escape this debt. People are always so shocked when they see a story on the news about someone killing their entire family, but for me that kind of story hits close to home. I know it's wrong, but I've thought about it many times. And I've lost a lot of weight recently. There's this pawnshop that I go to, with this nasty old man. He's like the pawnbroker from Dostoyevsky's *Crime and Punishment*. He is completely heartless. Anyway, he always carries a wad of cash with him, and in the ceiling of the pawnshop is a vent sealed with steel bars. One day while looking at the tiny vent, I thought to myself that I might be able to fit if I lost sixty more pounds. I wasn't actually planning on doing it, of course. But ever since that day, I've gotten thinner and thinner and thinner. All I did was imagine it, but look how thin I've got.

Life was so futile. When my husband left for work, I had nothing to do, not even a child to look after like the other women. Money – well, that wasn't an issue. As long as I had enough to eat and clothe myself, I was fine. But not my husband, or his relatives, or any of my relatives. I couldn't understand why they obsessed so much over money. Anyway, I took a poetry writing class at the culture center and even thought about going to graduate school, even if it was a bit late. But everything just felt so pointless. I'm a bit of a hypocrite for saying this, but I felt silly wearing education and culture around my neck like other well-to-do women, as if it were some accessory. So I would just sit in my apartment alone and cry. I can't talk about it when I see old classmates. Who am I to complain when so many other people are struggling just to get by? I know there are people who have tough lives, but my life is tough like hell, too. It feels like I'm living in a void. Do you get what I'm saying?

I worked for several years as a greeter at the entrance to a department store. I had to wear a wide smile on my face for ten hours straight. Then one day, I lost the ability to stop smiling. Even when I was angry or sad, I couldn't stop smiling. My smile just wouldn't go away. Even at my mother's funeral I couldn't stop smiling. Tears kept falling from my eyes, but on my face was still that bright smile as always. "Welcome, enjoy your shopping," my smile was saying. And because of this, my smile is a cheap one. It's a smile from a bargain sale. My smile is always discounted, always at dirty-cheap prices. Is this a disease? Have I gone crazy?

"Am I a symptomer?"

"No, you're not a symptomer. Not yet. Don't worry. You can still make it in this city."

PART 3
Boobytrap

BOOBYTRAP

There is a bomb named the Massive Ordnance Air Blast (MOAB). Born in 2003 in the US, this 9-meter-long, 9.5-metric-ton bomb is as large as Totoro, that creature from the Miyazaki film. Of course, stuffed with all manner of explosives, the MOAB isn't quite as cute as Totoro. Indeed, being the most explosive conventional bomb ever, the MOAB is second only to nuclear bombs. And when this bloodthirsty fucker is released, it creates two blasts, and obliterates every living organism within a one-kilometer radius.

The first explosion creates a blast radius of 350 meters, no less. Anything within that radius is killed either from the shockwave or the heat. Then, when the aerosols from the first blast have sufficiently diffused into the atmosphere, there is a second explosion creating temperatures exceeding 1,000 degrees Celsius, effectively burning all the oxygen within 1,000 meters of ground zero. Those exposed to this second blast are killed either by the back blast or the ensuing burns. Anyone lucky enough to have a deep underground bunker to hide from the back blast and heat, will eventually die from asphyxiation.

The MOAB is more commonly known by its nickname: the "Mother of All Bombs." Who knew bombs had mothers? Sometimes I wonder how the warm and tender word that is "mother" could be attached to something so horrific as a bomb. American soldiers chose the name probably because

251

they lacked the imagination and vocabulary necessary to think of a better substitute for the acronym. They could have chosen anything else. Monkey of all bombs, mouth of all bombs... Heck, even that would have been better than mother of all bombs.

Not being a fluffy anime character or a missile, the MOAB cannot fly on its own. And because it's so fat, you can't load it onto a plane. Ignoring its thin shell, this fat fucker is 100% pure explosives. If they made a nuclear bomb as big as the MOAB using today's technology and detonated it, the whole world would be turned to ash.

The first reason they made such a large and immobile bomb was because it was cheap to build. The second was that, at least compared to nuclear weapons and chemical bombs whose use in war was heavily criticized by the public, this bomb had a relatively good public image. Despite the fact that the MOAB releases aluminum oxide and other harmful chemicals into the air when exploding, making it a sophisticatedly devastating bomb, as far as the public is concerned, the MOAB is just another conventional bomb and, in fact, an improvement over the napalm bombs of the Vietnam era. In fact, if it could talk, the MOAB would probably try to convince us of its banality: "I'm not a nuke. I'm no different from the cannonballs Napoleon used at the Battle of Waterloo. I'm based on the same principles as the Molotovs used by university demonstrators. I'm a proper and fair weapon. Admittedly, I do contain more explosives than the cannons at Waterloo. But that was two hundred years ago."

Hansen Brown is a nice fellow. He's an honest husband, a good father, and has volunteered to help immigrants and impoverished children in his community since he was a young boy scout. Once he was even featured on the front page of the local newspaper for donating half of his fortune to save a local girl from heart disease. And every morning, Hansen Brown goes to work at the munitions factory to build MOABs.

One day, Hansen Brown's daughter came home from school in a fit.

"People say you make the biggest bomb in the world," she said. "Is that true, Daddy?"

Hansen Brown's face went white as he thought for a moment.

"Yes," he finally answered. "Daddy's job is to make misfortune. But if Daddy didn't make misfortune that explodes on the other side of the world, that misfortune would end up in our sitting room or somewhere like your savings."

There's a boobytrap called PERSCOM. This anti-personnel, anti-tank boobytrap, which is laid around M114 155 mm howitzers, or dropped by planes and helicopters, is a series of eight landmines. If any one of its eight tripwires goes off, all eight landmines will detonate in succession. Whereas most anti-personnel mines only take the life or leg of the soldier who steps on it, this boobytrap can massacre an entire squadron if one person makes a mistake. One detonation trips the detonation of the next mine, which detonates the next mine, and so on and so forth until everything has been turned to dust. If it could talk, this boobytrap would probably try to warn us of trusting others: "Didn't you say teamwork was important? If that was the case, you should have made sure the guy backing you up was dependable."

In an odd way, this boobytrap mimics misfortune. Just as one unfortunate event is connected to the next, tripping one wire will set off an explosion of unfortunate events.

Boobytraps are thrown out like bait on a fishing line: you only need to wait. But, unlike with fishing, the person who casts a boobytrap has little interest in food or sport; people who set boobytraps are only interested in the amount of misfortune they can create. Indeed, the more unhappiness they can bring to their prey, the better. Another difference is that, when it comes to fishing, there is at least a contest between the caster and the fish – albeit an unfair contest, as is often the case in life. But boobytraps present no contest. Indeed, the despicable thing about boobytraps is that, by hiding in anonymity, the setter makes contest impossible.

Boobytraps work via the principles of temptation and error. According to the ROK Military Field Manual, rice, canned foods, guns, maps, compasses, and water are common incentives used to lure people into making contact with a landmine detonator. Death awaits anyone who removes such an item from the top of a boobytrap. Survival awaits those who don't. Now, let's imagine the case in which someone does take the bait, causing the detonators that have been waiting so long to go off; was their death due to temptation? Or was it due to error?

Had we the power to see the future, we would be astounded by just how many spiderweb-like boobytraps are lain throughout the world and our daily lives. Indeed, you would begin to wonder if avoiding such a dense web of tripwires were even possible. Won't I eventually be lured in by one of these temptations and make an error? And if not me, what about the person in front of me? Or the person behind?

When people go bankrupt or suffer some unexpected disaster, they lament how life and misfortune happen so suddenly. But life is not as simple as that. In fact, the boobytrap wire is tripped way before we become aware of the misfortune. A moment as simple as making a left turn instead of a right could have caused a crack to form on your brakes, starting the countdown to your inevitable misfortune. Something as simple as giving your boss a firm "no," or telling yourself, "What could go wrong?" as you get up to accept an unassuming handshake from a shadowy hand. Something as simple as being merely unlucky. And sometimes, without any provocation, for no reason whatsoever, the tripwire might one day decide to just snap, all on its own.

We can never escape this web of misfortune that blankets our lives. It is just too expansive, too intricate. The history of power is a story of boobytraps. Or, to phrase it slightly differently, the history of humankind is a story of boobytraps. Out of fear and anxiety, we keep laying boobytraps, even if they might harm us. Countless wires rigged with detonators, wires of misfortune that multiply ad infinitum. Surveillance cameras and thick legal dictionaries demanding restrictions and regulations. Order necessitates thousands, millions, billions of boobytraps. The person in front of me, the person behind me, my lover, my enemy – if any one of them trips on a single wire, there will be a cascade of unfortunate events. It's not enough just to be careful myself. You and I both have need to avoid temptation and making a mistake. After all, there's a man with a kind face all the way on the opposite side of the globe who goes to work every morning to build giant bombs for us.

The Book of Genesis is also a story about boobytraps. When God made the universe, God also made boobytraps. And in the Garden of Eden, God placed a trap in the form of the forbidden fruit. Through the serpent, God created an elaborate plan to tempt Adam and Eve. And according to this plan, the two were caught in the boobytrap. They triggered the detonator, setting off a cascade of unfortunate events. Work, labor pains, hate and regret, shame, murder and theft. Not to mention good and evil, which never would have existed if it weren't for God.

But, through this boobytrap, what did God hope to learn about humanity?

WILL EXECUTION INC.

Professor Kwon had been in a coma for several days. According to the doctor, he wasn't going to wake up again. Sitting inside the hospital room, I stared at Professor Kwon's face for a long time. I tried not to get emotional. I had seen the face of a dying person before. At some point, their face goes from holding on to life to giving up on everything. It's then that they've died. It was clear that Professor Kwon was going to die in his coma. And if by some miracle he did wake up, he wouldn't have much time before he died anyway. And yet, his face still looked as though he was holding on to something. I couldn't understand why.

The day before, I had been visited by an employee from an odd company named Will Execution Inc.

"Will Execution Inc? What kind of company is that?" I asked.

"Founded in 1653 in the Netherlands, Will Execution Incorporated is an international company that specializes in executing the wills of deceased people. In other words, we make sure that a person's will is faithfully carried out after their death."

"Isn't it that a lawyer's job?"

"When the items in a will have various stipulations or require an extended period of time to be executed, it is sometimes necessary to have a separate entity monitoring the process. When wealth and power are being transferred, it's only natural for people to appear who covet that wealth and power. So, if the deceased's money is to be donated to a charity, we monitor whether that money is being used as prescribed in the will; or we can make sure offspring do not receive their inheritance all at once and are instead given manageable monthly allotments – just to name a few examples. And in the instance of a sudden accident or tragedy, we also offer a type of compensation. Of course, we do more than that, too. And we offer these services regardless of the size of the inheritance. That's because we're able to make a profit from investing the inheritance."

Listening to him speak, it dawned on me that there were all sorts of ways the dead could meddle in the lives of the living.

"What happens to the families when your investments go bad?"

"There's no chance of that happening. You see, founded in 1653 in the Netherlands, our company offers a certain amount of security and–"

"OK, OK. So, what does this have to do with me? I can't imagine your company would have any reason to contact me. I don't have any connections to that industry. Nor do I have any wealthy relatives."

"You are mentioned by name in Professor Kwon's will. Under the condition that you take on the work of managing Professor Kwon's research data, you will be paid a million won monthly. And that amount will be adjusted each year according to inflation. Other business expenses will also be paid for, of course. And there is one more special clause. In the event you find yourself in peril, you will be provided with a safe house. Our safe houses are recognized as some of the most secretive and secure in the world. Needless to say, Will Execution Inc. will cover the cost."

"A safe house? What exactly would I need to be kept safe from? A nuclear weapon? A volcanic eruption?"

"The safe house is for you to escape to when people with ulterior motives threaten to assassinate, blackmail, pursue, or detain you."

Hearing this, I burst out into laughter. He had said the words assassinate, blackmail, pursue, and detain with such seriousness.

"This is all terribly interesting. But ordinary people like me don't have to worry about things like being assassinated, blackmailed, pursued, or detained. Those things only happen in the movies."

"I'm only reading what was written in the will."

This guy seemed stubborn and stiff.

"Anyway, I'm sorry to have to tell you this after you've come all this way, but I'm not capable of looking after Cabinet 13, nor do I have any desire to."

"The decision is yours, of course. I'm just fulfilling my obligations."

"Was Son Jeong-eun mentioned in the will?"

"Unfortunately, I am not at liberty to discuss other parts of the will."

The man took out a piece of paper for me to sign. When I asked what the document was for, he told me it was to acknowledge that I had heard the will and promised to keep its secrets. I signed the document. The man gave me his business card and told me to call him if I changed my mind.

Will Execution Incorporated – it sounded like Professor Kwon. I had thought he was joking when he offered to pay me a million won a month to look after Cabinet 13, but I guess he was serious. I started to wonder if that old man had any sense of how much things cost nowadays. He couldn't possibly expect me to buy and house and raise a family in an unforgiving city like Seoul on a million won a month, could he? But then again, what would a man who was single his entire life and ate castella and cup ramen every day known about finances?

I had no idea what would happen when Professor Kwon was gone. Nor did I know what was going to become of all the hundreds of symptomers who depended on him. Did Professor Kwon really think such a pathetic attempt to bequeath Cabinet

13 to me would work? This wasn't something that was going to go away just by pushing it off on me. How could Professor Kwon not know that? And what could I do for that cabinet and all 375 of those weirdos? Maybe he expected me to team up with Jeong-eun? If that was true, he was more foolish than I had thought. And besides, there were countless matters Professor Kwon had handled in secret – things that I knew almost nothing about.

Things were going to work out, regardless of what I did. Death was as common as falling leaves in the autumn. The world wasn't going to end just because someone died. After Professor Kwon's death, the symptomers of Cabinet 13 would disperse and continue to live their lives as they always had.

Suddenly, smelling something foul come from his sheets, I lifted Professor Kwon's blanket. The bed sheets were thoroughly soaked with Professor Kwon's runny excrement. Even when unconscious, his body knew how to take care of business. They say the last thing condemned criminals do when being hanged to death is soil themselves. They spend the last moment of their lives shitting themselves. Thinking about it, it's both kind of funny and a bit horrifying.

I took off Professor Kwon's pants and removed from them his shit-stained diaper. Then with a wet towel, I wiped his anus and genitals. Boredom must have overcome me because I decided to lift Professor's penis with my thumb and index finger and asked in a serious tone, "Hey, Mr Penis. Have you ever been used for anything else besides taking a whiz?" Of course, Mr Penis didn't answer my question. But then again, what would I expect from such a shy-looking penis.

Lying in the bedpan beneath the bed, whether by the nurse's mistake or by design, was an unused diaper. I changed his diaper then took the bed sheets, soiled diaper, and bedpan out into the hallway where there was a special bin for used diapers. The bin was already full of the excrement of patients who had lost the ability to tell the difference between number one and number two. I threw the diaper in the bin and went to the restrooms to clean the bedpan. Despite being stained with Professor Kwon's loose stool, it smelled more strongly of medicine. The doctors had given him enema medicine called Monilak to prevent his liver, which was having trouble detoxifying his blood, from being overwhelmed. Forcing him to have diarrhea right after every meal prevented his body from producing ammonia, which needed to be processed in the liver. And so, he would eat only to immediately have diarrhea. And because not eating wasn't a choice, he would have to eat again, which would make him have diarrhea again. It was a truly wretched cycle.

When I returned from the restrooms, K was waiting for me in front of Professor Kwon's hospital room. Looking calm and relaxed as always and with a sneer on his face.

"I heard the news. I guess he's not waking up again."

I didn't say anything, and just nodded my head. I thought to myself that the syndicate's showing up here now was ideally timed to take advantage of me. After all, I had no pride in Cabinet 13 and wanted to free myself of it as quickly as possible. Getting a large sum of money would make things even better. Unfortunately, I had nothing to sell them.

"Have you thought more about our offer?" K asked.

"I don't think this is the best time to talk about it."

"I disagree. Now is the most appropriate time for you to decide. Things will only get more complicated once Professor Kwon passes. His office will be cleared out and the research data dispersed."

"You should go. I don't know anything about it, and I don't want to be involved anymore."

"Please reconsider. You have no need of those files."

"I'll be frank with you. If I did have those chimera files, I would have sold them to you. As you say, I have no need for them, and two billion won is no small amount of money. But Professor Kwon doesn't have the chimera files. And if he did, I wouldn't know anything about them. He didn't leave me with any clues. So, it seems to me like we have nothing more to talk about."

"Then it appears our deal is off?"

"We never made a deal in the first place. The only thing we've exchanged is your business card."

"This is quite befuddling. And very regrettable."

K politely bowed to me then left.

Once K was gone, I started worrying about the things that would happen after Professor Kwon's death. Would I really be able to leave behind Cabinet 13 irresponsibly like that, like nothing over the past several years mattered? Regardless of how conflicted I might be over it, it seemed like that was what was ultimately going to happen. After all, there was absolutely nothing I could do for the damaged souls of Cabinet 13.

Perhaps the true reason Professor Kwon chose me as his assistant was because I was an idiot capable of doing absolutely nothing. Perhaps all he truly needed was a janitor. He didn't need a scientist or a flask or a test bench; all he needed was a librarian—in fact, a simple cabinet. But why? Why did he need an empty cabinet like me? I was nothing more than an empty tin can.

"I once saw this article about the Amazon rainforest. I guess giant fast food chains like McDonalds are burning the Amazon rainforest just to get beef for their hamburgers. Each hour in the Amazon rainforest, there are seven thousand forest fires. This means that at the current rate, the Amazon rainforest will disappear in a hundred years from now. It means the lungs of the Earth will disappear. It means it will slowly get harder and harder to breathe. It means life itself will disappear from the Earth. But is anything changing? Is anyone able to stop McDonalds? And why do you think that's the case? It's because there are selfish people like yourself on this Earth. If only people like yourself were gone from the planet, everything would return to peace."

"And what about you? Don't tell me you've never had a hamburger."

BLUE LITMUS PAPER

I was on my way to work waiting for the bus when a man in his mid-fifties approached me.

"Excuse me, are you Mr Kong by any chance?" he asked.

The man was handsome, somewhat like a salesman, but his spray-on smile, which was cheap to the point of looking obsequious, made him seem a bit simpleminded. I answered yes.

"Thank goodness it's you, Mr Kong. Thank goodness," the man said, sounding like a child. He looked so ridiculous I couldn't help but scoff.

"What's so good about that? And what's it to you?"

"It's very good. Very good, indeed. If you weren't Mr Kong I would have to look all over this city again for him. I'm sorry for coming to you like this so early in the morning and without notice, but could you spare me a minute? It won't take long. I'm sorry about this, but the work I do always has to be done immediately. If you're afraid of being late to work, we can talk while I drive you to work."

The man pointed to his car in the distance. It was a compact car and very vintage.

"No, if it won't take long, we can finish our business here. I'll just take the bus to the subway when we're done. After all, I don't even know you."

"Then perhaps I can give you a ride to the station. I think we'll have enough time on the ride there."

The man still had yet to reveal who he was. But even so, I did need to go to the subway station, and it was ten minutes by bus; if that's how much of my time he was going to take, I didn't see much of a problem. I accepted the man's offer and got into his car. His movements were quick as he hopped into the driver's seat. After starting the car, the man said, as if humming a tune, "I would be very thankful if you could fasten your seatbelt. Belts save lives!" "What a square," I muttered to myself as I buckled my seatbelt. The man tried to remove an object from his suit's breast pocket, but it seemed to be caught on something. I assumed he was trying to remove his wallet to give me his business card. However, the thing he pulled from his pocket looked more like an electric shaver.

"What's that?" I asked, a little suspicious

"Nothing. Just an electronic device of sorts. It's made in Germany, but the engineering is just average. Do you want to see for yourself?"

The man held out the device. Despite not being too interested, I craned my neck as I pretended to give it a perfunctory look. The man then suddenly put the device to my neck. All I saw before passing out was a flash and some sparks.

I was in an office when I regained consciousness. My body was tied to a chair and my hands were restrained by handcuffs. Because the blinds were closed, I couldn't tell where exactly I was, but hearing the sound of cars honking from below, I guessed it was some tall building downtown. The office was clean. There was a telephone, a fax machine, and a desk, as well as a reception room, just like a regular office. A shelf on one wall was packed with books. In the room opposite that wall was an operating table and several tools that looked like medical instruments. It seemed to be a dental office of sorts.

Watching TV was the man I had met that morning. Skinny and of average height, he looked to be in his fifties, and had dull eyes. Because of his gentle and good-natured appearance, he didn't seem like the sort of person who would stun you with a taser or kidnap you. Then again, I had no idea what a professional kidnapper would look like.

It seemed like he was watching a comedy program. With his arms crossed, he stared at the TV and knitted his brows as though he couldn't understand something. I had never seen someone watch comedy with such a grave look on their face before.

"I don't get it," he muttered to himself. "Why do people find that funny?" He then turned to look at me. "Awake, are we?" His voice was calm, as though he was asking his coworker how they had slept the night before.

I sat there in silence. The man took a cigarette from his coat pocket and stuck it in his mouth. As he brought the lighter close to his face to light the cigarette, his face turned to shock as he exclaimed, "Right!" as if he had just remembered something. "I've tried to quit several times, but I always end up failing because I forget that I've quit. Habits are a scary thing. Have you experienced that?"

Holding the unlit cigarette, the man made a look of embarrassment, as though he pitied himself for forgetting that he had quit smoking. It was a bit absurd, though. He had tased, kidnapped, and handcuffed another man, and all he had to talk about now was how he couldn't quit smoking?

"What do you think you're doing? I already told that K guy I know nothing about the chimera files," I shouted. The man looked shocked by my shouting.

"Ah, yes! We'll get to that in a bit. There'll be a phone call any minute now. I think it best only to talk once I've heard from them. To be honest, I'm also not quite sure what we're doing here. Anyhow, what was it that we were discussing? It's going to kill me if I don't remember it."

The man tightly knitted his brows, trying to recall what he had been talking about. Looking at him, I couldn't help but think he was an idiot. Then suddenly, the man began speaking again as if he had finally remembered.

"Ah, yes! I asked if you had ever tried to quit smoking but failed to quit smoking because you forgot that you had quit smoking. That was it. So, have you?"

"Never."

I answered his question despite how ridiculously he was acting.

"That's very strange. Everyone's tried to quit smoking at least once. Sometimes just for kicks, you know."

"If you've quit smoking, why do you carry around cigarettes?" I asked testily.

"Not carrying around cigarettes makes it unclear whether I've ever quit smoking at all. And I can't stand things that are unclear."

"Do you know how serious what you're doing is? This is a crime. It's kidnapping. I hope you have a good plan to get out of this."

"I already told you; we'll talk about that later. After I get the call."

The man said this with a smile. He then returned to the TV, sat down on the sofa, and focused on the comedy program as if he weren't bothered in the least by the crime he was committing. Each time audience laughter roared out of the television set, the man's face went cross. "What on Earth is so funny? Damn, this is getting on my nerves. Everyone's laughing and I'm here alone missing the joke," the man muttered under his breath. Listening to him talking to himself, I thought to myself, "That's because you're too stupid to get it." His face looked so naïve as he focused on the television.

The man would look at the clock from time to time as he watched TV and make a "What's taking so long?" sort of face. He had been waiting for several minutes now. But I couldn't tell what it was exactly he was waiting for, and I wanted to know. Only when the thing he was waiting for arrived could my situation change, be it for better or worse. And if my situation didn't change, I would have to continue sitting here with that man watching a comedy program with a grave face. To make things worse, my hands were numb because the handcuffs were so tight.

"Maybe you're right," the man spoke up suddenly. "Maybe quitting smoking is a fool's errand. After all, you're more likely to die in a car crash than from smoking."

When he finished, he took out another cigarette and lit it. Then sitting back and relaxing, he took a long satisfying drag on the cigarette before blowing out a stream of smoke. The cigarette smoke had a very pleasant aroma.

"Oh, how rude of me. Do you want one?"

"I'd rather you take these handcuffs off me."

"No can do, kiddo."

"Then at least loosen them a bit. My arms are going numb."

Initially, the handcuffs had actually been quite loose, but by wriggling my fingers around I had accidently tightened them to the point where I couldn't move. The reason I had moved my fingers so much was because of the silly hope that I might be able to unlock them myself. But because of the teeth on the inside of the cuffs, once they ratcheted tighter, there was no going back. In other words, the handcuffs could move only in one direction, and that direction was tighter. The man came over to me, fiddled with the handcuffs, unlocked them with his keys, then loosely handcuffed me again. He also stuck a cigarette in my mouth and lit it for me.

"Do you know what handcuffs and quagmires have in common?" the man asked as he lit my cigarette.

I took a long drag on the cigarette before saying, "What do they have in common?" Truthfully, I had little interest in the commonalities between handcuffs and quagmires.

"The more you struggle, the deeper you sink."

The man grinned slightly as if to tell me he knew the handcuffs hadn't become tighter on their own. At that moment, the phone rang. The man turned off the TV with the remote and answered the phone. He stood there for a while with the receiver next to his ear. The person on the other end of the line was doing most of the talking.

"Yes, yes. And that's as far as I'm going. I don't want any more involvement in this."

The man then hung up the phone. As far as what...? The man peered through the blinds with his finger, then lit another cigarette.

"I like this place. It's in the city; it's high up and the view is nice; it gets a lot of sunlight; and all the cars and people look like ants from here. It's much better than talking in some dark dank office. Conversations go much more smoothly in a place like this. If you decide to get revenge on me after all this is over, you should start looking for me here. I always do my work here. But it won't be easy. Seoul's a big city with lots of skyscrapers and lots of offices."

"I guess it's the syndicate who's ordered you to do this, but you've got it all wrong. I don't know anything about the chimera files."

"I see you're going to make me repeat myself. I have to do things in order. If I don't, everything's going to get out of whack. And if that happens, I'm going to get pissed. Besides, I have no idea who you are or why you've been brought here. How do you expect me to know about your situation? If this job required me know the reason for your being here, I'd know all about it, sure. But it doesn't, so I don't. I'm sure there's someone who's paid to know why it is you've been brought here. After all, there's a job for everyone. If you want an answer to your question, you should talk to them. That's all I'm going to say about that. It's not my job to answer your questions, so don't even ask. All I've been hired to do is interrogations. Receive instructions and debriefings, know what's permissible and what's not, and the occasional beating or use of torture – those are my duties. There's no need for me to make any tough decisions. I'll say it once more, I don't know why you're here."

Beating or torture? Not being able to process the man's words, my eyes glazed over for a moment.

"Coffee?" the man asked.

I didn't answer. Having taken my blank expression as a yes, the man brewed two cups of coffee. He placed the two cups of coffee on the small tea table, as well as an ash tray and some cigarettes. To allow me to drink, the man uncuffed my hands from behind the chair, brought my hands to the front, then handcuffed them again. The whole time I let him do as he asked.

"Cream? Sugar?"

He sounded as if he was talking to a houseguest. I shook my head slightly to indicate that I wouldn't have either. After all, was this really the time to have a friendly cup of coffee with sugar and cream?

"So, what is it you're going to do now? Are you going to torture me, or something?" The moment I asked this, the fear suddenly became more palpable.

"I don't particularly like hitting people or making them scream. I prefer having a nice, calm conversation. Besides, brute force isn't that effective."

"That's a relief."

"If I can believe what you tell me, they'll be no need for all that cumbersome stuff. The most important thing is trust. But trusting another human isn't easy. Don't you agree?"

I nodded slightly to show that I partially agreed with him.

"Have you finished your coffee?" the man asked.

Actually, I hadn't even touched my coffee. Regardless, after glancing at the clock, the man took the cup from my hands. He dumped the coffee into the sink, rinsed out the two cups with water, placed them on the rack, and dried his hands with a towel.

Tearing open a sealed envelope, the man read a piece of paper for a moment before jotting something down in a notebook. He then opened the closet and changed into a white gown. Going into the operating room next door, he picked up a few medical instruments and inspected them under the fluorescent lights. He brought over a medical cart and placed six medicine bottles and several different sized syringes on it. He also placed forceps, scissors, and a scalpel on the cart. After placing a few more things which I couldn't identify on the cart, he positioned it next to the operating table. Seeing the mysterious medicine bottles and tools, I became even more frightened. What was he planning to do to me? Was he going to perform brain surgery on me? My heart began to pound violently. The man walked over to me, lifted me to my feet, then led me to the operating table. Now that I was closer to the cart, I could see a terrifyingly sharp scalpel and pair of shears, the kind used to cut branches. At that moment, indescribably surreal and horrific thoughts started to dance in my head. The man laid me down on the operating table. To restrain me to the rails on the operating table, the man uncuffed me. But as soon as he unlocked the cuffs with his keys, I lunged forward with my fists. I never thought I was capable of such a thing. Perhaps it was the man's somewhat small frame that propelled me forward, or perhaps it was the unconscious desperation knowing that now was going to be my only chance. But the man easily avoided my first, which I had thrown at him with all my strength, and quickly countered by sticking out his thumb and jamming it deep into my larynx. His movements were nimble and practiced. I let out a heaving gasp as I fell to the ground. My head was spinning with vertigo and I couldn't breathe.

"You're more fun than I thought you'd be. I like that," the man said with a smile.

The man lifted me up as I gasped for air, leaned me up against the operating table, then with one hand pressed down gently on my chest as he grabbed my belt with the other hand. Then, as if he were a cornerman standing in front of his boxer at the end of a round, he pulled my belt toward him as he said, "Breathe–"

After he did this about ten times, I finally raised my hand to tell him I was fine. The man laid me down on the operating table and restrained both my arms and legs to the rails. This time I didn't fight him. To be honest, I had no more strength left in me, so I didn't really have a choice in the matter. Once I was resting on the table, the man started inspecting the drugs and operating tools. He then shoved the cart to the wall, went over to the blinds to look out as he had earlier, and lit a cigarette. He came back toward me after he finished.

"Let's get started, shall we? Quick and easy, for both you and me. The longer things like this take, the more uncomfortable and tiresome it'll be. I'm not asking for any help. Let's just do what's best for both of us. I know this isn't the most pleasant situation for you, but we should avoid making it any worse. Don't you agree?"

I couldn't quite place my finger on it, but the man's gentle tone was somehow reminiscent of a soldier's.

"Here are the rules for this little tête-à-tête. First, I want short answers. Avoid as much as possible any unnecessary modifiers or conjunctions like 'but,' 'however,' 'nevertheless.' And, if possible, don't use adverbs or adjectives. I don't like overly descriptive language. So, answer in the simplest, most concise sentences you know how to make. Understood?"

Lying on the table, I nodded my head.

"Second, tell me as much as you can. And if you have any secrets that you must guard, you better hope they're kept perfectly hidden in a place I can't find them. Because if I get even the slightest inkling that you're hiding something, it's going to be a long day for you. And you *will* tell me all your secrets, believe me. Just for your information, I've been professionally trained for this. From my experience, there's only a handful of people in the whole entire world who could walk out of this room with their secrets. In other words, if you aren't one of those people, you better just tell me everything from the get-go. If you make me wait, you're going to pay the price. Understood?"

Again, I nodded my head.

"Third, don't change your story in the middle. If you change your story, we're going to need to start over again so I can get the real story. That means we'll need to go through everything a second time. It's only going to result in more pain, for the both of us. Understood?"

I nodded my head once more.

"Please remember these rules. If you follow them closely, we'll be able to finish this without any pain. My teacher taught me that good questions result in good answers. I'll try my best to ask you specific questions. I only ask that you try your best to give me good answers. Are you ready?"

I nodded my head. But ready for what? I had no idea what I was nodding for. The man walked over to the desk and brought over a document. He then began his interrogation.

"Are you familiar with the chimera files?"

"Yes."

"Have you ever seen the chimera files?"

"No."

"Do you know a man by the name of Kim Woo-sang?"

"Yes."

"Do you remember for how long you were in contact with Mr Kim?"

"From July of 1998 to October of 2001. We met once a month."

"Good. You're doing great. Just keep answering just like you are now. According to the report I have here, you managed Mr Kim's lab data for three years. Is this correct?"

"Yes."

"The name of the file you managed for Mr Kim – its title was 'CHIMERA D303417 – GINKGO TREE MAN KIM WOO-SANG.' Correct?"

"Yes."

"Well, isn't that strange. Didn't you just say you have never seen a chimera file? So, which one is it?"

"The documents I wrote up were consultation logs and records of observation. Basic documents. They're not the chimera files the syndicate is looking for. What the syndicate wants are documents containing genetic engineering technology for hybrid humans, right? I've never been involved with any such research. I didn't even know Professor Kwon was doing such research."

"So, let me get this straight, you did basic research together, but you didn't know the goals of that research or where the data is? Is that right?"

"I'm not a scientist, so I was never actually capable of doing any research. I didn't do any basic research together with Professor Kwon; I only organized the files."

"You're the only assistant to Professor Kwon, are you not?"

"I am."

"There were no other assistants?"

"None."

"That must mean he destroyed forty years' worth of data. And because you were only his assistant for seven years, you don't know whether those files still exist?"

"Yes."

"You're aware that those files are immensely valuable, yes?"

"I don't know how valuable they are precisely. But I was offered two billion won."

"Were you aware that fourteen years ago, Professor Kwon attempted deals with the former Soviet Union once, and with a German company three times?"

"I was not."

"Then what exactly *do* you know about the chimera files?"

"I know that they no longer exist."

"How can you be sure they don't exist anymore?"

"Because Professor Kwon told me that he burned them all."

"I'm a sensible man. And a sensible man would not be able to understand the things you've told me up to this point. Professor Kwon cancelled the contract during negotiations with the

German company because the price and terms were not to his liking. And you're telling me he just threw them in a fire?"

"As I said, I wasn't aware that he tried to make deals with the Soviet Union or some German company, as you say. I wasn't even employed at this company at that time. All I told you was what Professor Kwon told me."

"Then why did he burn them?"

"He thought that they weren't of use to humanity. He might have thought that the syndicate would use them for evil; or maybe he finally realized later that he had made a monster, like Frankenstein."

"How romantic. Fourteen years ago, he tried to sell them, and then over the next fourteen years he changed his mind and burned them – those files that were worth trillions, maybe tens of trillions of won. I have a hard time believing that."

"Believe it or don't, that's what he told me."

"Then I'll ask you again. Are there any chimera files?"

"I told you, they don't exist anymore."

"Perhaps they do exist, and you just don't know where they are."

"They don't exist."

"Professor Kwon didn't give you – his only successor – any clues?"

"How many times do I have to say it? He gave me no such thing."

"And everything you told me is the truth?"

"Yes."

"And you have no interest in changing your story?"

"Obviously. It's the truth."

"Tell me, do you know that hot water freezes faster than cold water?"

"Come again?"

"It's really strange. How can boiling water turn to ice faster than water that's been sitting in the refrigerator? I've never been able to wrap my head around it."

"What are you talking about?"

The man didn't answer my question. Instead, he dragged the cart with its surgical tools next to the operating table. He then put on some latex surgical gloves. On the cart were an assortment of surgical tools, six neatly aligned bottles of medicine, and an icebox with packs of blood used for transfusions.

"It says you're type O blood on the chart. Is that correct?"

"What are you doing?"

My question clearly made him annoyed.

"What I asked of you was simple. Anyone could do it with a bit of care. If you followed my rules, no harm would come to you. Just give me straightforward answers. Everything in order. Is that such a difficult request? You're really starting to get on my nerves. You better watch it. I'll ask you again. Are you type O blood?"

"Yes."

"Good. I'm now going to perform a little experiment with you. Don't worry. I'll use anesthetic so you won't feel any pain. I don't like playing stupid games by beating people to a pulp with a club or giving them electric shocks. It's a waste of time. And that's because easily repeatable injuries never made someone talk. No, I plan to cut off a part of your body. But don't worry, it won't be a vital part. I'll take a toe, a finger, an ear, your nose, then your cock – in that order. Think about it carefully. Think about whether what you're protecting is worth it, Mr Kong. Think long and hard about how much you can take. If what you're saying is true, you better try everything in your power to convince me of it. If I believe you only after I've cut off a finger or a toe, it'll be a damn shame for the both of us."

At that moment, I should have spoken up, but everything the man was saying was so unreal, and I was so overcome with fear. As my surroundings started to fade into blackness, all I could see was the man's lips as they moved on their own like some cartoon character. I couldn't understand what he was saying anymore. Strangely enough, I thought to myself how good of a talker he was. Why was he explaining everything to me in such detail? The man lifted my foot and stuck my pinky toe with an anesthetic needle. He then poked at my toe with the needle and watched my expression. All the feeling in my pinky toe had been lost. He picked up the shears. I heard a metallic snip come from the shears as one of my toes fell to the floor. As there was no pain when the toe was severed, it didn't feel like it had been my toe that had dropped off. I looked at the toe, then back at the man with utter astonishment. The man had no expression on his face as he picked my toe up off the ground with a pair of forceps and showed it to me.

My god. He had really cut if off! My toe!

"Felt like nothing, didn't it?" he asked with a smile. I just continued to look at him with a blank stare. Everything felt so surreal.

"I use anesthetic," the man began, "because I value efficiency. The pain caused by cutting off toes willy-nilly only wastes a bunch of time. People kick and scream and do all sorts of unnecessary whining. That only prolongs the interrogation. And I hate loud noises. It all makes for a very tiresome and bothersome experience for me. But if you numb them, they can approach pain and loss more rationally. To help you, I'm going place each of your severed body parts here for you to see."

The man placed my severed pinky toe atop a white illuminated table. The toe, which changed to a strange color in the fluorescent light, was still trickling blood. The man took off his latex gloves and went over to the blinds again for a smoke. I continued to look at my pinky toe on the illuminated table. As I stared at it, my chest felt like it was going to burst with fear. The man returned to the operating table after he had finished his cigarette.

"Let's start from the top again. Where are the chimera files?"

"Just tell me what to do. I'll do whatever you want."

I was discombobulated and desperate.

"All you need to do is tell the truth. That's all I need. I'll ask it again. Where are the chimera files?"

"I don't know. But if they do exist, I can find them for you. Really."

"I hate when people repeat themselves. And you changed your story. That'll cost you. This time, it'll be a finger as punishment."

The man put anesthesia in my left pinky. He then checked with the tip of the needle to see if the anesthetic had kicked in. "I'm sorry! Please give me another chance," I screamed as I twisted my body. The man didn't answer. Instead, he started to scowl as though my screaming was annoying him. The man took the sheers and cut off my left pinky with another metallic snip. He then picked up the finger with his pair of forceps, showed it to me, and placed it alongside my pinky toe on the lit table. And just as before, he took off his gloves, went over to the blinds, peered out for a quick glance, then began smoking another cigarette. When he finished the cigarette, he read the document on top of the desk again, then tapped the document twice with his finger. Walking over to me again, he adjusted the operating table by raising my legs and the arm rests. He then tied a rubber ring tourniquet around my ankle, and then my wrist.

"To stop the bleeding. Well, shall we? From what you divulged just a minute ago, it seems there's a possibility there are some chimera files after all?"

I thought for a moment about how I should answer. My mind was working faster than it ever had. I thought about countless scenarios, my speech habits, his possible reactions. What did he want? Did I have what he was demanding from me? How could I avoid losing all my fingers today? If I said now that there were chimera files, won't he chop off my ear? On the other hand, he'll probably chop it off if I say there aren't…

"Yes, there might be," I said shaking.

"Since I've already cut off one of your fingers, let's get things straight before continuing. First, you said there were none. Now you say there might be. So, which one is it? Are you going to stick with that there might be some chimera files?"

I nodded my head.

"So, the chimera files could exist; you just don't quite know where they are. There are only two people who handle Cabinet 13, but, being one of them, you still have no idea where they are. Is that what you're telling me?"

"At least until now. I mean, until now I haven't really given the chimera files much thought."

"A man named K offered you two billion won for the files, and you're telling me you still didn't give the chimera files much thought? You didn't even try looking for them?"

"I did think about it, but I didn't try too hard to find them. I thought they might not even exist. And because I have a steady income, I didn't really need all that money. Of course, if I did have them, I would have sold them. But Professor Kwon's such a scrupulous person that, if he had decided to hide them, they'd probably be hidden in a place I'd never be able to find them. And–"

"You're talking too much; you're not getting to the point; and you're contradicting yourself. Tell me the truth. That's the only way out of this. You're going to leave this place in pieces if you play tricks trying to save a few fingers."

The man numbed another toe and cut if off with the shears. I closed my eyes as he cut off the toe. My entire body was shaking. When I opened my eyes, another toe had been added to the growing collection.

This torture continued for the better part of a day. The man asked the same question again and again, and I said whatever I could trying to get out of the situation. Sometimes I spoke carefully, sometimes I fumbled with my words and contradicted myself, sometimes I mumbled to him in utter despair, and sometimes I cursed at him in vain. Sometimes I said I knew where the files were, sometimes I said I didn't, sometimes I said I was sorry or asked for forgiveness, and sometimes I said I would get revenge on him if I ever got out of there. And each time, the man just shook his head as he cut off another one of my fingers or toes. After several hours of this, five toes and four fingers were congregating on the table. The man showed me his collection of fingers and toes as he spoke:

"It's been five hours and I still haven't heard any of the answers I've been looking for. You have five toes and six fingers left. Do you know what that means? It means if you can't figure it out soon, you're doing to lose all your toes and fingers. How many fingers can you have cut off before you cease to be human? In my experience, about four. Up until that point, you're still a human, but once you've lost five or six, you're more monster than human. Mr Kong, how do you see yourself now?"

I was so paralyzed by fear, so foggy in the head with disbelief. I was lost in a maze. It felt like I was playing a game of Russian roulette and had lost more than half my fingers and toes in the process. I was so beaten down. I didn't answer the man's question. I had no answer to his question, nor could I even understand what it meant. I couldn't form thoughts because all the words in my head were shattered like broken glass.

"You bastard, you should have just cut off the whole fucking arm," I spat at the man.

The man turned my face toward him and look into my eyes. He then shook his head in disapproval. The man took the cart to the wall cabinet and took several minutes to pick out more medicines. The vials he returned with were different from what he had been using so far.

"This serum was designed to help extract secrets. It was first developed during the cold war by the Americans and the Russians. It also helps the individual who takes it to have a conversation with their inner ego. Today I'm considering using serum made in Russia and Germany. The Americans think theirs is the best, but the CIA doesn't know as much about fear as they think; the KGB, they know what fear is."

The man gave me an injection. Immediately my mind went fuzzy. My body became light as if I were in a dreamlike state, and my mood even seemed to improve. The man asked me how I felt. I told him I felt great. He then asked me if I was ready to talk. "Of course. I feel like I could ramble on for hours!" I said. The man continued to ask me questions, and my tongue began to move on its own. It felt like magic. As he continued his questioning, he suddenly stopped and said, "This isn't working," and brought over the shears again. Intoxicated from the serum, I begged in a weak voice, "No, please don't." He ignored my pleading and cut off another finger. I tried counting my remaining fingers, but I kept losing count. When he placed my severed finger atop the table, I thought to myself the absurd thought that I wished I could feel the pain when he cut off my fingers.

"You're a cruel person," I said. "Actually, you're a nice man. Always kindly explaining everything to me in such detail."

"It's what I do," the man said politely. "I'm a janitor, a public servant, and a delivery man."

"Right, the modern job market is very diverse," I said. Thick rain clouds were forming and floating inside my head. Rain fell, and lightning struck, and I could hear thunder. The falling rain turned to snowflakes and fell backwards up into the sky.

It was nighttime when I awoke. I had a skull-splitting headache. The man must have given me pain medication because I still couldn't feel the pain from my missing body parts. The man was watching television. After I let out a groan, he came over to me to speak.

"I guess you don't have the chimera files after all. I'm sorry that things have turned out this way. As I said at the beginning, it's not easy for humans to trust one another. I know you don't have the files, but I'm not so sure they will believe that. If the syndicate isn't convinced by the report I'm going to submit to them, they're going to send another person. You need to be careful. If you can't find the chimera files, you'll be on the run for the rest of your life. Get some more rest. While you're asleep, I'll call a doctor to stich up your hands and feet. Unfortunately, the doctor I usually work with is away on a business trip right now. He could have made your hands look pretty again."

The man stuck another needle into my arm. I slowly drifted into sleep. I probably would have fallen asleep even without the medicine. I was so tired and beaten down.

UNFAMILIAR CITY

When I awoke, I was on a park bench. I opened my eyes to see yellow gingko tree leaves falling on my head. "Fucking ginkgo trees," I muttered to myself. I turned to look at the base of the tree and swore again.

"I said, fucking gingko trees!"

My skull felt like it was going to split from all the drugs. The freezing early morning October air was penetrating straight into my bones. I tried to remember what had happened to me. It felt like something awful, but because my head was full of cotton wool, I couldn't remember exactly what that was. Nevertheless, it was clear that it was terrible indeed.

And yet I was still alive. The man spared me. He could have killed me, had he wanted to. But then again, I really had nothing to thank him for. The only reason he hadn't killed me was because killing me would have been more trouble than not. Perhaps I wasn't even a human worthy of killing.

They had performed surgery on me while I was asleep and stitched five of my fingers back to my hand. The bandages were soaked with blood, and the knot with which the bandages were tied looked somewhat shoddy. What kind of doctor had he called? Some deprived surgeon whose license had been revoked? Or maybe some barber-turned-illegal-doctor who had never gone to medical school? After all, what kind of doctor would take money to reattach a tortured man's fingers? My fingers, which were wrapped tightly in bandages, were shooting with pain and unable to move. Part of me wanted to take off the bandages and see how my fingers had been reattached, and another part of me was too scared to look. Perhaps, I thought to myself, I had become some sort of Frankenstein's monster.

I stood up to leave the park and took a few steps before losing my balance and falling. The drugs probably hadn't worn off yet. Had they reattached my toes, too? If they had done my fingers, they probably had done the toes. The inside of my shoes was soggy, most likely from all the blood. I wanted to take off my shoes and check, but fear of what I might find stopped me again.

I stuck my hand in my coat pocket to find some cigarettes. What I found was not a packet of cigarettes but two bags of medicine. One looked to be a painkiller and the other looked to be an antibiotic. *Nice guy. Giving me painkillers for the fingers he cut off.* Suddenly feeling the pain in my fingers worsen, I took two painkillers. My dry throat made it hard to swallow. I waited for the pain to go away. But even after waiting a while, the pain refused to subside. Impatient, I opened the bottle to take ten more.

Even after eating twelve pills, my fingers still ached like they had been bashed with a hammer. As the pain became more acute, my consciousness became fuzzier until I found it hard to know where I was or where I was going.

"Am I really that fortunate to have survived?" I asked myself.

"Of course, it's fortunate you survived," answered another me.

"You're optimistic," I said.

Perhaps what I should have been most thankful for was the fact the drugs still hadn't worn off. It was good that half of me was coming back to reality slowly while the other half of me was still stuck in a dream. If it weren't for that, the memory of that morning's horror would have put me in more pain. I thought about going to the police station and filing a report.

But for some reason, it felt like that was a bad idea. The police wouldn't be of much help, and going to the authorities would probably only anger my captors more. But then again, this was a serious crime. They had treated me like an animal. I was filled with indignation as I thought about how they had cut off my fingers and toes like a child catching bugs and plucking off their wings and legs. But this anger quickly extinguished itself like a cheap match. In its place was a growing fear. The thought of being dragged back to that office as punishment for letting my anger show scared me. I didn't want to go back there again. And besides, the police were never going to believe me. And even if they did, I doubted they would be able to find the man who did this to me. It's not like he and the people he worked for were amateurs. After all, they had purchased a dental office in a downtown skyscraper and tortured someone there in broad daylight; such people weren't going to be easy to lock up. They wouldn't have let me go if they didn't know they could get away with it. And to find that man, I would have to get a search warrant for every office in downtown Seoul: an impossible task. If I weren't able to produce any sort of proof, the police were just going to ignore my case. And that would only make my current situation go from bad to worse.

Thinking about this and that, I concluded that I should leave the park. They might change their minds and come looking for me again. After using all my strength to pull myself up, I staggered out of the park. In front of the park was a taxi stand, at which there were three taxis. I got in the second one.

I asked the cab driver where we were. He told me we near Gangdong-gu Office. "Gangdong-gu Office," I repeated to myself in a whisper.

"Where to?" the taxi driver asked me.

I thought about where I should go. But I had no idea. I told the driver I didn't know where I was going because I had just experienced something very confusing. The driver stared at me through the rearview mirror. He looked to be in his late-fifties and had gentle eyes. "Take your time. I don't mind," he said. "For now, just start driving. In any direction," I finally said. And with that, he started driving.

"That happens to me sometimes, too," the man suddenly spoke up. "Before I was a taxi driver, I used to own a small business. Then one day I went bankrupt. Within an hour, the debt collectors showed up at my front door – I don't know how they knew. I just needed to get out of there. So I took a taxi. But I had no idea where I was going."

The taxi driver continued to ramble on about his life experiences. But suddenly, my ears became filled with a mechanical hum, making it hard to understand what he was saying.

"Please go to the Y Research Center in Hongneung," I told the driver.

The driver nodded his head and began to accelerate. A few moments later, he glanced at me through the rearview mirror and mentioned that blood was leaking from the bandages wrapping my hand. Nonchalantly, I replied that it was because someone had cut off my fingers with a pair of shears. When I said this, the driver's eyes widened, "You're joking." I didn't answer him.

When we arrived in front of the research center, there was a black luxury sedan illegally parked in front of the stone wall. Inside the vehicle were two burly men eating bread and drinking milk with smiles. Seeing them frightened me. They looked as though they could be more professionals hired by the syndicate to kidnap and torture me. Perhaps the syndicate thought it was a mistake letting me go and had sent these people to take me in again. Or maybe they were just average salarymen parked in front the research center for a quick bite. In fact, come to think of it, cars frequently parked illegally in that spot.

"Sir, we're here," the driver said to me.

I contemplated for a moment whether I should get out of the taxi or not. Actually, it would be more accurate to say I was spacing out, unsure of what I should do.

"Sorry, but can you take me to Seogyo-dong?" I said to the driver.

He gave me a somewhat suspicious look.

"Didn't you tell me to go to Hongneung?"

"Yes, but now I want you to go to Seogyo-dong."

The taxi driver shook his head as if to say he didn't understand, then stepped on the accelerator. Feeling again the pain in my fingers and toes, I took out six more painkillers and swallowed them. Seeing me take the medicine through the rearview mirror, the driver offered me some bottled water. I drank the water as I stared out the car window. People were on their way home from work, as if it were just another day. The sight of people going home felt unfamiliar and somewhat unbelievable.

When we arrived at my house in Seogyo-dong, there was a small van parked at my front door. Inside it were another three burly men. Adhered to the inside of the van's window was a sticker that read, "Pipes, plumbing, and blockage removal." Seeing this van, I again became frightened. They might have been dressed like plumbers, but the men looked more like hitmen. The smooth-talking man from earlier that morning should have reported that I didn't have the chimera files, but it seemed like the syndicate hadn't believed him. If that were the case, the syndicate would have sent a new team to my house to torture me again. On the other hand, maybe they were just plumbers here to unplug a clogged drain. The faces of the men in the van made it look like this was actually their line of work.

"Sir, we're here. Are you going to get out?" the taxi driver said, clearly irritated.

Not answering his question, I continued to peer inside the van. One of the men inside the vehicle was holding a spanner as he joked with his friends. Seeing him wave the spanner in the air, I became even more scared than I had been while being tortured earlier that day. My body reacted to this fear by shaking violently.

"Sir, are you OK?" the driver asked as he looked at me with a cold sweat.

It didn't seem like I was OK. If I couldn't go to the office or into my own home, where could I go? Where could I go to avoid being monitored and tracked?

"Take me to Gwangmyeong City, right now. No, take me to Uijeongbu or Dongducheon City," I blurted out.

The driver pulled up the hand brake and slowly turned to face me.

"Sir, the fare is already over 40,000 won."

What did he mean by that? I couldn't understand what he was trying to say. Obviously, I knew how much the fare was; it was displayed clearly on the meter.

"And?" I replied.

"I'm fine with it; I just can't understand why you keep jerking me around for no reason. And my shift for this taxi is about to end, so I can't take you all the way to Uijeongbu."

For no reason? How could he say for no reason? This was my life we were talking about. I guess it was of no concern to him. And he was about to end his shift, after all. He would have to give this taxi to another driver soon. I opened my wallet. I only had 50,000 in cash. I gave all 50,000 won to the driver.

"Just drive a little bit longer and let me off at a good place," I said.

The man took the money and stepped on the accelerator. Five minutes later, he let me off in front of the old World Cup stadium. Picking a random direction, I limped aimlessly away from the stadium, dragging my aching legs behind me. It crossed my mind that someone might still be following me. Dipping into an alley lined with unlicensed homes, I crouched next to the corner of a rock wall and waited there for a while to see if anyone was coming after me. After a while, I concluded

I probably didn't have a tail. But then it crossed my mind that they might have attached a tracker to my clothes, like they do in the movies. I stole and changed into a set of old sweats hanging from a clothesline. I then took my suit and cellphone and threw them into a dumpster.

Crouching again by the edge of the rock wall, I thought for a long time about where I could go to hide safely. Then it struck me. If the syndicate was aware of Jeong-eun's connection to the cabinet, they would be monitoring her apartment as well. But there was no way they knew about her involvement with that cabinet. If they had, the man who had tortured me would surely have asked about her. And besides, I had learned about her knowledge of the cabinet only just recently myself.

I got on the subway and went to Jeong-eun's apartment. Passersby glanced suspiciously at the blood oozing from my bandages and shoes. My fingers and toes stung like they had been sliced with razors, and I still had a splitting headache. I sat on the stairs on the eleventh floor next to the door to Jeong-eun's apartment and waited for her to arrive. I was famished, still high off the drugs, going mad from the pain in my fingers and toes, and unable to rid myself of that man's voice which was still ringing inside my ears.

When I awoke, Jeong-eun was sitting next to me and crying.

"Mr Kong, what happened to you," she said with a look of shock on her face. I burst into tears as soon as I saw her expression.

"I was kidnapped. They cut off my fingers and toes. No one's chasing you, are they? Did anyone come to the research center? You need to be careful, Jeong-eun. They're after me. Actually, they're after the chimera files, but I don't have them. This is all because that irresponsible old man left without doing what he needed to do. They don't believe a word I said. They're dangerous people, Jeong-eun. They cut off your finger if you change your story. They cut off your finger for talking too much. I shouldn't have talked so much. I shouldn't have changed my story. But I'm not getting a second chance. Next time, they'll slit my throat. You need to be careful."

I was shaking violently as I said this. Jeong-eun gave me a big, full-bodied hug. Being held in her embrace, I cried for some time.

THERE'S A CROCODILE
AFTER ME

Jeong-eun went to work the following morning. But when exactly it was that she left, I wasn't sure. Because she walked with such soft steps, she rarely made a sound. She was a silent human, so to speak. Perhaps her ancestors were ninjas. Or maybe it was just because I took too many sleeping pills.

I lay on the sofa all day and stared at the dog. It was a massive dog that didn't bark and didn't seem to like me. Its ancestors dragged sleds across the Alaskan ice in -60°C weather. What was a dog with genes like that doing in a cramped apartment like this? "What on Earth are you doing?" I said as I firmly tapped the dog's nose. The dog stared at me for a moment with a blank expression before sauntering off into the corner.

There were times when I would suddenly remember something frightening or be overcome with anxiety for no reason. When this happened, I would grab a kitchen knife and hide in Jeong-eun's closet. I spent several months at Jeong-eun's place. Since being kidnapped, I wasn't able to leave this apartment even once. Jeong-eun said that she had seen men dressed in black suits in front of the research center. But she also said she couldn't be positive that those men in black suits were the same men in black suits that I had seen.

Fear and lethargy took turns attacking my body until I was

like a boxer down for the count. Each day, my emotions faded from bone-shaking apprehension to utter lethargy. And on days when I was most lethargic, I would just lay down next to that dog that never barked and stare up at the ceiling. By the way, did I mention the dog didn't like me? Because Jeong-eun didn't have a television set, the only sound in her house was the occasional dripping of water droplets from the sink. When I got hungry, I would eat the food Jeong-eun left out for me on the kitchen table. It's embarrassing to admit, but because it was impossible to lift a spoon with my fingers, it sometimes took more than an hour to finish a single bowl of rice. Sometimes, having forgotten that I had taken a bite of rice, I would just sit there drooling.

The fingers that had been reattached were in poor condition. Three of them had been reattached successfully, but both of my pinky fingers turned black and rotted. I was now convinced the doctor didn't have a license. One day I stuck my hand into the sunlight, and like a dry leaf, one of my pinky fingers fell off with an audible snap. The other one fell off too, but when it was that it fell off, I couldn't be quite sure. And even the fingers that had been successfully reattached still couldn't be considered normal.

Jeong-eun was silent. She didn't speak much. After cooking me dinner, she would go into her room and sleep. Sometimes I thought about whether we might have sex, but for some reason, after being released by my kidnappers, I couldn't get even the slightest of erections. It could be because I wasn't attracted to her sexually. But it could also be because I was suffering from PTSD.

"Is it uncomfortable having me here?" I asked.

"It is. I've never had someone live with me before. But it's OK. It's not as bad as I thought," she said.

"That's fortunate, that it's not as bad as you thought."

And it was fortunate. If she had asked me to leave, there wasn't a single place on Earth I could go. But I couldn't stay here indefinitely. If they found out I was staying here, they would kidnap her too. They would take her to that half-dental office, half-corporate office place. And then that smooth-talking man would cut off her fingers. Who knows, he might even cut off other parts. He was more than capable of it. When I explained all of this to her, Jeong-eun made an unabashed smile saying, "It's fine. I can spare a few parts." Another thing that worried me was that, as someone who didn't talk much, Jeong-eun would have trouble answering the man's questions. And that would put him in a bad mood. And if that happened, the result wouldn't be good. The extreme anxiety from imagining what might happen to Jeong-eun prevented me from sitting still and would force me to pace about the living room.

I kept thinking that I had to leave this place, both for Jeong-eun's sake and my own. But there were eyes everywhere. I didn't have the strength to keep running. And because my toes were completely shot, I wouldn't be able to run away from someone chasing me. I had no strength to fight, nor did I know how to fight. I tripped a boobytrap. I had no idea I had already boarded the Misfortune Express. I had lived my life forgetting that things completely unrelated to me could suddenly insert themselves front and center into my life. I was an idiot. But what had I done wrong?

One morning, after Jeong-eun left for work, I picked up the bottle of sleeping pills by my bed. It was empty. I had started with just one pill, then two, then three. These days I needed six to fall asleep. If I kept this up, I'd eventually never wake up. I stared at the empty bottle of sleeping pills for some time before finally picking up the phone and dialling the number for Will Execution Inc.

"I'm in need of that safe house. There's a crocodile after me."

"Are you leaving in search of a new world?"

"No, I'm on the run."

"How long can you keep running?"

"I'm not sure. I'll run to the end of the world. But I'll get caught eventually. The world's too small to run from fear forever."

THE ISLAND

This island is uninhabited. The only things here are the incessant blowing of the wind and the monotonous sound of crashing waves. And yet the island is quiet. It's so quiet, in fact, that sometimes I get the feeling everyone on Earth has migrated to Mars. My only friend is a stupid dog that barks at the sun all day. It's a dachshund, and, because its legs are so short, its belly drags on the ground. I named it Crazy after the way it runs around in circles trying to bite its own tail. Stupid dog.

The island is shaped like a peanut. At one end is my cabin, and at the other head is a dock. In order to get to my cabin, you have to walk two kilometers from the dock up a deserted hill. Because I can see the trail from my cabin, I will know if someone is coming for me. Behind my cabin is a steep cliff. I've prepared a rope that extends from the top of the cliff to the sea below. If someone comes for me, I must take the rope and descend 100 meters down the cliff. Remembering the unfortunate prisoner of Saint-Pierre, Andre Droppa, who fell to his death because his rope was too short, I've tested my rope by dropping it over the side of the cliff several times. It is long enough. But I hope I never need to climb down the cliff.

I also have a rifle with a scope. Sometimes I line up empty cans and practice shooting targets, but my aim isn't good. There is also a security system surrounding my cabin. Each morning, by surveying the island and checking the security system, I take a peek at the crocodile secretly growing inside me.

Everything necessary for a person to survive is inside my safe house. It's not necessarily cultured, but neither is it primitive. Thanks to my wind turbine generator, which spins round and round making electricity, I can make toast with my electric toaster. All my fishing needs are satisfied by the island's shallower cliffs, which provide good places to catch fish. All in all, this place is a perfect place for someone to hide. But it's boring. I wish I could invite people here, but that would be dangerous. If I told anyone where this island was, my chasers would get here faster than you could look it up on the map. They think I'm hiding some secret, and their eyes are bloodshot looking for me. My soul is pure – light and airy like a piece of fluff left out to dry in afternoon sun.

It's absurd, but recently I've been thinking that was all some ploy orchestrated by Professor Kwon. Perhaps there were never any chimera files to begin with. And if there were no chimera files, that would mean there was never any syndicate trying to get their hands on them. Perhaps K, with his elegant business card, and the smooth-talking man who cut off my fingers were both sent by Professor Kwon. Maybe everyone had conspired to banish me to this god-forsaken island. As I imagine such things, it all starts to make sense, and I begin to feel like I've been duped.

Someone had to devote their whole life to guarding those abandoned stories. And that someone, at least in Professor Kwon's eyes, was me. I was perfect for the job: stupid, naïve, gullible, and afraid.

But this wasn't a bet I was willing to take. There really could be a syndicate looking for chimera files, and there really could be men in black suits chasing me. If I were caught by them again, I wouldn't be able to make it out of there with just a few fingers missing. Perhaps this was all because of that god damn Professor Kwon. Because of him, I'm living on this forlorn island with no friends, no women, and no alcohol.

* * *

Unsurprisingly, there's a cabinet on this island. Organized in this cabinet are files from the original Cabinet 13. They're all the leftover symptomer files that the syndicate or investors must have deemed worthless. Despite everything that's happened, they're still unbelievable. But not having anything to do, I often take out the files on sunny afternoons and quiet, lonely nights to read and organize – just as I always have.

I read those files, again and again – that's what I do. I leave records of my doing this in various ways. Sometimes I make codes that no one can understand, and sometimes I rearrange the order of the files into a labyrinth. There's no real purpose for any of this. I just do it for fun. However, because symptomers are a little different from other people and, in some ways, unique, I always think it very important that I find diverse and accurate ways to describe them. I do this because form is sometimes all that matters. The Russian formalists of Korea who were so deeply enamored with the beauty of form, once said this:

Cold noodles in a bowl for beef broth are not cold noodles.
It's just really poorly made beef broth.

I like this quote. Keeping these words in the back of my mind, I'm always trying to think of the most appropriate bowl in which to put these odd humans. But it's not easy.

Sometimes I miss those absurd humans. Had the 290lb Mr Hwang lost weight and transformed into a nimble cat? Had the Mr Ko of Alien RADCOM received a reply from his home world? Had the torporers who were in a long state of torpor finally woken up? They must be getting annoyed that no one is answering their calls at the research center. Was the poor formerly conjoined twin still cremating her split soul on the weekends?

Each night I think of them. It's not because I miss them, but because this place is so utterly boring. I think about their lives from my island and write about the things I've read. It's similar to how Ludger Sylbaris in the middle of the Mexican desert sought out revenge little by little on the people of Saint-Pierre who had turned to ash.

This is how I'm spending my time, at the end of the world, in the middle of nowhere, with a stupid dachshund that chases its tail all day long. Aside from the discomfort of trying to reach the shift key without any pinkies, everything is all right. There are people in much worse circumstances in this world than me.

However, I don't know how much longer I can last here. With nothing but the waves and the seagulls and the ridiculous stories of Cabinet 13, this island is so monotonous, so boring, so tedious. My life is full of that I-would-rather-eat-dog-treats-than-suffer-this-boredom boredom.

Perhaps you know. I don't deal with boredom well.

"How's it going?" Professor Kwon asks from heaven.

"Bad. Very bad. What am I supposed to do on this god-forsaken island?"

"I'm not sure there is anything to do. Just endure your time. Life is nothing but time that's been momentarily placed in a bowl."

"You mean, like a cabinet?"

"Yes, like a cabinet."

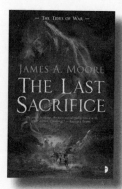
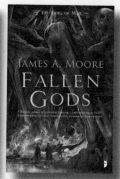
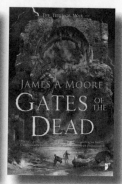

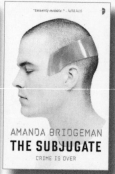

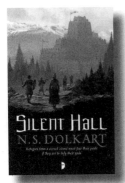
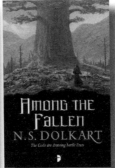
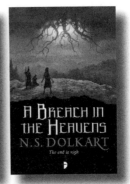

Science Fiction, Fantasy and WTF?!

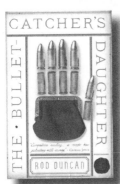

@angryrobotbooks 📷 🐦 📘

ABOUT THE AUTHOR

Un-su Kim made his debut as a writer in 2002 through the Jinju News Fall Literary Contest with short stories, *Easy Breezy Writing Class* and *Dan Valjean Street*. His first full-length novel *The Cabinet* won South Korea's Munhakdongne Novel Award in 2006. His novel *The Plotters* was published in English in 2019

ABOUT THE TRANSLATOR

Sean Lin Halbert was born in Seattle, USA, and holds a BA in Korean Language from the University of Washington, and a MA in Korean Literature from Seoul University. He has been awarded the Global Korean Literature Translation Award, the Korea Times Modern Korean Literature Translation Award, and the Literature Translation Institute of Korea Award for Aspiring Translators. He currently lives and works in Seoul as a full-time translator. *The Cabinet* is his first translated novel.